D0597021

DON'T WANT TO BE YOUR MONSTER

DON'T WANT TO BE YOUR MONSTER

DEKE MOULTON

tundra

Text copyright © 2023 by Deke Moulton
Jacket art copyright © 2023 by Matt Rockefeller

Tundra Books, an imprint of Tundra Book Group, a division of Penguin Random House of Canada Limited

Library and Archives Canada Cataloguing in Publication

Title: Don't want to be your monster / Deke Moulton.
Other titles: Do not want to be your monster
Names: Moulton, Deke, author.
Identifiers: Canadiana (print) 20220226644 | Canadiana (ebook) 20220226652 | ISBN 9781774880494 (hardcover) | ISBN 9781774880500 (EPUB)
Classification: LCC PZ7.1.M68 Don 2023 | DDC j813/.6—dc23

Published simultaneously in the United States of America by Tundra Books of Northern New York, an imprint of Tundra Book Group, a division of Penguin Random House of Canada Limited

Library of Congress Control Number: 2022937912

Edited by Peter Phillips
Designed by Andrew Roberts
The text was set in Minion

Printed in Canada

www.penguinrandomhouse.ca

1 2 3 4 5   27 26 25 24 23

Penguin
Random House
tundra   TUNDRA BOOKS

For Gleno, who kept my eyes pointed to the stars

1

ADAM

I know my brother is evil, but that has nothing to do with him being a vampire.

"We're sneaking out for *this*?" I ask as I peer down from the rooftop Victor has finally stopped on.

It's not like I don't know *what* my brother brought me to. Even though my eyes sting from the lights of downtown, nighttime Olympia, one sign draws my attention. Under neon letters spelling out "Capitol," the theater marquee reads *The Lost Boys—Sat Jan 13—7pm*. Which is today. Right now. The question is *why* we're here.

Victor lowers his hands. He's done one of those ta-da gestures, like he's brought me to something a lot more fun than an old theater. It's the kind that plays movies that have been out for decades. Pretty much the most useless place to risk getting in trouble for sneaking out to, since we can easily see the movie from home.

"*This*?" Victor asks, fake-offended over the way I said the word. "This is the best movie of all time, Adam."

That is totally a matter of opinion. *The Lost Boys* is Victor's current favorite movie. A movie we watched *last night* from our very own couch. It can't be the only reason we snuck out.

"If the moms knew—" I start to say.

"They're at work," Victor says. "They'll never know."

"But the mortals . . ."

That has to work. The street below us is filled with them. Sure, they aren't acting all that scary. Laughing and waiting in a line. Taking selfies. The least threatening anyone could be . . . *nowadays.*

But I know that mortals also hate vampires. *Hunted* us.

"Exactly. The *mortals*," Victor says, grinning wide enough that I can see his fangs. Everything about Victor reminds me of an icicle. His blond hair is perfectly styled around his pale face, and his blue eyes sparkle as he grins. Not at all worrying about death-by-moms. "After watching the movie, they're going to be so easy to scare."

Seriously? Sneaking out to watch a movie is one thing. Sneaking out to scare people? "I'm going home."

Victor latches onto my arm.

I squirm but can't get away. Partly that's because I'm only ten and he's fourteen, but also partly because I'm skinnier and scrawnier and all around more puny than Victor. Which isn't fair, because we've both been drinking the same blood for the last nine years. But somehow, he's grown up to be so much stronger than me.

"Don't worry," Victor says. "You really think your big brother's going to let a bunch of mortals get you?"

I scowl. We aren't related. Not by blood, as mortals would say (which, I need to point out, is the weirdest saying). It's not like vampires can be born. We're brothers because our moms run what is pretty much a vampire foster home, rescuing anyone they can from more dangerous situations. Victor has never told me how he ended up bitten and in the Rossi house when he was only four, but I know my own story. Mom turned me herself when I was only a baby. Who my mortal parents were, I'll never know, but if mortal brothers are as annoying as vampire ones, I hope I was an only child.

I try again to pull free from Victor's grip.

"Fine," I give up.

"Follow me," Victor says, the grin back on his face.

No one notices us leap clear across the alley onto the opposite roof.

The giant mural on the wall spelling out "OLYMPIA" gives us enough cover when we hop down from the multistory building next to some dumpsters. We peek around the corner. At least we're dressed for moving around in the night. I'm wearing my comfy black hoodie and jeans. Victor has been dressing differently lately and tonight is no exception: a black button-up shirt and dark-wash jeans. Not at all prepared for if the sun comes up, but at least his clothes are dark.

I pull my hood back, pushing my wavy brown hair out of my eyes. I scowl again at the theater marquee.

"The movie hasn't even started yet," I say.

"Your point is?" Victor asks.

"Aren't you going to scare the mortals . . . *after* the movie?" I ask.

"We," Victor corrects. "*We* are going to scare the mortals. Together. But there's no way I'm missing *The Lost Boys.*" Victor laughs. "I thought you knew me."

"It's rated R," I say. "They're not going to let us in."

"They will if I"—Victor wiggles his fingers in a spooky way—"tell them to."

I groan, realizing what Victor's grand plan for sneaking into the movie is. *Charisma*: using our natural vampire charm to encourage mortals to think whatever we want them to. Like that two kids are actually old enough to watch an R-rated movie without their parents.

"Tell me, Adam," Victor goes on, either not noticing my lack of enthusiasm or ignoring it. "Do you want a beard? I'll make you a big, burly guy."

"This isn't going to work," I say. "You don't even know how to use charisma. Neither Mom nor Mama has ever taught you how—"

"Watch and learn, then," Victor says, as he begins sauntering toward the ticket booth. "I'm going to be a natural."

It's no use arguing with him. I pull my hood back on, tugging it as low as it goes, and hurry to catch up with Victor.

My heart is in my throat, beating hard. The streets have emptied—Victor, despite his bravado, waited until the mortals in line had gotten their tickets and the sidewalk in front of the theater was empty. But still, my heart races.

I clench my teeth so I don't accidentally reveal my fangs. Sure, Victor has tried to explain "cosplay" to me—that mortals dress up as characters from shows they like, which means no one will think we are actually real vampires watching a vampire movie if they see our fangs—but there is no way I'm going to take that risk.

Victor, on the other hand? Grinning the widest grin possible.

The mortal on the other side of the glassed-in ticket booth doesn't look impressed.

"Two tickets, please," Victor says. He drops the tone of his voice, trying to sound older, and I nearly laugh at him.

"Isn't it past your bedtime?" the mortal asks.

Victor clenches his fists. I can see them trembling. "We're eighteen."

The mortal laughs so hard that Victor storms away. He retreats into the alley, and I follow him up onto the rooftop.

"So . . . charisma failed," I say.

"Really?" Victor asks. "I'm so glad you pointed that out. There's no way I would have realized that didn't work if you hadn't just told me that, right now. Thanks."

He doesn't say anything else as he takes off, jumping from rooftop to rooftop, heading east. Heading home. I might have felt bad for Victor. It isn't the first time he's tried to do some cool vampire thing and failed. But I also know that for us to really tap into all our powers—to be able to convince a mortal that two kids are actually grown-ups, for example—we need at least two things we don't have: lessons, for starters, and a *lot* of blood to drink. A lot more than what our mom is usually able to sneak home.

We settle to the sidewalk once we get to the I-5 underpass. We never jump over the interstate—there's too many cars and not enough trees. And cars have dashcams. It would be too easy to get caught. Now that we've slowed to a stop, I can actually talk to Victor. I catch up to his side.

"Look, maybe—"

My head snaps up at the same exact moment as Victor's.

"Do you smell that?"

Of course I do. It's the best smell in the world. *Blood*.

Our eyes meet and, without a word, we're off. Under the bridge, back onto rooftops, following our noses. I almost can't think. I'm sure Victor isn't thinking at all.

We are close to Huntamer Park when the flashing red and blue lights of about a dozen police cars, fire trucks, and an ambulance stop us. Victor pushes my head down, and even then, he only risks his eyes peering over the ledge of the building.

"It's a murder," he whispers, ducking his head down as well.

"A murder?" My voice cracks. "How do you know?"

"You can't hear them?" Victor asks.

I don't want to admit that the only thing I can hear is my pulse hammering against my eardrums. I shake my head.

"They're talking about setting up a perimeter," Victor says. "You can smell it though, right?"

I nod. I can't see the body, but from the smell of it, I know it's a middle-aged man. There's a lot of different blood I can smell too: bright red, oxygen-rich blood. Thick, dark, oozing veiny blood. All of it smells absolutely delicious.

"He's been slashed apart," Victor whispers, peering over the ledge again.

"Werewolves?" I ask.

"Nah," Victor says. "Werewolves don't kill people. It's definitely mortals. It's the way they are. They don't even need to kill. Not like us. They just hate each other."

"Maybe we can help?" I ask. "You know, look for the killer? We heal way faster than mortals do, so we could try to stop the murderer, and even if they try to—"

Victor cuts me off with a laugh. "They hate *us* more than they hate each other."

He looks back at the scene and shakes his head, disappointed. "What a waste of blood," he says. "Come on." Victor pushes himself away from the ledge, away from the smell and the flashing lights. "Race you home."

2

ADAM

"Get off," I say from under Victor's butt. Or, at least, I talk as well as I can while being sat on.

"Not until you give it back."

"GET OFF."

"I'll fart on you," Victor warns. It's a bold thing to say for someone who doesn't digest. But we both watch enough TV to know that mortals fart, and that it's unpleasant. And it's a good enough threat to use if you're sitting on someone.

"I'll tell Mom."

"Mom doesn't get home for another hour," Victor says, leaning forward enough so I can see his face. Victor pulls back his lips, as if going out of his way to show off his fangs. They're sparkling white in the darkness of the living room. I really don't think sitting on someone is enough to kick off bloodlust. Vampires can't eat other vampires anyway, but it's not like I want to find out if I'm wrong.

"Dude, give the remote back," Victor says. "I promise, we don't have to watch the end this time. We will absolutely skip the part where they kill all the vampires. You just need to see all the cool parts."

"Get *off*, Victor," I growl back, showing off my own fangs. "You're breaking my jaw!"

"You talk great for a kid with a broken jaw."

"I'm serious!"

"Then you better hope Mom brings home young blood today and not stuff from someone with osteoporosis."

"Fine, take it," I grumble, and push my hand out from between my chest and the couch. Victor jumps off me and is instantly all smiles, like always, now that he's won control over the TV.

"Jerk," I mumble, wiping my hair out of my eyes. I know Victor can hear me, but he pushes Play on our ancient DVD player, combing his fingers through his hair and getting it back in style. If he couldn't watch *The Lost Boys* in a mortal theater and scare a bunch of people, then he was definitely going to watch it once we got home. But I'm not in the mood to watch a movie where a bunch of mortals get eaten.

I push myself off the couch.

"Where are you going?" Victor asks, tilting his head in my direction but not taking his eyes off the screen. "Look, look! See? That mortal thinks he's so tough, but just wait for it..."

I don't answer. I shouldn't have to. There's no way Victor completely forgot that we stumbled upon a real-life murder not even ten minutes ago.

Unfortunately, it's hard to get away from Victor in our house. Even though the couch and TV are tucked away in one corner of the first floor, the whole house is wide and open. Bookshelves line the walls, and there are a few squishy black armchairs Victor and I have used more for making forts than sitting on.

I stop at the closest lamp to the TV and turn it on, the red light from the bulb illuminating the shelves. All of our lamps have red lights in them, just like all of our walls are painted in dark colors. White lights bouncing off of white walls? My eyes hurt just thinking about it. I don't know how mortals deal with that.

The bookshelves contain a little bit of everything. My eyes skim the spines of the hundreds of books: journals and novels and *so* many travel books. Black porcelain vases dot the spaces between the books, filled with dried roses and snapdragons.

And then there are the tchotchkes from all over the world. Random little knickknacks. All of them mementos of the other vampires who have passed through these walls.

What would any of them do if they saw a murder?

Victor laughs at something in the movie.

I want to say something, like asking my brother why he drools over a movie that does vampires so wrong... that makes vampires *evil*. The only people we know are other vampires, and none act like the mortal actors pretending to be us on screen.

It wouldn't have mattered. Victor's answer never changes: "At least they look cool."

My brother has a point. Compared to what our moms do—a nurse working night shifts at a hospital and an astronomer at the local university—prowling an amusement park looking for kids to freak out and blood to drink *is* much cooler.

"I'm going to go there someday," Victor calls out to me.

I cave. I walk back over to the couch and glance at the screen. The clan of teenage vampires is strolling around on the Looff Carousel.

"They're not even playing the ring game," I say.

Neither of us has ever been to the Santa Cruz Beach Boardwalk, but since Victor is obsessed with this movie, we've spent hours on Google Street View, pretending to be there (but let me say how completely unfair it is that there's no nighttime option). We've learned all about the boardwalk. And we learned that the carousel the vampires in the movie are on right now has a game you play while you ride. You grab a ring on one side and then throw the ring into a clown's mouth on the other side, all while the carousel is spinning. You don't get anything if you win—maybe bragging rights with your brother—but that at least looks more fun than scaring people.

"When we go, you have to promise we'll play the ring game," I say.

"Who says I'm going for the rides?" Victor says.

I narrow my eyes. "Why else would you go?"

As if on cue, some security guard starts screaming in the movie and running away from flying vampires. I scowl. Thinking jerk teenagers were cool was one thing, but . . . in the movie, that screaming guy got all his blood drunk. Got *killed*. Just like the guy who got murdered tonight.

Victor laughs. I scowl, but Victor doesn't seem to notice.

Look. I get it. It's a movie. It's not real. But I don't want to even think about eating people the way mortals think vampires do. Hunting. Killing. Biting viciously into mortal necks while they scream. Not like how Mom does it. How *all* vampires used to do it: gently, respectfully, taking just a little at a time, just what we needed to live. We used to be friends with mortals, but one look at the movie is all I need to remember that they forgot.

"Just think about all we could do if we had that much to drink," Victor says.

"We *just* saw a murder," I tell Victor.

"Don't remind me," he says, but he goes to hold his stomach like he's hungry. "What a waste."

I push past Victor, even going out of my way to bump into him, and stomp to the stairs leading up to my bedroom.

"What gives?"

I don't answer.

My foot stomps echo in the old and drafty Victorian two-story house. I bet you could hear it from outside, but no one is around to listen. Our house is in the middle of a rainy forest of towering Douglas fir, down a long, dark gravel road no one even uses to turn their cars around.

Victor and I aren't the only ones home, though we might as well be. I walk past my other sibling's door. It's not like Sung is available to vent to. The sign on their door saying "*FINAL SEMESTER: Knock and I take your hand*" is a warning I'm going to pay attention to. I'm sure my vampire healing skills are powerful enough that I could probably reattach my hand if it got lopped off, but that's a theory I'm not about to test.

Though it makes me feel even more alone that I've got family all around me and no one to talk to.

I flop onto my bed, the bottom bunk of the bunkbed I share with Victor. I know the myth is that vampires sleep in coffins, but we don't. I can kind of see where mortals are coming from, though. We sleep during the day, which is the opposite of what they do, so they've got to think it's weird. Plus, we sleep deeply enough that we probably appear dead. Maybe that's why mortals think we're "undead," but it's not like we're zombies or so evil we're not allowed to die or whatever weird stuff they came up with.

I pull my black-and-navy quilt over me like a tent. Without thinking, I reach over to my nightstand to grab a magazine.

My mom brings home old magazines, the ones that the hospital keeps in the ER waiting room for people who forgot to bring a phone charger. I used to pore over them, looking at all the people in the photos, always searching for one thing I could never find. It wasn't in the pictures of kids in school. Or women kicking a soccer ball. Guys sitting on a couch, cheering about something. Ballet dancers. A bunch of people standing around a construction project.

I'm looking for space where a vampire could fit in.

Not in the world as it is, that's for sure. The whole "drinking blood" thing has always made us different from mortals. Different enough that they could be convinced to be freaked out over it. Hundreds of years ago, they *did* get freaked out over it, and started to think we were too dangerous to live around, and tried to kill all of us. Every vampire they didn't kill went into hiding. We did such a good job at it that mortals think we're "extinct" now, but that doesn't stop them from making movies about us when they want some surefire monster to be scared of.

A knock at the door shakes me out of my thoughts.

"Look, you got the remote," I growl. "What else do you—"

It isn't Victor.

"Hi, Mom," I greet her gloomily.

She steps into my room, as graceful as a dancer. I could never get a straight answer out of her about whether or not old-timey moviemakers had based their vampires off of her, but she fit the picture perfectly: pale skin, hazel eyes, brunette hair always pulled back into a bun or a braided crown, and high, super-noticeable cheekbones. She buys any lipstick or nail polish that uses a blood pun. She is in nurse scrubs now, but once she's done checking in on everyone, she'll be in a huge maxi skirt.

At least I can get away with looking like a normal kid. I have a mop of messy brown hair, brown eyes, and my skin ... all vampires are just a *bit* paler than our mortal counterparts. No sun and all that. But I'm still more tan than Victor. Tan enough to look mortal. Victor is so pale he could get away with looking like a ghost.

"Are you and Victor *fighting*?" Mom asks.

As if I can say anything. Victor and I aren't supposed to leave the house (remember what I said about vampires tricking mortals into believing we are extinct?), which means I'd have to admit to sneaking out if I let her know I'm upset about seeing a murder. I'm not about to tell on Victor either. Even if he's joking about eating people— that's high on Mom's no-go list.

I shrug, and finally settle on, "Victor's being a jerk." It's a solid complaint. "He doesn't want to do anything I want to do anymore. He's seriously watching *The Lost Boys* again. It's the fifth time this week."

Mom sits on the corner of my bed and smiles.

"He's trying to find his place in the world."

"And he's got one. Like, right here. This house. Lacey, Washington State. Pacific Northwest. United States of America."

Mom laughs. "He's at the age where that's not the right answer. And I know that's hard when you two have always been so close, but it's part of growing up."

"Easy for you to say. You're like three hundred years old!"

"After forty, you stop counting."

I groan and throw myself back into my pillow. It's just my luck that I have to put up with Mom jokes *and* Victor going ultimate vampire jerk mode in the same night.

"I wish I didn't have *one* person to hang out with," I say. "Sung's too busy with school. They don't play anymore."

Mom doesn't get the hint.

"I'm sure . . . I could find some mortal kids," I say. I've never actually seen them, but know there are definitely mortal kids in this town.

"We have to keep our secrets," Mom says, getting the hint now. "Mortals don't trust us. We can't risk our family being put in danger for you to find a mortal kid to play with. I'm sorry, I know that's rough to hear—"

"Okay, but then . . . you know . . ." I glance at the ground. "You could bite another kid?"

The look on Mom's face? She isn't angry or upset. But she *is* surprised, which hurts more.

"Someone my age," I go on quickly before she responds. "It's not fair Victor got to have a kid brother and I don't. And if you bite someone, I wouldn't be alone."

Mom smiles.

"You aren't alone, sweetie," Mom says. "And I know that you might not feel that, especially when you and Victor used to do everything together. I'm not saying being a vampire is anything to be ashamed of, but I can't just go around turning people. That's not fair. And especially another kid. I know you were bit so young you don't remember mortal life, but mortality is something very special. I couldn't take that away from someone."

I shrug. "You still bit me."

"You were turned for the most special reason of all," Mom says. "I'm sorry. I know you'd love another friend, Adam, but I can't."

"It's okay," I say, even though I can't take my eyes off the ground.

"You know what?" Mom says, way too cheerfully. "I know something you can do with your brother."

My eyes fall on the bag Mom has with her. I know what's inside.

"Oh, right . . . ," I say. "Time to eat."

3

VICTOR

Mom *hates* it when we ask "who" is for dinner. So what's the first thing I ask every time we sit down to eat? "Who's for dinner?" Boom.

Mom gets mad every time, but then she goes on to explain pretty much everything anyone would want to know about the person whose blood we are drinking that night. She says it's to teach us "empathy." To see that the stuff that ends up in our cups is coming from a person, not much different from us . . . but it's a lost cause. Mortals are nothing like us. What am I supposed to have empathy for? Mortals being weak? And getting sick? Yeah, *so* much sympathy for that.

I know the real reason she explains it: to squash any questions on why the blood she brings us tastes the way it does.

"This was donated by a wonderful young man named George," Mom says as she pours the blood into mismatched coffee mugs. She's careful not to let any drops go to waste or stain her white-and-black striped skirt or her denim blouse.

I'm not fooled by the word "young." Every mortal is a baby compared to Mom, so she's never wrong.

"What's he dying of?" I ask, calling her bluff.

"A combination of diabetes, heart disease, and what'll probably do it, pneumonia."

"All that and he's still alive?" Adam says, looking at the thick, dark red liquid. Adam *would* find it scary that a mortal—someone who can literally die at any time—could have so much sickness and not go down. Of course, mortal diseases have absolutely zero effect on us.

"Why do you spoil us so much?" I scoff.

"Because I love you," Mom says, smiling at me sarcastically.

Mom doesn't have fangs. Or, she used to, but she filed them down. To look human. To blend in. And every time she flashes me a smile, I think about how mortals force us to live. Mom doesn't even hurt mortals, but that wouldn't matter if anyone were to discover she's a vampire.

"It's always old people," I say. "Why do you *always* have to get old-people blood?"

"They never ask any questions on why you're taking so much of it," Mom says. "Now sit down, before it gets cold."

"You mean colder," I mutter.

Everyone else pulls out their chairs all nice and slow, like it's totally fine that we have to eat junk, but I yank back on my chair, slamming my elbow into the wall. The wooden table, with its deep mahogany wood and elaborate carvings, is far too big and grandiose for the room, let alone the five of us (four now, seeing that Mama isn't home) that currently make up my family.

My older sibling, Sung, joins us to eat. Dinner is the only time I see them anymore. They sit cross-legged in their chair, wearing white shorts and an oversized burgundy college sweatshirt. They've got dark bags under their eyes from staying up all day attending online classes (of course *they* get to use the internet anytime they want, unlike me and Adam). Their short hair is always messy, like they just tried pulling it out. It makes me never want to go to college. There has to be such a thing as a vampire plumber, right?

I grab my mug, which has the NASA logo on it and says "I NEED MY SPACE" in huge letters. I go to drink, but Mom reaches out to cup her hand over my mug.

"Victor . . . ," she warns.

Mom lifts up her coffee mug, which is orange and has a Dracula Mickey Mouse on it, and the others copy her. I rest my chin in one hand and pull my mug off the tabletop with the other.

"I would like to offer a blessing of thanks," Mom says. "For this portion of blood that will keep our family sustained." Adam holds up his mug in classic "toasting" fashion, Sung says "Jal meok-ge-sseum-ni-da" before they drink, to thank Mom for preparing our meal, and Mom makes the sign of the cross before taking a sip.

I guzzle most of it down in one slurp.

"I can taste the medicine," I say as I put my cup down and smack my lips.

"Good, then you won't ever need to complain about your pancreas," Mom says.

Adam laughs into his cup, and I kick him under the table. If we heal fast enough to keep us from catching any mortal diseases, our vampire blood is just as good at neutralizing their medicine. That doesn't mean I can't taste it. The medicine adds a gross, sharp, fake sourness to the delicious metallic taste of blood.

I reach over to tap on Adam's shoulder—the one farther away from me. And, like a dork, he turns to look. He still catches me pouring the last bit of my blood into his cup.

"Since you like the flavor of medicine so much," I offer as an explanation. Because "you really should be drinking more blood than I do" sounds way too mushy.

"Victor has a point," Sung says to Mom. "This guy tastes like he was embalmed already. Don't they have anyone in the hospital who is, I don't know ... more ... organic?"

My head snaps up. "Yeah, like someone who got murdered tonight, right?" I notice Adam's eyes going wide, so I quickly add, "We saw it on the news. That's why I know there was a murder. Why couldn't you get that blood?"

"Hmm," Mom hums, looking up like she's thinking. "I guess I could have gone down to the ER and asked if I could drain the blood out of the dead body. Maybe ask the coroner to help. Emily makes a lot of jam and stuff ... I probably could have asked if she had a spare mason jar lying around."

My shoulders slump. Mom is always this annoyingly sarcastic.

"Imagine all that blood going to waste." I groan.

"Imagine getting killed," Adam says with a shudder.

"Who are *we* going to get killed by?" I ask.

"Vampire hunters!" Adam interjects immediately.

I knew it.

Just last week, Adam watched *The Lost Boys* with me for the first time. And later that day, he woke me up—he'd had a bad dream about vampire hunters coming to hurt us. I get it—just about every movie with vampires has them getting slayed in the end—but I guess this one really hit him hard.

I smirk and curl my right arm, flexing. "Drink up, then, bro." I nudge his cup closer. "I keep telling you, you've got to get that vampire strength. Come on, flex."

Adam's pitiful little stick arm doesn't bulge or change shape at all when he flexes it. I laugh and go to take another sip of blood, but I forgot I'd already emptied my cup. Not that I regret sharing, just that I can totally still feel the emptiness all the way deep in my veins.

"When are we getting more?" I ask, licking the inside of my mug.

"Later," Mom says.

"Later tonight?" I ask. "You can still go get that murder blood."

Mom laughs, which is the worst parental "no" ever.

"Okay," Sung says, draining their cup and standing up. "Well, this was over quick. If only my paper gets written just as fast." Sung is *royalty* when it comes to masking their frustration with bad jokes. "Bye everyone. Jal meo-geo-sseum-ni-da." Which is their way of saying "thanks for the blood."

"Good luck, Sung," Mom says, and then points at me and Adam. "Don't either of you go anywhere. You have homework to finish."

The worst.

I watch Sung disappear upstairs and I get up from the table too.

I drop my mug into the sink and slip out the back door without making a sound. It's drizzling out. January is normally the best time of the year to be a vampire. Long, dark nights? Check. Cool temps? Check. If it wasn't for the rain ruining my style, tonight would be perfect. Our house is surrounded by a canopy of evergreens, so I'm spared most of the rain. Still, there's dampness on the air . . . better make this quick.

My feet creep over mulch and dead leaves as I sneak around to the side of our house. I move like a shadow. The blood I drank should be giving a power boost to all my vampire abilities. Stealth. Strength.

I glance up at the windows. The light in Sung's room flickers on. I jump up, clear to the second-story window of my sibling's room.

Score. I pull off surprising Sung.

"What the—!" they yell once I land softly on their bedroom floor. "I have way too much studying to do to put up with you right now, Victor."

I ignore their annoyance. "Hey, you left your bedroom shutters open."

"For fresh air," Sung says. "It's not an invitation! I have so much to read and—"

"Why do you even *want* to go to school?" I ask, jumping up on their chair to keep them from sitting down. "You're a vampire! You can literally do anything in the world, and you choose the most boring, mortal thing."

"Get out of here, Victor!" Sung yells again.

"Not until you teach me some cool vampire stuff," I say. "Come on. You used to live like a real vampire before Mom found you, right? Are Korean covens different from American ones? Teach me how to use charisma on a mortal."

"*Get out!*" Sung says.

"Okay," I say, but I'm not giving up. I notice a book propped open next to Sung's laptop.

"Oh no, don't you dare," Sung starts. They dart forward, but it's already in my clutches. Before they can stop me, I jump out the window.

I lunge from trunk to trunk in the dense, dark forest. I keep listening for any hint that Sung is chasing after me, but all I can hear are a thousand branches creaking in the breeze. It's a windy night, which totally works against me. I try to time my jumps, but the tree trunks are swaying wildly. I miss a tree by more than a few feet.

Thankfully, I can handle a fall. Sung's book? Not so much.

"Oops," I say as Sung lands on the ground next to me, their jaw hanging open at the sight of their expensive college book lying in the mud.

"Victor, I'm going to murder you until you are dead," Sung mutters.

"Oh, cool!" I scramble to my feet. "Does that mean you can teach me to fight? Come on, we used to wrestle all the time."

Sung rolls their eyes at me as I make fists and start to shadowbox.

"You want to learn something so badly?" Sung asks. "Why aren't you getting ready for school?"

I groan as loudly as I can, leaning my head back and looking up at the sky.

"You're really going to tell me that?" I ask.

"Yeah, so you can become a phlebotomist and get blood from mortals without killing anyone and without getting caught," Sung says. It's what Mom expects me to go to college for in four years, since I'll be eighteen and I've been growing up at the same rate as a mortal kid.

Mom always tries to make it sound like she's doing something cool and sneaky when she's drawing blood. Like a cat burglar.

"All that means is never doing anything even remotely resembling the vampires we are," I say. "I have all this . . . promise right under my skin. I can feel it. But I'm doing nothing with it. I could be so much *more*, but I might as well be a regular kid. Even a nerd like you has to admit going to school is a total waste of immortality."

"Believe me, Victor," Sung says. "There's more to life—even an immortal life—than being a vampire."

My shoulders droop. So much for putting what's bothering me out there. I pick up Sung's book from the mud and hand it over.

"Sorry," I say.

The book makes a squishy sound as I press it into Sung's hands.

A smile pulls at their lips and they shake their head.

"Well," they say. "I'm going to have to use some charisma to convince the bookstore to buy this one back. Might as well tell you how it's done."

"Really? You mean it?" I ask, straightening up.

"Yeah, once I can convince *you* to let me finish my paper, I'll know I can do it," Sung says with a smirk. "*Then* I'll be able to teach you."

"Come *on*," I growl, and chase them back home.

4

ADAM

The smell of rain seeps into the house through our open fireplace, filling the air inside with pine and mud and damp. A chill prickles my skin. Raindrops tap against the windows in a constant, soft pattering, but it doesn't matter. I can still hear the car crawling toward the house over all of it.

I recognize the sound of the motor and I know whose car it is—nothing to be alarmed about. Still, my heart puts on a burst of speed and feels all flighty in my chest. I immediately chide myself. What did I think was going to happen? Someone was coming to catch us? Am I still so shaken by that murder?

I push out all the air in my lungs in one long blow. *Mortals don't think we exist anymore*, I tell myself. *Vampire hunters are only in movies.*

"It's so quiet!" Mama's voice calls into the house so brightly you can hear the smile behind her words. "Is it schooltime?"

"Hey, Mama." I'm resting my head on my arm on the table. "Not exactly."

If Mom is the classic movie vampire, then Mama is the one who counters spending all of her time in the dark by wearing the most brilliantly colorful clothes possible. She has dark skin and eyes that are such a deep brown they are nearly black—they reflect every light so that, no matter what, it always looks like they are filled with stars. She shrugs off her hijab, loosens her ponytail, and shakes out her hair, simple acts that let us know she's officially home.

"Hey, welcome home, Samira," Mom says graciously, getting up from the table to give her a welcome home hug and kiss, her skirt sweeping after her.

"Good"—Mama looks at her watch—"morning, Beatrice." I love the way Mama says Mom's name. The Italian way: Bay-a-tree-chay. Mom's lived in the United States a long time, so long that her accent's gone and she uses the Americanized way of saying her name. But Mama always, *always*, pronounces it the Italian way.

"What is this?" Mama asks, gesturing to me doing nothing at the table.

"Waiting on Victor," I grumble.

"Ah, I guess he wanted to do recess first again?" Mama asks.

"Maybe he's not coming back this time," I mutter under my breath as I tear a strip of paper from my notebook, fold up a little origami frog, and bop the back of it, trying to get it to jump up into my mug. It's something my foster sister Michelle taught me to do before she moved to Chicago.

Mom shakes her head but doesn't say anything. She's looking up at the ceiling, and in a moment, I can hear it too. The sound of feet suddenly landing on the floor, laughing, teasing.

Another minute later and Victor jumps down the stairs and comes back to the table like he hadn't left at all. He ignores the earful he gets from Mom and goes right to giving Mama a heartfelt greeting.

"Today's lesson isn't even that bad," I whisper as Victor slumps into his seat.

"Oh, so we're learning some cool, very-specific-to-being-vampires stuff?" Victor asks me, his voice dripping with fake enthusiasm.

"Geography, actually," Mom says as she joins us at the table, opening the notebook she uses to keep track of all the blood we drink. "But don't worry, Victor, we'll make it specific to vampires. Find something in the house that's red. Once you figure out where in the world it came from, research that country in the encyclopedia set and its history in treating its vampire citizens."

"Mama!" I call out. "Your cardigan is red! What about Sudan? Could you tell me about—"

But Mama just waves me off. I know better than to ask her, but it doesn't stop me from trying. She has never liked talking about her past.

"Ooh, how about . . ." Victor snatches my coffee mug off the table. "Eilat, the Red Sea. Famous for . . ." He rotates the mug in his hands, looking at the painting of palm trees, jumping dolphins, and beachside resorts. "Not being red.

And beaches. Hmmm, darn, look at that sun. Not a place I'd ever go to, so I don't need to know about it. The end."

"Allora," Mom huffs out, tapping her pen against her notebook, showering George's blood type in angry, inky dots. "Wash that mug before the blood dries."

Victor shoves my mug into my chest so hard that I tilt back in my chair. "Hey!" I shout, but he's already out of the dining room. I chase him to the bookshelf.

"Something red, something red . . . ," Victor says, ignoring me and scanning the shelves.

"Don't give this back," I growl.

"That's *yours*," Victor says. "I'm not doing *your* chore to clean the stuff *you* use." He wraps his hands around mine, squeezing my hands against the mug, and smirks in the most condescending way ever. "Enjoy washing it."

"You were the last one to touch it!" I argue, holding out my mug. "You only gave it back to me because Mom said to wash it."

"I only had it because it was a prop for a joke," Victor says, picking up something red and scaly off a bookshelf. "Remember when Mason came to visit from Ireland and convinced you this rock was a dragon egg?"

"Don't change the subject," I growl.

"How am I?" Victor asks. "This is literally the thing we are supposed to be doing now. This *is* the subject."

I hold up the mug. Victor ignores me, picking up things off the shelf and turning them over in his hands.

"Hmmm . . . this daruma is red," Victor says. Why he's saying his thoughts out loud, I have no idea, but I swear it's

30

just to annoy me. "Dala horse . . . ? Wait, which of our siblings is from Sweden?"

"Johan," I mutter.

"I can't remember people I've never met," Victor says dismissively.

"They're our family," I say.

"They're people I've never met," Victor repeats. "Someone crashing here for a few years to figure out how to be a 'nice vampire' isn't the same thing as a family. Plus, Mom's been doing this for like, over a hundred years. How am I supposed to keep track of them all? Hey, check it out, another Red Sea mug. Looks like there was another Adam here before you."

Victor picks up a mug from the shelf that's covered in artwork of Moses crossing the Red Sea. He makes some joke about the water still not being red and how it's false advertising when you're doing a school project involving colors, but I glance at the bookshelves, a wave of dread hitting me.

One day, am I going to grow up and move out? I look down at the mug in my hands, tightening my hold on it. It's the mug Mom bought when she brought me home. That's Mom's thing—she buys coffee mugs when she rescues people. So we have something to drink out of, sure, but it's something personal, unique to us. But . . . what happens when I grow up? Will I just leave one day? And end up being forgotten? Nothing more than a souvenir on a shelf that a future-adopted vampire won't even be able to attach a name to?

"Well . . . ," I say, stammering against the thoughts in my head. "I mean, this is our home. All the other vampires Mom and Mama rescued were like . . . teenagers. Or already grown-ups when they became vampires. So that makes sense why they'd only be here a little bit. Like, Sung was a teenager, right? That's why they're going to move back to Korea after they graduate. But we were kids when we were bitten—"

"*I* was a kid," Victor interrupts, picking up a matryoshka nesting doll with a red babushka painted around her head, his fingers tightening around it. "*You* were a baby." He brightens up immediately. "I just had a thought. Imagine if mortals were right about us—you know, how they think vampires can't grow up?" Victor teases. "Could you imagine if that was real and you had to stay a baby and poop in your pants forever?"

I cringe. "Mom probably would have just let me die as a mortal then."

Victor's playful grin drops off his face.

"Oh, yeah," Victor says. "Mom does say you're the only mortal she's ever turned . . . but I'm glad she did. I would've hated to grow up without you."

My chest flutters and I smile. "Me too."

"Hey, come here," Victor says. Before I know it, he wraps me up and crushes me in a massive bear hug.

"VICTOR!" I shout in warning. A crackling pop snaps in the air and I push Victor away, but it's too late. The coffee mug comes apart in my hands and the wooden living room floor is suddenly white with porcelain shards.

"Shinu hadith?!" Mama calls out from the dining room.

I stand frozen in shock, unable to tell Mama what has happened.

"Oh, whoops, I forgot you had that," Victor says, looking around at the mess. "Check your hands and see if you're bleeding. It'd be an awful waste of blood if you were."

"That was my mug . . . ," I whisper.

"It's okay, we've got a cupboard full of—"

"No, you don't get it," I stammer, anger getting the better of me. "That was *my* mug. You broke it, I—"

"At least you don't have to worry about washing it now," Victor says.

"Jerk!" I shout, shoving Victor's shoulder. He stumbles back into the bookshelf. Before he can retaliate or answer, I storm out of the house.

It's chilly outside, and that's good. I need to cool down. I didn't grab my hoodie, but that's okay. I could have walked out there in my underwear and not shivered in the wet, forty-degree night. That doesn't mean I would— I would die from embarrassment way before I'd have to worry about hypothermia.

"It's a clear night tonight, masha'Allah," Mama says. "Gemini should be right over the house by now."

I turn to see Mama stepping out of the house, wrapping her floral patterned hijab casually over her head.

"There it is," Mama says, pointing up.

I look up at the night sky. It looks pretty. The rain has stopped and, over our house, a patch of deep navy night sky opens, dotted with stars sparkling golden, crimson, and white, my view ringed by the tops of blacked-out pine trees. Moments with Mama are always like this—poetic, somehow.

Which doesn't mean Mama is letting me off the hook.

33

She takes off her leopard-print glasses, wiping the dots of rain from them before putting them back on.

"You did not come out here to look at the sky."

"I know," I say, though honestly, I would rather stare at the stars for the rest of the night than stand here trying to figure out what to say. "Victor's just . . . being a complete a-hole tonight."

Mama gives me a mischievous glance. "What a wonderful coincidence you decided to come outside! People have used the stars as a guide for thousands of years."

I glance at the constellation above us.

"Seriously?" I ask.

"*Seriously*," Mama echoes and laughs. "Do not worry so much! Gemini is a good sign. It represents dual natures. Opposing forces."

Dual natures. Yeah, that sounds about right. Victor and I are growing more and more different each day. *Opposing forces*. All the pushback I get from Victor? Whether it's scaring mortals or watching movies, he's always fighting against me. And if all of our struggles are fate? It can only mean one thing.

We're doomed.

"But they stay together," Mama is saying. "Even if they have all of the sky to move around in. They may be different, but they are walking the same path, and they do so together."

That does it. Mama's words all but destroy any chance I had to talk about my brother. I wish hearing that didn't hurt as badly as it does. Lately, we've hardly done anything together, let alone "walking the same path."

"You know everything about the stars?" I ask. Hopefully Mama doesn't pick up on my diversion.

"They are a good companion to keep," Mama says. "No matter where you travel, they are always there, traveling with you. Funny, I used to not care so much for the stars until they were all I had left. They are special in that way. No matter what we do down here, we can never change them. Never harm them or distort them. Never let them down."

I crane my neck back once again and look at the constellation. *Gemini.* And if Mama is trying to tell me that was supposed to be like the relationship between Victor and me? I really want to be hopeful, but the only thing I can think of is how Victor really *is* like those stars. No matter what I might try, Victor will always be out of reach.

"But what about when you're feeling...," I start. My mind drifts on my broken mug. All my siblings who move away. The imaginary empty spot on the bookshelf that will now never hold my coffee mug when I'm gone.

"*Scared*?" I ask.

Mama straightens up when she hears me say that. "Habibi? *Scared*? What of?"

I kick at a rock, and I finally get the nerve worked up to admit it. "Being alone."

"With our big family?" Mama asks. "How can you ever be alone?"

"Oh, jeez, I don't know," I snap. "It's hard to feel like you belong anywhere when everyone's going to leave you."

And I vanish into the woods before I feel bad about yelling at my mother.

5

ADAM

The more Mama calls my name, the further I press into the forest.

I just want to get far enough away so I can't hear anyone. I get it; it's weird to want to be alone when you're scared of being alone, but I just need to think. I need space. I groan out loud remembering that that's the slogan on Victor's coffee mug, and I pick up my pace.

I shoulder my way around giant tree trunks, my feet slipping on the wet, decaying leaves that lay several inches thick on the forest floor. I trip about a billion times over the ferns that hug the ground. Still, I don't turn back.

I don't know why I'm so confused. I'm grateful for my family. For my moms. For being bitten. It meant I survived.

As far as I know, I'm the only vampire ever to get bitten as a baby. Mom and Mama had been on a date in downtown Olympia when they heard something explode. They went to help. Someone had driven a semi-truck into the synagogue downtown... on purpose. And not only did the building get wrecked, but the driver rigged it up so that the stuff the truck was hauling got thrown into the air. Mom said it was chlorine. Like the stuff people put into pools, but when it's in the air? It stops people from breathing.

The moms are vampires, so it didn't stop *them* from breathing. The vampire blood pumping in their veins kept healing them, over and over again. Mama and Mom tried to help. Mama pulled some of the people far enough from the scene so they could breathe again.

Mom found me. A baby, covered in dust from the rubble, unable to breathe. Even though she got me away from the gas, I was too little, my lungs too weak. Mom said she couldn't watch me suffocate. That she'd only done it because she had rescued Victor when he was four, and Victor had continued to age.

Even vampires who are bitten as teenagers grow up a little bit more. Something about how humans are "at their peak age" around twenty-five, so that's where all vampires grow up to (or down, I guess, if they were bit when they were older). So Mom bit me.

You'd think she'd be happy about saving me, but you wouldn't believe how much she apologizes for turning me into a vampire. I never cared before.

I don't really care now, either. I just—

I stop.

The forest comes to an abrupt halt. I squint my eyes, but I can't see anything in front of me except a wall of gray fog.

I take one step forward, and I can make out soft, brilliant green grass, beads of sparkling dew shining on the blades. The grass is cut nicely and even, and that can only mean one thing: I'm in a mortal place! And that's when I see it—a new forest emerging from the fog. A forest of tombstones. An icy fist grips my heart. *A cemetery*. Like a scene from a horror movie. My heart lurches up into my throat, but what am I scared of?

Ghosts, I tell myself. Mortals don't send their dead friends and relatives off to the afterlife with hopes that they "rest in peace" for nothing. If I annoy the dead, will they rise up? I groan, imagining that if Victor were here, he would tease me so much.

I creep around the grave markers, cringing as I stir up the fog. *Get over it, Rossi*, I tell myself. *You'll never die.* Even if there were such a thing as vengeful spirits or zombies, I would survive anything they could throw at me.

Survive.

It's weird and kind of hard to put into words. I almost had a mortal life. I glance at the tombstones around me. Or a mortal death. I could have ended up here, buried under the wet soil. And that . . . that kicks off a morbid curiosity that pulls me forward.

I can't say what I'm looking for. All these graves aren't exactly it. What's in them, maybe? I mean, not literally, but . . . I take a deep breath. I just saw a murder. And someone had tried to murder me as a baby.

Why did I get to escape that? Why was I lucky, while these other mortals didn't get another chance?

"AAH!" I cry out.

I trip over a tombstone and fall flat on my face.

I push myself up to my knees with a grumble. I shouldn't have screamed like that—what if a mortal heard me? I can see their houses behind the hedge surrounding the cemetery. Even though it's dark out, the sun will be up in an hour or so. I hold my breath and listen, wondering if anyone heard me. I pull myself up to my feet and crane my neck around. There aren't any street lights or lampposts around the cemetery. Everything I'm wearing is black, just like the shadows.

And now that I'm standing still and quiet, the cemetery is actually kind of peaceful—in a silent, otherworldly kind of way. Just another thing mortal movies get wrong, making something that isn't scary into something that is.

Creeeeeeeaaaaak.

I cringe at the grating sound and turn to look where it's coming from. Two big brick pillars stand on either side of the single-lane cemetery entrance. The gate is sealed shut with a heavy chain, with a big lock hanging from it, but the gate sways slightly in the breeze, creaking each time. I push out all the breath in my lungs (okay, I'm just relieved the creepy sound was *not* a ghost) and step closer to the gate. Between the two pillars, there's a wrought-iron banner making a little arch. Words are spelled out with iron, which are pretty much impossible to read from behind. I squint as I rearrange the words in my head.

Until the day breaks and the shadows flee away.

I turn away, weaving my way through the grave markers, my head hanging down. *It's not like the gate is wrong,* I tell myself. A little light will be climbing over the horizon in a few hours to chase me away. No one would even know I'd been there.

"Of course I laid a bunch of pillows under my blankets. How do *you* sneak out?"

I have never in my life fallen to the ground as fast as I did just then, dropping behind a tombstone.

It's *mortals.*

Every muscle in my body is tense. I'm thankful for the shadows, for my black clothes. I try as hard as I can to not breathe.

Two kids have stopped at the cemetery gate.

"It's locked," one says.

"I mean, sure, if you want to call it that," the other says.

"What does that mean?"

And just like that, one of them pushes the gates as far apart as the loose chain will allow, and they both squeeze their way through the gap.

One wears a bright purple puffy jacket, big yellow rain boots, and a skirt that hugs at her hips. The fur-lined hood is pulled up over the kid's head even though it's stopped raining. I forgot for a moment that tonight is probably cold to mortals.

The other one wears jeans, a dark jacket, hiking boots, and a bright blue baseball cap. He stomps around loudly enough to wake up the dead.

"Luis, wait up!"

"Right here!" Luis, who I'm guessing is the kid wearing the baseball cap, stops in front of a tombstone and gestures at it with both of his hands. "See? What did I tell you, Shoshana? Perfecto."

"No," the other one, Shoshana, says, shaking her head.

"What's wrong with it?" Luis asks.

"I'm not raising a ninety-year-old grandpa," Shoshana says.

"He's a veteran of *two* wars," Luis argues. "Look, they even tell you. World War II. Korea. Like, if we're going to raise a ghost to help us stop a murderer, I want a dude that is advertising on his tombstone that he's gone on a trip to kill people. Twice."

Stop a murderer?

Did I hear them right?

"Yeah, and I do a séance to raise a dead old man and he sees he got summoned by kids, he's going to be as impatient with us as *my* zayde was when we couldn't find the afikomen fast enough," Shoshana says.

"What does any of that even mean?" Luis asks.

Shoshana huffs. "It's an analogy. I'm talking about how you can't finish the Pesach seder without the kids first finding the afikomen, and if I know anything about old men, it's that they like their rest. So he's going to see our murder investigation as the seder and us catching the killer is the afikomen. So if we—"

"Your analogy is taking too long," Luis cuts her off. "If you're such an expert, then who do you want to raise?"

A cold bolt of sheer terror cuts into me because Shoshana begins to walk in my direction. She stops right on the other side of the tombstone I'm hiding behind.

"You have got to be kidding me," Luis says.

I don't dare to peek at what tombstone they're looking at.

"No, I'm not," Shoshana says. "Luis, listen to me—this is perfect. It's a ghost that will *want* to be raised. It will want to help us."

"Hiring you was a mistake," Luis says, his voice dripping with annoyance.

"Okay, one, you didn't hire me," Shoshana says. "You just came over to my house, at five in the morning, mind you, tapped on my window, and asked me to help you stop this murderer. And second, it's not a mistake. We do a séance, we raise this ghost, we give it friendship and a name—"

"A name, *exactly*," Luis says. "Don't you have to raise up ghosts by name? Like, how are you calling for this ghost?"

"I'll ask what one it wants," Shoshana says.

"Pena ajena." Luis face-palms.

"Look, if it doesn't work, we'll do it your way," Shoshana says with a sigh. "Okay?"

I hear the sound of paper ripping.

"So, like, what do we do now? Turn our backs to the tombstone and then check the note? How long does a ghost need?" Luis asks.

"You want me to do this *now*?" Shoshana answers. "It's not even sunrise."

"Yes, now, it's time-sensitive."

"I didn't bring any of my stuff."

"You need stuff?" Luis asks. "You can't go get it now?"

"I have Hebrew school today," Shoshana responds. "Also, I'd like to point out, if you want my help so bad, you better stop pretending like we don't know each other in regular school tomorrow—"

"Fine, we'll meet back here when you're done!" Luis cuts her off, and a moment later, Shoshana and Luis are walking back to the gate, arguing back and forth.

"Not right after class," Shoshana says. "It needs to be night..."

"Why? Do ghosts get sunburns?" Luis asks.

"They don't come out during the day," Shoshana says. "Seriously, have you never heard a spooky story in your life?"

"Alright, then *tonight*. And I mean like, the minute it goes from to*day* to to*night*. We're doing this conjuring stuff early." Luis yawns. "Are all witches like this, or just you?"

"Like what?" Shoshana asks, insulted, and that's the last thing I hear from them before they're out of earshot. I let out a sigh of relief. They didn't see me.

A smile starts to creep onto my face.

They want to *stop* the murderer.

I stand up. Even though I hadn't seen which grave they were talking about, I knew it the instant I saw it—just a tiny little slab of rock, smaller than a shoebox. There are only two things carved into the stone: "Baby Boy, 1 DA—1923."

A baby's grave. Like there might have been for me. A morbid shiver runs down my spine... and then I pause.

Under a rock, placed on the corner of the tombstone, I see
a piece of paper fluttering with the rising breeze. A note?

I hold my breath as I read it. Handwritten on the paper,
Shoshana had left a message:

> I'm sorry no one named you.
> What name would you like?

6

VICTOR

'm not saying I'm freaking out but . . . I'm starting to freak out.

I climb to the top of the tallest tree I can find. Over a hundred feet up off the ground has to be a good vantage point, right? I scan the forest. It's foggy, and even vampire eyes can't see through that. Smell? Nothing but wet. I keep my ears open. A breeze brushes through the forest, and the sound of billions of pine needles rattling against each other makes the wind sound like a hurricane. I've got nothing.

Where could Adam be?

Okay, no lie, at first I thought Mama was being over-protective or something. She came back into the house and said Adam had been talking about how he was scared (of vampire hunters?!) and didn't want to be alone (he doesn't think I can protect him?!), and he stormed off into the forest and wouldn't come back when she called for him.

I was out of the house before anyone else in the family.

Not like the head start has done me much good.

I glance over toward Ruddell Road—the cars speeding by, their headlights blinding the night. Would Adam cross it? No . . . he's too scared of mortals, and crossing the road would put him right in one of their subdivisions. He'd stay away from that. Which means he has to still be somewhere in the seventy-four acres of forest our house is hidden in. I squint through the needly boughs of the firs, looking for the next tree I'm going to jump into, when I hear it . . .

"Aah!"

I lunge out of the tree. My feet skip lightly off branches as I let gravity pull me back toward the earth. I hit the ground soundlessly, but Adam still jumps and wheels around.

"Victor?" Adam isn't scared. He isn't hurt.

I sigh, both frustrated and relieved.

"You have a good trip?" I ask.

Adam smiles shyly. "I didn't go anywhere."

"I meant, you had a good *trip*," I say, pointing to the splatter of wet pine needles stuck to Adam's shirt. "How many times did you fall down? You have half the forest on you."

"Oh," Adam says, and looks down at his clothes. "A few times, I guess. Is everything okay?"

"You tell me," I say. "Mama said you got mad and stormed off. You've been wandering around the woods for almost an hour."

"I had to find a pen," Adam says.

I blink a few times. "A *pen*?"

"The church had some," Adam goes on. "*And* it was unlocked. I tried the funeral home first but—"

"Hold up, I'm still stuck on the pen," I say. "What did you . . . no, wait, I'm over the pen. You broke into a church? A *mortal place*? *Why*?"

Adam fidgets. "I wanted to leave a note. In the cemetery. You know . . . just to scare them. But don't worry, no one was there."

"But what if there was?" I hiss, ignoring the stab of betrayal. He went to pull a prank on mortals . . . *without me*? "You have any idea what they'd do if they had caught you? And you were all alone? You know they could've staked you right in the heart and there would have been no one there to protect you."

"But mortals don't believe in us anymore," Adam says.

"Yeah, but let them get one good look at your fangs and they'll figure it out," I say. "They've been taught their whole lives to hate us. Every movie, who do the mortals cheer for? The vampire hunter. Every single book, who's the bad guy? *Us*. They don't like us, Adam. When we get killed in movies, the audience is supposed to feel relieved. 'Another monster gone.'"

Adam nods glumly.

"Hey, look, I'm not mad," I try. "But you have to promise me you won't go off alone without me."

"Wow," Adam says. "You really went full Mom-mode on me."

"*Big-brother*-mode," I correct. "It's not at all the same thing. I can be protective of you too."

I feel a twinge of guilt as Adam hangs his head, looking thoroughly defeated.

"Hey." I try my nicest voice.

"I guess . . . ," Adam says. "That's why you like the vampire movies so much . . . even if it's not really what we're like? Because the movies say to hate them, but they're *us*. So you root for them, like, to stick up for them?"

"Of course," I say.

Okay, so honestly? I'd never really thought of it that way, but it sounds noble. Defiant. Like I'm fighting the mortals and their hatred of monsters by cheering all the movie vampires on. I don't want to mention that the vampires in movies are also decked out in the best clothes. With the best hair. And the coolest confidence.

"Come on," I say. "We need to get home. Everyone's wondering where you went. Mom's forgotten all about homework, though, so don't bring that up."

It's a good thing Adam's a vampire, because I'm pretty sure he needs to heal after the crushing hugs he gets from the moms. That's one attack I'm not about to rescue him from, so I sneak off into the house.

It's almost dawn and no one's even locked the place up yet. Every window on our house has heavy, wooden shutters. We open them at night to let the cold air in, but during the day, they are a perfect seal, keeping the sunlight out. I get it, everyone was out looking for Adam, but still . . . the sun doesn't wait for anyone. I walk around to all the windows, pulling in the shutters and locking them tightly.

Mama must be getting in my head, because I realize these shutters keep us safe from more than just the sun— no one can break in easily either. The shutters lock from the inside, so the only way mortals can get to us while we're sleeping and vulnerable is if they chop into them with an axe.

I'm walking past the bookshelves when pain shoots into my foot. I almost yell—that's how bad it hurts. I pick up my foot just in time to watch my cut heal and push out what I'd stepped on. It's a porcelain shard from Adam's shattered coffee mug.

I'd cleaned up the mess without thinking, but Adam had been pretty upset about it breaking.

I curl my fingers around the shard and grin. I have a plan.

7

ADAM

I wake up right after the sun goes down.

I grab a black-and-white plaid flannel shirt and black jeans, pull on my boots and a hoodie, and stuff a pair of black gloves and a scarf into my pockets. If there is one bit of vampire-mom-worrying that I can never forget, it's "if you're going out, be prepared in case you get caught in the sunlight."

And tonight? I have to be prepared for anything.

I sneak out of the house as quietly as possible. I left a note for Victor telling him I was out and to cover for me. I really hope he doesn't come looking for me.

I pick my way through the forest, walking through the wet pine needles and moss, stepping carefully so I don't squish a banana slug or a newt. It's not raining, but with the drizzle in the air, all the wet animals are out soaking it in. I keep my head down and trace the same path I'd walked the night before. My heart is racing in my chest.

The mortal kids said they'd come back to the cemetery tonight.

Did you forget mortals hunt us? I take a deep breath. That's definitely why Mom has her strict don't-leave-the-house rules, but it's not like those kids are even going to know I'm there. I'm going to stay a very safe, very far distance away from them and just make sure they actually do get to raise a ghost to help them stop the murderer. That's it. Then I won't really be breaking my parents' stay-safe-by-staying-home rules. I won't get too close to mortals.

The cemetery is completely empty. Empty of lights, empty of fog, empty of sound (okay, that last one kind of made it more scary, though), and definitely empty of people. There's no shortage of puddles, though. There's at least a hundred of them forming around the headstones.

I get there just in time.

I see Luis's and Shoshana's silhouettes crossing the cemetery grounds. They head straight for the grave marker Shoshana had left the note on. I crouch down behind a sword fern on the forest's edge, hoping that being a vampire will help me be extra quiet. Or sneaky. Shoshana picks up the note while Luis looks over her shoulder.

"No. Way." Shoshana's piercing voice carries over the cemetery.

"What?" Luis asks.

"No. Freaking. Unbelievable. Way."

"What, Shoshana? What happened?"

"The baby wrote back."

"What? No, it didn't."

"Look at the note! Yes, he did. *He*, don't call him it. He wrote 'Adam.' He wants us to call him Adam."

"Or the cemetery dude is pranking you."

"'The cemetery dude.' Who's that?"

"You know, the guy that does the grave-digging."

"Okay, Luis, look, you begged me to summon up some ghosts to help you and I'm not getting any support here."

"Okay, okay, jeez . . ." And then after a pause, "Where does a dead baby get a pen?"

"It's not a pen."

"Yes, it is. Look." Luis licks his thumb and then smudges the wet fingerprint across the paper, showing the black ink on his hand as evidence.

"No, it's not. The ghost baby . . . listen, Luis, the ghost baby had to project his message to us through the ethereal plane. He chose to put his message on the paper in a way that looked like a pen because that's what *I* used to write *my* message."

"That is so convincing, yet so wrong."

"Look, I schlepped all this stuff over here. Now, do you want to do this conjuring or not?"

"Fine."

Shoshana sits down, puts a stubby white candle on the tombstone, and lights a match. She waits a second to make sure the candle won't go out before she pulls a notebook out of her pocket, holding it open in her lap.

"BY THE LIGHT OF THE MOON, REACH THIS LIFE TAKEN TOO SOON—" Shoshana booms.

"Where'd you find this, anyway?" Luis asks, crouching down next to her.

"I wrote it."

"What if he doesn't like poetry?" Luis says, picking up a pebble from the ground and tossing it onto a neighboring tombstone. "You really want to risk raising a dead baby from the grave *and* making it angry?"

"It's not a poem. It's a spell. And it's to help direct my focus. But you know what's *not* helping my focus?"

"Thinking about how a ghost baby is going to move?" Luis suggests. "I mean, are we going to have to carry it, or is it going to zoom around in the air like someone let go of a balloon?"

Shoshana's face sours. "Your negativity."

"Hey, all I'm saying is two-wars-dude can walk."

"Do you do this?" Shoshana asks. "Do you create spells? Do you raise the dead? No. I do. Or I'm going to. Try. And it's hard. *You* were the one who asked *me* to help, remember, and now you're making it difficult for me for no reason! I could go home right now and it wouldn't mean anything to me, but then you'd be stuck here without anyone helping you. So, do you want me to get a ghost to help us or not?"

"I want ghost help . . . ," Luis said. "Alright, let's do it. Ghost it up."

Shoshana huffs and looks back at her notebook.

BY THE LIGHT OF THE MOON,
REACH THIS LIFE TAKEN TOO SOON.
WE WANT TO HEAR YOUR STORY,

DON'T APPEAR ALL GROSS AND GORY.
BE AWOKEN BY MY WORDS, MY SOUND,
ARISE, ADAM, FROM THE GROUND.

The silence in the cemetery sounds even *more* silent, somehow, after Shoshana's booming chant. The two kids look around, as if a ghost might appear from anywhere, and . . .

"Well, that's kaput," Shoshana says, slamming her notebook shut.

"Alright, so do you need to, like, do a reset or something, or do we get right to work on two-wars-dude?" Luis asks.

"We admit it's not going to happen, Luis," Shoshana says. "We aren't raising any ghosts."

"What does that mean? You're giving up?" Luis asks. Shoshana doesn't answer him, but she blows out the candle and starts putting her stuff in her bag, clearly giving up.

I can help, I think to myself. I'd even told Victor last night how a vampire would be perfect at tracking down a murderer. Except Victor didn't want to help. But there are mortals who do—they're standing right in front of me. I decide it. Right then and there. I'm going to help.

I wrap my scarf around my neck. I make sure to cover my mouth extra tight. The last thing I need is it slipping and revealing my fangs. Hopefully the scarf isn't going overboard and I pull off "mortal human is cold" and not "why is he being weird." I barely make a sound as I creep from the tree line through the cemetery. My feet are silent no matter what I step in, whether it's crushed gravel or soppy mud. I have to be quiet just in case, at the very last second, they do something that rings my vampire-alert bell. To give myself a chance to run away and hide. But they're . . . really just kids. No wooden stakes peeking out of their back pockets or anything like that.

I take a deep breath and step out right in front of them.

They both jump to their feet and stare at me. Okay, so that might not have been the best idea. Emerging from the darkness? Too late to go back and try again. I don't know what to do, so I just wave awkwardly.

"Hi, I'm Adam."

8

ADAM

"I DID IT I DID IT I DID IT!" Shoshana cheers, bouncing up and down, her hood falling back and her dirty-blond hair spilling all over her face. She grabs Luis in a death-grip hug. "It worked! I summoned a ghost! I didn't think that was going to work..."

Now that I'm standing in front of them, I realize exactly why Mom never lets me or Victor out of the house. She never told us how much I would be able to *smell* them—not *them*, necessarily, but their blood. The scent oozes out of them and wafts in the air and makes my brain a little dizzy. Their *youth*. It's so young it even makes the breeze feel more alive. For a split second, it's impossible not to see them as paper-thin skin-bags holding what I need to survive. One bite... the smallest puncture. I could be slurping up their blood. Just with one—

I quickly refocus on their faces.

Shoshana is pale—not pale like Victor but more like me—with a round face and hazel eyes. Luis is a lot more tan and has a little cleft in his chin, with warm brown eyes that I can tell are looking at me suspiciously.

"I don't think that's a ghost," Luis whispers sideways to Shoshana, but loud enough that I think he wants me to be able to hear him. "It's just a regular kid."

"That's right," I say quickly. "Just a regular kid. Like you. Uh, walking . . . breathing."

"That's totally something a ghost would say," Luis says.

"Ooh," Shoshana's eyes lit up. "Or maybe Adam's appearing like a kid our age because that's how we appear and—"

"No, I'm alive, I breathe. I *can* breathe," I say, and take a big breath. But with the scarf around my mouth, I breathe in a bunch of scarf lint and start to cough. "See?" I say, my voice strained. "No ghost would cough, right?"

Both Shoshana and Luis exchange glances.

"What do you think?" Luis asks Shoshana. "We came here for ghosts, but you summoned some kid . . ." His words trail off while he holds out his two hands, as though weighing the coolness of each one.

"You're really just a kid?" Shoshana asks me, her voice heavy with hurt.

"Uhhh . . . yeah, see? I have a pulse," I say, offering my wrist, hoping that it wasn't too weird a thing to do. Did mortal kids know where human pulses were?

"Yup, checks out," Luis says, reaching out to touch my wrist. "Unless he's projecting warmth from beyond the ethereal plane. You know, how ghosts like to connect to our—"

"Forget that!" Shoshana says with an accusatory tone, pointing at me. "You pranked us!"

"Uh...," I say, taken aback. "You mean the note? That wasn't a prank. I saw that note asking for a name, and I thought, well, I have a good name. But... why're you trying to make a ghost appear?" I did not want to let on that I'd been eavesdropping on them.

"It's a very important mission," Shoshana says.

"*Secret* mission," Luis hisses at her.

"*Most* secret," Shoshana agrees.

I look between them, waiting for someone to elaborate.

"And that secret mission is...?" I ask, cringing a little. Maybe if I feed them some lines. "It's for something real dangerous, right? You wanted a ghost, so you need someone to help you that can't die. Well, I can't die—" I cut myself off and wince at my fumble.

"... easily," I add.

Thankfully, mortal kids must think they are immortal too, because neither Shoshana nor Luis react to my claims of being death-proof. Instead, Shoshana's face lights up.

"You spied on us!" she says.

"Sorry," I apologize.

"And we didn't notice," Luis says, in a tone that I immediately recognize as not being angry or accusatory, but full of awe.

"And you weren't even far away," Shoshana goes on. "You came out from behind that tombstone! Like, that's pretty high-level sneaking."

"How'd you do it?" Luis asks.

"... Sneakily?" I answer.

"No, give us some deets," Luis says. "We need details."

"Okay," I say, and point to the trees. My hand drops a little bit. Shoot. I was just about to give away where our house is! "Uhh . . ." *Come on, think, Rossi!* Why else would I be coming out of the woods? "I was uhhh . . . collecting rocks! To paint! You know how people paint rocks and hide them around Wonderwood Park? Yeah, I was going to do that. And there's a lot of river rocks. In the forest. In the dark. Phew, okay, so I was in there, and I heard someone shout my name, I guess that was you . . . and then I snuck over to that tombstone, then that one. And then I crossed the road and then—"

"You crossed the road?" Shoshana asks.

"And you had to do it fast enough for us not to see you!" Luis says.

"I'm wearing a lot of black," I hurry to say. Did I just give away how un-mortal-like I am?

"We didn't hear you either," Shoshana says.

I start feeling all itchy everywhere, like my skin wants to get out of here as bad as I do. "I'm light on my feet?"

"Those are boots." Luis points to my feet, impressed. "And when you crossed the street, where did you hide?"

"There," I say, pointing to a tombstone.

"*That* tombstone?" Luis asks, pointing to the grave marker as if really wanting to make sure. "There's no way. I should have seen you! Or at least heard you."

I pick at the loose threads of my hoodie. Shoshana and Luis exchange glances.

"Maybe . . . ," Shoshana says. "Maybe he *can* help us."

"You mean it?" I ask, standing straighter.

"You'll have to prove you're serious about helping us first," Luis says.

"Okay!" I say. "What do I need to do?"

"Pass our spy test," Luis says.

"You have a spy test?" I ask.

"Yes, it's very technical," Luis says. "If you want to be our spy, you need to prove that you'll be good at . . . hiding. And if we can't find you, you pass."

"Oh," I say. "You mean hide-and-seek?"

"No, it's not a game," Luis says. "It's a very serious spy test."

"But you want me to hide so good that you can't find me?" I ask. "And you're going to look for me, so that's basically hide-and-seek."

"Dude . . ." Luis shakes his head, disappointed. "Shoshana, you should hide too. Maybe we can test how good Adam can find you after I find him? That's, like, a spy skill, right?"

I nod, clenching my teeth to keep myself from biting my lip. I've seen movies with mortals in them. They are definitely nowhere near vampire-level at doing stuff. But how am I supposed to know what would impress Shoshana and Luis? There is a very fine line between "impress the two kids you want to help" and "tip them off that you're not one hundred percent like them," and I have no idea where that line gets drawn.

I look around the cemetery for the best hiding spot. It's not too hard. There are grave markers everywhere, with faded fake flower arrangements dotting the grounds. Pines rise up beyond the tombstones like the walls of a fortress.

"No, that's out of bounds," Shoshana says, following my gaze to the forest.

"*Okay*," I say. "Though if I needed to hide in real life? The first place I'd go is—"

"You hide in the forest," Luis says. "And you're going to keep on hiding cuz no one's coming to find you."

"Fine."

"You better hurry up because once he gets to fifty, he's looking for you," Shoshana says.

I don't wait to get told again. I sprint as slow-as-a-mortal as I can, nearly spinning out as I round a corner. I find a wide tombstone to hide behind, way closer to where the tree line is. Just in case I need a quick getaway. Shoshana comes running up a half a minute later, out of breath.

"How'd you run like that?" she asks, scooching next to me in my hiding spot.

"Like what?" I ask, hoping if I sound naive enough, she'll forget that she inadvertently told me I'd failed at guessing where the line between mortal-speed and vampire-speed gets drawn.

"Like a ghost," Shoshana whispers.

"I'm not a ghost," I mutter. "Shove me or something. I'm very solid."

Shoshana grimaces for a moment and then pushes me with her hand. Her touch is quick, and she moves her hand away even faster. "Yeah . . . but then—"

"THIRTY-EIGHT! THIRTY-NINE!" Luis calls out loudly.

"We can't both fit behind this," Shoshana whispers. "Hurry! Find another spot. You're faster than me."

"But I'm supposed to find you next. How—"

"We'll both find a new spot."

"FORTY-FOUR!"

I jump to my feet and scan the cemetery, quickly finding the next best hiding spot. I hate this. I either run at vampire-speed and hide really fast, with Shoshana probably watching me, or I mess up the spy test. And if I can't help these mortals track down the killer?

Running fast like a vampire it is.

I curl up behind a tombstone just as I hear Luis say, "Oh my God, Shoshana, you're the worst at hide-and-seek!"

"It's not my fault! Me and Adam picked the same spot."

Luis just laughs as if that's the funniest thing in the world. "Well, help me find him."

"He can't have gotten too far. We were literally just right here."

I gulp. I'm now on the complete other side of the cemetery. I'm going to need to sneak closer. It takes all my vampire stealth to not get spotted by the two kids looking for me as I weave my way between the headstones, ducking and sneaking and rolling, until I find a new spot. Luis spots me the next instant.

"How did you make it *way* over here?" Luis says, his voice full of awe. "I don't even think the Flash runs that fast."

"Who?" I ask.

"It doesn't matter," Luis says. "Bet you could win a lot of races running like that. You ever think of doing cross-country?"

Shoshana crosses her arms over her chest. "I thought you wanted a spy, Luis, not a sports guy."

"A 'sports guy,'" Luis says flatly. "You mean an athlete?"

"An athlete is still not a spy," Shoshana says.

"He could be both!" Luis argues. "Like James Bond. James Bond is a spy *and* an athlete."

"He's also not real."

No, no, no. They can't start thinking of things that aren't real! Because when it comes to mortals? Vampires have been gone for so long that we might as well not be "real." I need to stop them from making that connection, and fast.

Quick, think of something mortals do. Something real, something real, something real.

"I think I need to . . . ," I say, thinking hard. "Uhh . . ." I take in a deep breath and smell their blood again. "Eat! I need to eat. But like, the food that you . . . regular food! No . . . umm . . ." This is getting way too awkward. "I'm getting kind of hungry."

"I have some chocolate," Luis says, reaching into his pocket and pulling out a little bag of M&M's. The wrapper is covered with tiny purple bats. I grimace. Everyone always thinks vampires turn into bats (we can't). And seeing a "vampire myth" while I'm trying to *prevent* these mortal kids from realizing I'm a vampire? I recoil a little.

"Still from Halloween," Luis admits with a shrug. "Your family do Halloween?"

"Oh, yeah," I say, grimacing and lying through my teeth. "It's the best, pretending to be—"

"The trick is," Luis goes on. "Before you get home, you have to load all your pockets with candy. That way, when your parents confiscate the bag, going all, *candy is a treat, you can't have it all the time*, you have your own stash."

"But . . . it's January now?" I question skeptically at the candy he rattles in his hand.

"He's got a bissel of it everywhere," Shoshana whispers.

I take the candy.

I have never eaten chocolate before. Mom said we can't eat anything except for blood, but what if that was just some kind of weird Mom thing? I've never tried anything else. But also, it isn't like I've ever felt hungry for mortal food either. What's there to lose?

I rip open the wrapping, scattering half the pan-coated chocolate disks all across the ground. I apologize—though to who, I don't know. Luis? The wasted M&M's? I am so nervous.

I clamp my lips together so I don't accidentally reveal my fangs and I pull my scarf down. Luis and Shoshana just look at me. I smash my hand, full of M&M's, against my closed lips and, using my hand as cover, very sloppily open my mouth. It makes a weird, wet, smacky sound as I try to get them all into my mouth before I can risk taking my hand away.

The hardest part is controlling my face. It is so *disgusting*. It probably tastes like what farts smell like. Immediately, my stomach starts churning.

I double over and spit them out without so much as dwelling on how weird I'm going to look.

"You should've eaten these in October," I say, gagging.

"Wow," Luis says. "I don't think I hurl like that until I've eaten at least a hundred—"

A shrill, loud buzzing from Shoshana's wrist interrupts him and my hands go up to cover my ears. They both give me a look and I wince at my vampire sensitivity, giving me away again.

"Alarm," Shoshana explains to me. "Lets us know when we got to get out of here."

"Why?" I ask, pulling my scarf back up over my face. "But we just got started?"

"Luis's dad always comes by here to—" Shoshana starts before Luis cuts her off.

"Do nothing!" Luis shouts over her. And then he lowers his voice to a normal level. "He's not doing anything or checking on anyone. Seriously, maybe you need to take a spy test, Shoshana."

"It's cool," I say, trying to hold back a laugh. Mortal kids must think they're going to die every second to be so secretive. "My moms don't know I'm sneaking out either."

Luis grins. "See? Perfect spy. Case closed."

"Just wait, what?" I ask. "But . . . I didn't prove I could do *any* spy stuff."

"Are you kidding? You did like a million times over," Luis says. "You're in." He offers his hand to shake. "Luis Espinosa."

Shoshana copies him. "Shoshana Fridman."

I shake both their hands at the same time, which gets me two raised sets of eyebrows. I grin back awkwardly, hoping they still just mistake me as a weirdo and not a never-been-around-mortals vampire kid. "Adam Rossi."

"Same time tomorrow?" Shoshana asks.

"Definitely," I answer. Though hopefully I can brush up on how to act more mortal before then.

9

VICTOR

The door creaks open and I let out an aggravated sigh. Alright. When I get a moment alone with Adam, I need to teach him how to *not* give off one-hundred-percent-guilty vibes, especially after *specifically* asking me to cover for him. He pushes the back door open slowly and looks around before stepping inside. He might as well be wearing a ski mask because he's acting just like a cartoon burglar.

The family is sitting around the table staring back at him.

"Sorry," he starts to say.

"Adam! You can't keep disappearing like this!" Mama says, jumping up to give him a shaky hug. "What were you doing out there?"

I can tell from Adam's wide eyes that he didn't even bother to come up with a cover story for if he got caught.

"I was looking for rocks!" he blurts out.

"Rocks?" Mama holds him out at arm's length, looking him in the eyes with so much confusion in hers.

"Yeah, you know, painted rocks, Mama," I say. I mean, Adam *did* ask me to cover for him. "I asked him to find some rocks to paint. We were thinking we could go to Wonderwood Park one of these days when you're not working and hide them like we used to."

Adam looks down suddenly at his hands, empty of rocks, and I groan.

"You left them all outside, right?" I ask Adam. "So we can spray them all with the hose and not bring mud in the house."

"Oh . . . yeah," Adam says. "Yup, that's what I did."

Mama bought it, which is a miracle in and of itself, but Sung narrows their eyes and shoots us both suspicious glares.

"Okay . . . okay, let me know when you're finished painting them," Mama says. "One of these nights coming up, we can all—"

"School!" Sung interjects.

"—most of us can go hide them," Mama says. "And yes, I'm going too," she says to my scoff. "You cannot visit mortal parks alone! Even if they close at sundown, you never know who might be there." She takes a deep breath. "But Adam, ya'allah, you scared us."

"Yes, we were all very scared," I say flatly, hoping that Adam would know to translate "scared" to "annoyed you snuck out without including me *again* after promising me you wouldn't."

"But now, we can finally begin," Mama finishes.

"We can finally begin" should never be said when a family of vampires is about to start putting together a jigsaw puzzle, but we're the most boring vampire family in existence and that is, in fact, what we're about to begin.

Mama doesn't ask any more questions about Adam's absence as he joins us at the table. Sung shoots Adam another glance but then returns their gaze to the puzzle pieces they're right-side-upping at nearly-the-speed-of-sound rapidness. Mom can't ask questions because she's at work and not here. I fold my arms across my chest, but I don't ask any questions either. I want to. Adam's taken off *twice* now. What is *up* with him?

But if he isn't ready to share, I'm not going to pry.

That's what good brothers do, right? Even if it hurts not to be let in.

Adam pulls his chair out nervously, kicking the Amazon delivery box our family's newest puzzle came in aside with his feet.

"Why do you suddenly think I'm going to do all your chores for you, Victor?" Adam mutters as he sits down.

"It's a box?" I ask.

"Breaking down boxes for the recyclables bin is a chore," Adam says.

I grit my teeth but don't say anything. I guess he's grown out of making spooky masks from boxes, like, overnight, just like he's outgrown hanging out with me.

"Let me set the timer," Mama says as she cues up the clock on her phone, a row of dots filling her screen.

"Can we instead take a moment to realize how pathetic this is?" I grumble, replacing my annoyance with Adam with annoyance for jigsaw puzzles. "We're only playing this game because, instead of learning stuff we might actually use one day, we're mindlessly passing the time like we have nothing better to do."

"This is not 'nothing'!" Mama says with a fake offended gasp, because she never takes my complaints seriously. "We might beat our record."

Mama is really good—and I mean like, really good even for a vampire—at noticing the smallest details. That's why she works with the astronomy department at the local university; she can catch the tiniest anomaly. A speck of a light that wasn't in the sky the night before. The most miniscule change in how a pulsar is pulsing.

Or seeing how a thousand different jigsaw puzzle pieces can fit together in mere seconds.

Cool vampire skill absolutely wasted on the most pointless thing.

"*Right* . . . ," I say. "And this is going to help us become better vampires by . . . ?"

"Coming together as a family," Sung says. "A bonded coven is a strong coven, and—"

"We're bonded," I interrupt them. "Who else could I possibly be bonding with? We don't know anyone else with whom *to* bond."

"Says the guy who doesn't even remember everyone in our family," Adam says under his breath.

"Hard to bond with people who *aren't here*," I hiss back, stressing those last two words. He doesn't answer me. Fine—I hope that means my message got through to him. For a kid who really prides himself on knowing all our siblings, he sure doesn't like spending time with the one right in front of him.

I can't wait until it finally dawns on Adam. See, I've always known stuff was temporary here. So many vampires coming and going? I got the hint early. Mom and Mama might be trying to make us feel like we're a real family, but in the end, it's all a ruse. One that no amount of wholesome puzzle nights can disguise. One day, we're going to leave and have to make our own way in the world. And I always thought that no matter what happens with the bigger family, me and Adam would stick together. Forever. Like we're real brothers.

But I guess not.

"*As* I was saying," Sung says, scowling a bit at me. "There's more to this than just doing the puzzle."

I give my sibling an unconvinced look. "Look, I know 'pretend we're a normal mortal family' when I see it."

"Are you so sure?" Sung asks.

"It's. A. Puzzle."

"But you forget, Victor! We are a vampire family!" Mama says. "If we truly try to work together, so many things can happen. We can pick up on each other's thoughts. Feelings. Without even needing to speak a word, we can know what each one of us is going to do. A thousand-piece puzzle like this? It would take mortals hours and hours. But for us? It's more than being fast—it's about seeing connections."

"You're saying if we're bonded and we do this puzzle...," Adam says, looking at all the pieces, his eyebrows scrunched together in concentration. "I would know what pieces someone else was reaching for?"

"Like we're one person, in one body," Sung grins. "Completely synchronized with each other."

I shrug, but my eyebrows raise in surprise. They pulled a fast one on me, but I wasn't about to complain. "Okay... that actually sounds kind of cool."

"Ah, that's good, because we only do cool things in this house," Mama says.

"With a bunny puzzle," I say, gesturing at the box that's covered in hundreds of fluffy baby rabbits, but Mama only laughs in her teasing way.

"Alright, we ready, then?" Mama asks, looking around the table. "Take a good look at this picture," she says, holding up the box.

Adam finally unwraps the scarf from around his neck and pulls his sleeves up. He's getting into it big-time. I crack my knuckles and wiggle my fingers.

"Hiya bina!" Mama says, and we start putting the puzzle together.

I give it my all. I need to. If Mama and Mom and even Sung have been trying to teach us vampire stuff all along? I need to show them how much it means to me, how much work I'm willing to put in to be the best vampire I can be.

"Oh, Victor! You got the spirit!" Mama laughs. I try to grin at the compliment.

It's just like they said. I can sense Sung's arm is about to move before they reach out to grab a piece. I can feel the flick of Mama's wrist as she secures two pieces together. I tap into that and don't let go. I don't reach out for pieces I can sense someone else's eyes on, and I can feel almost soft, unconscious pushes to pick up pieces that help me work on my own little corner. Every piece I look at, I can imagine exactly where it's supposed to go based on the image on the puzzle's box—the one I only glanced at for a moment. In some really weird way, I suddenly feel like I've got six extra arms and six extra eyes, but it feels so natural. So *right*.

Everything feels connected. Except for Adam.

He's got a piece in his hands. I can tell with a sideways glance where its place is. *The open spot is right there.* I try to send a mental message to Adam, except his eyes are scanning all over the other empty spots in the puzzle. Didn't he look at the box? Make a mental map of where everything was supposed to go?

I stare right at the empty spot. *Right. There.* But his eyes keep skipping over it. Yeah, well, what did I expect? He can't hear me. Maybe Mama was making that stuff up. It's easier to imagine that she'd lie to me to get me more interested in putting a puzzle together than the alternative. That me and Adam really aren't bonded.

It goes right there. Right in front of me.

And then I get why Adam can't find its spot. He's trying not to look in my direction.

I've had enough. I snatch the piece right out of Adam's hand. He yelps in angry surprise, but I ignore him as I snap the piece into the spot where it belongs. Sung pushes a few more pieces together, but I've lost my concentration. I don't have a link. I can't tell what anyone is going to do anymore.

They finish the puzzle without any more of my help.

Mama taps her phone to stop her timer and raises a fist in celebration. "We did it! Under fifteen minutes!"

I glance down at the collage of bunnies in front of me. Did no one even notice I'd lost our connection? "Is that a good time?"

"You don't even know," Sung says, looking at their own phone. "The best mortal time doing a thousand-piece puzzle is . . . guess?"

"More than fifteen minutes," I say.

"Two and a half *hours*," Sung says.

I laugh. Take that, mortals.

"Well, should we turn it over?" I ask, eager for more vampire training. "We could try doing the puzzle without the picture?"

"Why, so you can hog all the glory?" Adam asks.

"*What?*"

"You took that piece from me!" he argues. "Just so you could put more of the puzzle together than me."

"*You're* the one who wasn't paying attention," I say. "I was trying to tell you where the piece was supposed to go, but you wouldn't—"

The house phone rings and everyone goes quiet.

Yes, we have a landline phone. And even worse? It's one of those ancient plastic ones that is attached to the wall with a long spirally cord. It's the most insulting "you don't need a cell phone" excuse possible. Sung gets up to answer it.

"Yeoboseyo," Sung says into the phone. Which would confuse anyone who isn't Korean, but I guess some habits— like what you say when you answer a telephone—are hard to break.

"Hey, it's Jess!" Sung says to the rest of us. Adam scrambles out of his chair.

"Wait, who's Jess?" I ask no one, since I suddenly find myself at an empty table.

The phone is so old that there's no speakerphone on it, so Mama, Adam, and Sung all huddle around, listening to the receiver. Even with sensitive vampire hearing, I hear nothing from the mystery caller that everyone seems to know.

Except me.

I glance at my only company, the bunny puzzle, and I want nothing more than to crumple it back into its one thousand individual pieces, shove them all into the box, and never look at the thing again. I might as well—if I leave it on the table, Adam'll probably take it as some kind of an insult.

I fracture the picture, but that's all I get to do.

The door to the garage bursts open.

Everyone jumps. Mom's home, but this is the least characteristic entrance she's ever made. I stare at her, as if she might be wearing an explanation. My nose crinkles in confusion. Everything is off. The next beat, I realize something has burst into the house with her, filling the air with sparks and energy and . . .

I feel a tug deep inside my chest. I don't know how I know it, but I know exactly what Mom brought home with her.

It's young blood.

10

ADAM

hh . . . we'll call you back," Sung says into the phone before hanging up.

I don't blame them. I'm in shock too.

The back of my neck tingles. Something electrifies the air. Then I catch it, a smell I'd learned to recognize only a few hours earlier. The smell can only mean one thing.

Mom has finally brought home young blood.

My chest tightens. I want to lunge forward and slurp up every last drop. I'd never realized just how hungry I've always been until that moment but . . . I hold back. I made friends with two mortal kids. Kids whose blood this could've been.

I tremble as I wonder how Mom got this much blood.

"Where'd this come from?" I ask, my voice barely louder than a whisper.

"There was another murder tonight," Mom says.

"Another one?!" I ask.

"A young girl," Mom goes on. "There was nothing anyone could do. We tried to help but . . ."

I know what my mom wants to say.

Whoever's blood she has brought home, it's a life she couldn't save. And even if that blood smell in the air is making me drool, I know Mom would have rather it still be pumping in the person she got it from.

And it's not like Mom could have bit whoever it was. A kid dying in a busy hospital? With parents or guardians nearby? Hospital technicians? It isn't as simple as biting someone. Mom couldn't whisk that kid away to live a new life when there were so many people around. They'd think she was a kidnapper, and our family's cover would be blown.

Not like when I had been bitten.

"I . . . don't know, Mom, I'm not sure I'm . . ." I really don't want to end that sentence. What am I going to say? I'm not hungry? Everyone would know I'm lying. And what if they asked why I lost my appetite?

"I know it's a lot," Mom says. "You've never had young blood like this. There's a reason I've never brought it home," Mom says, and locks eyes with Victor. "It's intense. But we can't let blood that was lost like *this* go to waste."

I swallow back my guilt. Mom's right. There's nothing we can do about that kid now. We're vampires—we might as well drink it.

Victor looks down at the floor, but I can see him grinning. I can't blame him. Mom had listened to him when he complained about us only ever drinking old-people blood. That is the highest compliment a kid can get from their mom.

"You have to be home before the sun rises, of course," Mom says. "You'll . . . lose a bit of control, so don't wander too far. You'll feel quite unlike yourselves. Me and Samira, we'll . . . make sure you can't get into too much trouble."

"Like biting someone?" Victor asks.

"Oh, goodness, no." Mom nearly laughs but doesn't. "You're going to be perfectly satisfied with this. In fact, I won't need to bring home blood for a few days, but you might get a bit carried away with your . . . abilities. You might try to throw a car or something."

"*Cool.*"

"Oh, Beatrice, you're going to have to watch out for this one," Mama says.

"Parent chaperone on your first time with young blood. Good going, doofus," Sung teases.

"Fine, fine, no car throwing." Victor holds up his hands like he's surrendering. "And what are you going to do? Speed-read?"

"Speed-type," Sung corrects.

"Watch out," Victor says, with a grin. "You type too hard and you're going to break your keyboard."

Sung laughs.

At least Sung and Victor are excited. They're playfully shoving each other out of the way as they try to be the first to get coffee mugs out of the cupboard. I can't say I'm even close to their enthusiasm. If young blood is a roller coaster, I'm the person pressing my feet into the bottom of the car at the top of the hill. Victor, on the other hand? He looks ready for the plunge. He's pulling on his old, beat-up Converse sneakers and hands me my white Adidas Superstars. What does he plan to do that we need gym shoes for?

Mom wasn't kidding when she said she had a lot of blood. She hasn't smuggled it home in the normal little plastic tubes but in a bag.

And when Mom cuts the bag open? I need to lick my lips. I drool at the smell.

"Wow," I whisper under my breath.

Mom pours it out carefully, and the blood sloshes in the cups. They are full. Full cups! Victor has picked one out for me—a sparkly golden one that says "RISE AND SHINE!" on it. The cursive font perfectly matches the way the blood swirls in the mug. I don't even mind that I can feel the chill through the porcelain. I'm going to drink a whole cup!

Once everyone has a full mug, we raise our glasses and *drink*.

The blood is a billion miniature explosions on my lips. It tingles down my throat. It's absolutely nothing like the blood we usually drink. Everything inside me opens up, shakes off the dust, stretches. My heart grows larger. It's burning inside my chest, and the blood rushes everywhere, filling me up with magic, with *life*.

It *is* life. I am coming alive.

I'm outside before I realize I made that choice. I run. I have to. The young blood put a stallion in my chest, something straining against my body, pulling me forward. My feet fly over the ground. Silent, swift. Faster than a train.

With a leap, I'm halfway up a tree.

"Hey, catch me if you can!"

Victor is way up in the boughs ahead of me, but he looks different. I can see the force of life coming off of him. It's in my brother's eyes. They are red—blood red, and giving off a soft glow. Victor's teeth shine in the moonlight.

I leap after him, my feet in sync with my racing heart. It's pumping faster, pulling me further. I reach a hand out, but Victor rolls easily out of the way. He jumps up, launching himself into the branches high above.

I wheel in the air, changing direction, and kick off another trunk. I miss Victor again by inches. He's jumping from trunk to trunk, and I follow, always moments too slow. I catch nothing but air each time.

Gravity grows weaker as we grow stronger. I launch myself up the tree after Victor changes tactics and runs up the side of a fir. I chase. I see the bottoms of Victor's sneakers, slamming into the tree trunk, shaking bits of bark off with each step as he runs up into the sky. My pulse pounds in my ears, nearly making me deaf to the sound of my laughter.

I jump up, tumbling in the air, but Victor drops, patting me on the head as he falls. Fifty feet down, he lands on the forest floor as easily as if he'd only leapt from our top bunk. I fall after him, shooting through branches as though they are as weak as straw. Victor hurls himself the opposite way before I can catch him. I hit the ground running.

The smile Victor wears is one I've never seen on his face before.

"Well, come on!" Victor calls after me, and we are off again. Jumping over the road, running alongside the asphalt, laughing as the sound of wheels screeching echoes deep into the chambers of our lungs, the reverberation in my chest pumping my heart faster as we vanish once more into the night.

The trees standing in our way become sparse. We are chasing each other over buildings now, the concrete jungle, neon lights reflecting in our eyes. Sparking loud and electric, mimicking the crackling energy in my veins.

Cars race by beneath us and people walk from bar to bar and shop to shop but no one looks up. If they did, they would see nothing but shadows moving quietly in the night, the only sound an echoing laughter bouncing off concrete walls and into the starry sky.

The buildings come to an end and we make our last leap. We're at the Port of Olympia, squatting on the roof of the tall, wooden observation tower. Silence settles over the harbor. The water is calm, so there isn't even the sound of waves lapping up against the shore, against the boats.

I don't like it. I feel too exposed. The sky feels too big. Puget Sound stretches out in front of us, inky and black and still. The hills on the opposite banks are too far away, rising up like the sides of a bowl. Behind us, the great dome of the Capitol Building glows. And in front of us? The port's crane stands alone, tall and bright—because for whatever reason mortals like to put giant spotlights on things so they can see them when it's nighttime. A red flashing light on the very end of the crane's boom arm grabs my attention.

Victor follows my gaze.

"Bet you that's a hundred feet tall," Victor says.

"Probably," I say.

"Bet I could get there before you."

Victor doesn't wait for an answer. He jumps down from the observation tower and runs through the waterfront park. I grin and take off after him. I sprint through the park in seconds and clear the barbed-wire-topped fence surrounding the port as easily as my brother.

I run as fast as I can. The crane is surrounded by wide-open space in every direction: no cars, no lumber. I still hate the exposure, but I have to beat Victor. The concrete pounds under my feet and shakes my bones.

Victor is still in the lead. Of course, he's given himself a head start, the cheater. He throws himself at the building at the foot of the crane, scrambling from ledge to ledge straight up its towering side.

I'm not giving up so easily. I spot a lamppost next to the hook dangling from the crane's boom arm. I scale the post easily. The hook swings wide with my weight when I jump onto it, but I don't wait for it to settle down before I begin climbing the chain. Hand over hand over hand. The red light is right above me.

Victor is running up along the skeletal framework of the crane's boom arm. He slows as he gets to the top, a smirk on his face.

"I won," I announce. I've got my right foot planted on top of the red light.

Victor plants his feet on the beam too. For one wild moment, I wonder if we are going to wrestle for the prize, but no—my brother claps a hand on my shoulder.

"Hey, good for you," he says. And he's serious—not a note of sarcasm. My cheeks warm in a way that has nothing to do with the blood I drank.

I don't know what to say, and the longer I think of something that could match Victor, the more I like the silence settling between us. I look up at the night sky. The moon reflects brightly in Victor's eyes. I scan the stars for Gemini.

"We're going to live forever."

I'm surprised to hear Victor say that. It's not like it really *needs* to be said—we both know. But the way he says it. Like it finally clicked. That, I can relate to.

"Yeah."

"It can be like tonight for the rest of our lives."

I don't want anything else.

The only problem is, I can't stand still. My skin tingles, my heart races, the energy of young blood eggs me on. I bounce on the heels of my feet, ready for the next race.

I hear some mumbled confusion far below us. "Is someone up there?" Victor and I only grin as we turn and run to the other end of the crane, diving off the end of the boom arm, silently vanishing into the night once again. We land lightly on the concrete below, taking off at lightning speeds, leaping up onto roofs without so much as stirring the wind.

The sky is melting from black to deep navy.

"Come on!" I call. "Race you home!"

"Oh, I get it," Victor teases back. "You win *one* race and now you're Mr. Challenges."

We are tearing through the trees again, flinging ourselves over the road and back into the darkness of the woods. Weaving between limbs. Running so fast we could be flying.

Victor is always right in front of me, urging me on, laughing and disappearing and appearing again.

A car's wheels screech underneath us as we leap over College Street. We laugh and wonder what the driver saw— our red, glowing-with-young-blood eyes? Or just shadows? Fleeing shadows. Running until the dawn breaks.

The night can't end. Even if I can see the sky starting to lighten, the edge of the horizon warming to a yellow. The night can't end. Not yet. I'm not ready.

I can outrace the dawn. I can run forever if I have to. I will—my feet always running, taunting the sunrise, always a few steps ahead. The sun will be powerless to stop me. I'll—

I stop.

No. I won't outrace the sun. I'll *withstand* the sun. I'll stay up . . . I'll climb to the highest branches of the tallest fir tree. I'll watch the sun come over the horizon. I can't remember ever seeing its rays catching in my eyes. Warming my skin. I have no memory of it. But today . . . today, I will wake the dawn.

"Easy now, you're not as invincible as you think," Mom's voice shakes me out of my thoughts.

Where she'd come from, and how she'd found me, I don't know. And all it takes is a gentle tug to bring me back down. Stepping back from my place on top of the world. To bow my head under the weight of the darkness, to slip back under the shadows, like a blanket smothering out the promise of dawn.

Before I know it, I'm home.

I could have broken my face in two for how wide I yawn.

"And that's the last one back in the nest."

"Me?"

"Samira! I found him!" Mom calls out.

My mind gets fuzzy. My eyes are heavy. My arms feel like they are covered in weights. My legs are stiff.

Did I hear that right? I was the last one out? I outlasted Victor?

Young blood did that to me.

I yawn again and collapse onto the couch. I can hear my parents talking, but it's a meaningless murmuring. Someone says something to me, but my brain can't make the sounds into words. It comes at me like white noise, a lullaby in my overloaded mind. I fall asleep.

11

VICTOR

"Oh, look, here he is," I say.

I am talking way faster than normal. It's the young blood still crackling in my body. Adam is not on my level, and I laugh at the drowsy way he stumbles down the stairs.

"What are you waiting for?" I ask. "The sun's been down for over two hours now."

The TV is off. I'm perched on the back of the couch, while Sung sits on the cushions, in the way a couch is meant to be sat on. I am way too amped up to sit still.

"I thought I fell asleep down here," Adam mumbles.

"You did," I say.

"He brought you up to your bed," Sung says, tossing their head in my direction.

I can't handle any mushy caring-brother stuff right now.

"Hey, Adam, you're in luck," I say. "You're not the only one to break a mug."

"What?" Adam says. He's still waking up.

"In other words, Victor really needs to never try washing dishes after drinking young blood again," Sung says. They hold back a laugh. I can't. Adam's not in on our inside joke, so he just looks really annoyed.

"Victor? Washing dishes?" Adam asks.

"Hey, I couldn't sleep," I say.

That is true. Something about the young blood makes everything in my body feel brand-new. Every second. Running around but never getting tired. Staying up all day but feeling wide awake. It is the best feeling in the world. I'm practically vibrating with energy.

"You couldn't sleep, so you decided to wash dishes?" Adam asks.

"It's not like I could go anywhere. It was the middle of the day," I say. "And . . . I really couldn't sit through a movie."

"So you picked dishes," Adam says, still in sleepy disbelief.

"Mom's going to applaud the effort," Sung says. "The fact that now all the dishes are broken, not so much."

"All of them?" Adam asks.

Maybe I should feel bad about breaking all the cups. Vampires don't have a high need for tableware, and our kitchen reflects that. There's no fridge. No stove. No dishwasher. Just a very small cupboard above a very small sink, full of coffee mugs and wine glasses (for when the moms want to be fancy). We hand-wash all our dishes, but since there's only five of us? It's not like it's a lot of work.

"Okay, so, maybe after the first few broke, I might have seen if I could juggle," I admit with an innocent shrug. "The important thing is none of them went through the window."

"I'm sure Mom will appreciate that," Sung deadpans.

"What time is it?" Adam mumbles, looking up at the big grandfather clock that stands at the foot of the stairs. "Is that right?"

"Where do you have to be?" Sung asks, with a laugh of their own.

Adam answers with another yawn. How can he be tired? We drank the same exact blood. We ran around all night, clear to Olympia and back.

Adam slumps down into the couch next to our sibling and yawns again.

"It's really seven?" Adam asks and rubs his eyes.

"The moms are already at work, if that's what you're wondering," Sung says.

"Yeah, and hopefully there's another murder," I say, giving Adam another quick look. "Doesn't Mom have tomorrow off?"

"*Another* murder?" Adam asks.

"Duh," I say. I don't get what he's all confused about. Out of the three of us, Adam should be the one demanding young blood the loudest.

"You should be good for a few days there, high-speed," Sung says to me. "You nearly drank a full cup."

"And I'm ready for cup number two," I say. I jump off the back of the couch and dart to the kitchen and back, for no real reason other than to move.

"Victor, seriously, chill," Sung says. "There's a gallon of blood inside a person. And a vampire can go a month after eating a whole person."

"*Can*," I stress. "I also *can* drink blood whenever it's available."

Sung sighs. "If you actually paid attention to your math, you'd know that a gallon has sixteen cups in it, so drinking one cup should keep you happy for ..."

Sung pauses to do the math inside their head, but I scowl at the "happy" remark.

"... about two days," Sung says.

"I feel enlightened with this knowledge," I say with a fake-snooty tone to my voice, which I drop to add, "but not happy. I'm just saying it would be nice to stop feeling hungry for once."

"That's going to be a problem you need to work out, Vic," Sung says and stands up. "That's the price we have to pay to stay safe."

Sung gives me a look, but I don't speak. Let them think they've gotten the last word. I only nod when Sung says they are leaving to go study. I don't say anything until I hear their bedroom door close. Another minute, and their headphones will be on, and—

"It's not fair," I say.

"What isn't?" Adam says.

"You heard Sung. *We have to be safe*," I grumble. "And I bet that means we're going to have to wait *two* more days before Mom brings us blood again. And it's probably not even going to matter if there's another murder. Can this guy, like, not get caught until then?"

"You *want* the murders to keep going on?" Adam asks.

And he's shocked, as if I personally had something to do with it.

"How else are we supposed to get young blood again?" I ask.

"We don't!" Adam says. "We just go back to—"

"I am *not* going back to drinking old people blood," I say.

"But you don't care that a young girl died."

I laugh. "No, no I don't. Do you even know what mortals are like?"

"Oh, and you do?" Adam asks. "You see them in movies and you think it makes you know everything."

"And how many mortals do you know?"

Adam scowls and looks away, but of course he doesn't have an answer.

"Not all of them," Adam finally says. "There's got to be good ones too."

"They aren't even good to each other," I say. "We saw that murder. They do that kind of stuff to their own families."

"How would you know what they do to their families?" Adam asks.

I've kept this to myself all my life. My real life. My vampire life. I never wanted Adam to know before, but now it's different. He won't understand any other way.

I take a breath. And when I speak next, I'm not angry anymore.

"You don't remember your mortal parents, do you?" I ask. "Well, I do. You know how I became a vampire?"

I take another deep breath.

"My parents were vampire hunters."

Adam balks.

"Yeah, I know. It's not what everyone's parents do for work. But you know in some countries they still offer bounties on vampire heads so . . . that was their job.

"I was sick," I say. "All I remember from my mortal life is going to hospitals all the time. I had leukemia. And one day, when I was almost four, my parents told me they were taking me to see someone who could make me better.

"We traveled forever, to the middle of nowhere, way above the Arctic Circle. The people in the town didn't like strangers asking about the vampire, but my parents really acted it well. 'Our son is sick. We'd rather have him be a vampire and live than die.'"

I hate remembering that lie. How it felt when I was a kid, to hear it and believe in it, to think that my parents were trying to help me, and then realize it was all made-up. I hate this story so much. I swallow back my nerves and go on.

"They used me as a way to get in," I say. "I still remember what the house was like. Small, and everything inside was all dark, cramped. There was stuff piled up everywhere. And I remember what he looked like.

"He was *ancient*. Like, obviously, he looked young, but he felt old. His eyes were old. Mom says he probably was one of the oldest vampires still alive. He was like Mama, you know, more like a doctor. He believed my parents wanted to help me, and he tried to make me better.

"But my parents expected him to bite me. They figured I was going to die anyway, so if I got turned, they'd get two bounties for the price of one." The joke falls as flatly as my weak laugh. "They didn't change their minds, either, not even when they saw what he could do."

My shoulders are crumpling, caving in. I keep my eyes glued on my hands as I rub my palm with my thumb, because it's easier to pretend I'm just saying this out loud to myself than sharing it with anyone.

"My parents waited until he was absorbed in his work and his defenses were down. They stabbed him in the back while he was hunched over me. They missed his heart, and he fought back. It was all a blur. He didn't have any weapons or anything, and there were two of them fighting him.

"Sometime during the fight"— my voice hitches in my throat, and I wince at how this story unravels me—"the vampire needed blood. The only reason I'm not dead is that he didn't have the time to suck me dry. That vampire took enough of my blood to keep fighting, though.

"He didn't even manage to kill my parents. The best he could do was chase them out of the house. It was daylight, or else maybe he would have followed. I don't know what happened to them. They just left town . . . left me."

I laugh without humor. I don't like the way it sounds. "The last thing some ancient vampire wanted was to take care of a random kid he'd accidentally turned. I bet he would've eaten me if vampires could eat other vampires. Maybe I reminded him of my parents, but he hated me.

I don't know how Mom found out about me, but she did, and she came and rescued me."

I hate that story. I hate telling it. I hate remembering how I felt—unwanted and worthless. But I had to tell it. Adam has to understand what mortals are like, that mortals hurt everything they touch. Even if their lives are momentary, it doesn't make them treasure them more. Like that murder we saw the other night. Mortals don't *have* to kill—they just do.

"But vampires . . ." I take a deep breath. "We'd never do something like that. Hurt our own family? We look out for each other. That's what makes us strong. We always stick by each other, no matter what."

I wait for Adam to react, to understand. But I keep waiting. Staring. Analyzing the expression on Adam's face, looking for some kind of empathy. A breakthrough. Anything. Something's got to be clicking by now.

Finally, after what feels like years, Adam sighs. He doesn't make eye contact or turn to me or anything. He keeps looking out at nothing.

"And that makes murdering mortals right?" Adam asks. "Because you think you're better than them?"

"I'm done," I snap. I turn around and stalk toward the wooden stairs leading up to the second floor. "I can't talk to you when you're being *this* rude."

Adam calls after me, but I can't risk going back to argue with him. I'm angry, but tears are falling down my face. I have to get in my room. Now.

I slam my feet down as hard as I can with each step, hoping to push out some of this anger. Sung must have heard us arguing, because they yell from behind their bedroom door, "YOU TWO REALLY HAVE TO PICK A NEW MOVIE TO WATCH, OKAY?"

I get to our room and slam the door closed so hard it shatters.

12

ADAM

I don't want to stay home. I wouldn't stay even if Victor wasn't in our room. I don't want to be stuck within the same walls as him. I storm out of the house without another word.

The walk through the forest seems so different this time, and it has nothing to do with the fact that it's raining for the first time in two days.

Walking takes *so long*. Only yesterday I was practically flying through the trees. I look up into the boughs, remembering how powerful and unstoppable I'd felt. How much fun Victor and I had when we could simply laugh and be brothers again.

How could Victor possibly be unhappy with that? How could he want something *more*?

I reach the end of the woods, on the edge of the cemetery, and shake it off.

Shoshana and Luis are there, waiting for me.

Victor can't be right about mortals. The proof is right in

front of me—two mortals trying to find a way to stop murders. What's more noble and just than that?

I wrap my scarf around my face again, making sure I cover my mouth and, more specifically, my fangs, and run up to them.

"Hey, we said 'same time.' This is like a billion hours later than we met up yesterday!" Luis says, pushing up the hood of his rain jacket. "I'm wasting my night here. It's a school night. I have to go to bed early and—"

"Hey . . ." Shoshana drops her voice to a whisper. "Maybe it's not his fault he's late."

I don't get why she would whisper. Whispers are just as loud as anything else. I can hear it even over the sound of rain pelleting the black asphalt road that winds through the cemetery. Even as raindrops bubble and *blub* in the muddy puddles.

It clicks. Mortals probably can't hear as well as vampires. Shoshana doesn't realize I can hear her.

"Sorry I'm late," I say. "Though, you know, neither of you have told me what I'm spying for. I can't exactly get gigged for being late if I don't even know what I'm late for."

Luis and Shoshana exchange glances.

"There's a murderer out there, right?" Shoshana says. "Have you heard about it?"

I nod. "Yeah! My family's been talking about it, and . . ." I stop. I remember how we first met, and now I'm one hundred percent confused. "Why were you trying to summon a ghost to stop a murderer?"

"Not stop, spill," Shoshana says. "Like, spill the beans?

Anyway." She waves her hand like she could make her bad joke dissipate in the air. "We raise a ghost who could find the ghosts of all the murder victims. They schmooze, our ghost reports back, and bam! We know who the murderer is!"

"But . . . how is a ghost baby going to tell you anything?" I ask. "A baby can't talk?"

"Thank you," Luis says in relief, like he's grateful someone agrees with him.

"Why not just summon the ghosts of the people who *did* get killed?" I ask.

"THANK YOU!" Luis says.

Shoshana rolls her eyes. "They're in the funeral home. I'm not breaking in there to do a séance over their very real, very dead bodies. And it *needs* to be a ghost, because if we can just get a ghost to talk to the murder victims' ghosts, we can figure out who the murderer is and tell the police! But that doesn't matter now, does it? We have no ghosts."

"That's all you had planned?" I ask, and then I narrow my eyes. They had asked me to be a spy for them. "Just wait . . . you're not planning to kill me and make *me* the ghost?"

Luis laughs so much I realize it must have sounded like I was teasing her.

"Maybe we should forget it," Shoshana says. "Adam's right. There's no ghost, so there's no plan. We've got bupkis."

"I told you—I've come up with a new plan!" Luis says.

"You want us to spy on the murderer, I know," Shoshana says flatly. "Need I remind you that we are dealing with a person who *kills* people, and I am not interested in getting murdered?" Though she doesn't sound scared at the idea—just, like, mildly annoyed. Mortals really are wild.

"But we can't just give up! What kind of hero quits in the face of odds like this?" Luis says, then tilts his head and cringes, his eyes widening as he lists the odds. "Sure, we don't know who it is, or where he'll strike next, or even if he's a 'he' or if he's still in Lacey. But! We can't give up." Luis elbows me. "Adam agrees with me."

I nod quickly.

"I'm more worried about the odds of us dying," Shoshana adds.

"It'll be *fine*. Look," Luis says. "My dad says serial killers follow patterns. And so far, all the victims are people from like, fifteen to forty years old—"

"Fifteen is cutting it a *little* close, don't you think?" Shoshana asks.

"—*and* they've all been alone," Luis continues. "So we just need to stick together."

"*All*? How many murders have there been—" I start to say.

"Four," Luis answers quickly. "First two were in Olympia. And now they're happening here in Lacey."

"And what if the murderer gets desperate?" Shoshana asks. "You really want to depend on a murderer following 'serial killer rules' when, like, he doesn't even obey the law?"

"So self-centered, Shoshana," Luis says haughtily. "When we stand the chance of keeping others from dying!"

"Please?" I ask Shoshana, even though I can't exactly relate to her unease. It's hard to be scared about possibly getting killed when I heal super-fast. "We're trying to save people. I don't want anyone to die. And that's got to be worth the risk, right?"

Shoshana mutters. "For whoever saves one life, it's as if they saved the whole world."

"Ooh, nice quote," I say.

Luis nods. "Which, I might add, totally backs me up."

"Yeah . . . I know," Shoshana says flatly. "That's why I said it. I'm agreeing with you."

"What's that from?" I ask.

"The Talmud," Shoshana says, and then goes on, probably because she notices my confused face. "It's a Jewish book of—"

"Oh, you're Jewish?" I ask. "I am too! I think . . ."

"You . . . think?" Shoshana asks.

"Yeah, I'm adopted, but my mom told me that my parents got killed in this explosion at a synagogue and—"

"Just wait, *you* are a survivor of the Temple Beth Hatfiloh explosion?" Shoshana asks, cocking an eyebrow. "But they accounted for everyone, dead and alive. Well, there's that one baby that—"

Even though I'll live forever, I instantly know what it feels like to have a heart attack. My heart just stops beating altogether. Why did I have to say something? I had no idea that attack was a well-known thing, but duh, of course I should have known that! Olympia is a small city, and—

"You and your dead babies," Luis laughs, coming to my rescue completely by accident. "We have a murderer to stop here."

"Right!" I say, snapping back to the mission with more happiness than required. "Stopping a murderer."

I nod encouragingly at Shoshana, hoping that she'll just forget what I said, that I totally gave myself away.

"If only you could get your dad to give you better details," Shoshana says, dropping the subject. I cheer silently. "We'd have so much more to work with and—"

"¡Chitón!" Luis hisses.

"Why does your dad know about the murders?" I ask.

Luis shoots Shoshana a dirty look, as if she's done something hideous. A prickle of uncertainty runs up my spine.

"What are y'all up to?"

Someone new emerges from the fog and walks up to us. Whatever is coming off this new person feels like a punch in the nose. If I could smell the young blood in Luis and Shoshana, then this new person took that and ran with it. It isn't just life. It isn't just youth. The smell is somehow exactly that while being more than that. It's young, but like . . . double young.

The girl steps close enough that I can see her face. I can tell immediately that she and Luis are related. She has the same warm skin tone, and the brown eyes behind her glasses crinkle the same way Luis's do when she narrows them. She has bangs, and the rest of her long, brown hair is pulled up on top in a ponytail.

Trying to focus on her doesn't distract me for long, not like it did with Luis and Shoshana. My brain buzzes with whatever is in the air. And then it hits me—she's bleeding. There's a cut on her hand. I've never smelled blood like this—only blood that is hours old, cold, or filled with anti-coagulants. But . . . this? Fresh blood. Bleeding right out of a mortal body as I'm standing here?!

I don't want to freak the new girl out but my arms are suddenly really itchy. I know it's a risk, but I pull down my scarf. I need to breathe. It is getting harder and harder to keep my feet planted in one place.

"Does Dad know you're out for a walk in the middle of the rain?" Luis asks.

The girl, who I realize must be Luis's sister, rolls her eyes.

"You're the one playing in a cemetery and you want to talk?" she asks.

"You're like, in a cemetery right now?" Luis points out.

"Only temporarily. This is the quickest way to school."

"*School?* What kind of nerd breaks into school after—"

"It's open." She walks past us with a little wave of her hand. Luis watches her go, and after a moment calls after her, "You know there's a murderer out there!"

"It's raining out, remember?" she calls back. I cock my head a bit at the mention of the rain. "Besides, I left my project at school."

"You have to go get it right now?" Luis shouts.

She doesn't answer.

What did rain have to do with getting murdered? I don't bring it up. What if that's, like, common mortal knowledge? No murders can happen during precipitation . . . or something.

"She's strange," I say, not knowing how to put it into words that would make sense, and then I hurriedly tie my scarf back around my mouth. Where is my head? I can't be talking and opening my mouth and revealing my fangs.

"Good job using your vocabulary, Captain Obvious," Luis says. "She's a teenager. She's been like this since—"

"It wasn't how she was acting," I say. "I don't know, maybe that's how all teenagers smell?"

"If you say she smells like teen spirit, I'm going to—"

"Whoa, whoa, whoa, wait," Shoshana cuts in. "You *smelled* her?"

"Sure it wasn't the perfume?" Luis adds.

"Oh, right," I say with an awkward laugh. "Perfume. A lot . . ."

What I would give for something to break up the weirdness. Though police lights and a *whoop* sound isn't what I had in mind.

13

ADAM

"Let me guess, you didn't set your alarm," Luis grumbles at Shoshana as the door to the police car opens. "I leave my phone at home so no one can track it and you go and forget that you were our alarm guy."

Shoshana and Luis start arguing, but I can't speak at all.

It's like finding myself in a living nightmare. There's a cop here and there's nothing I can do. I can't run away. What if the cop freaks out and shoots at me when I suddenly move at more-than-mortal speed? I don't know what to do, so I stand there, awkwardly stiff.

The police officer stares at us a good, long, wordless minute before finally saying, in a deep, flat, emotionless voice, "Visiting the cemetery after sunset is going against the sign posted at the gate that says 'No visits after sunset.'"

I . . . think that's a joke? But I can't tell. The guy is absolutely deadpan. I glance nervously at Luis, but I get no hints from him.

The tall, broad-shouldered, unsmiling guy opens the back door of his patrol car.

"Get in," he says. "I'm driving y'all home."

I have half a mind to put all my vampire stealth to good use and vanish into the trees. But then I'd never be able to come back. There's no lie in the universe that would convince Shoshana and Luis that I'm not normally the kind of person who abandons their friends.

Acting noble doesn't help me calm down one bit. My pulse is in my throat. I walk all stiff-legged to the car. My shoulders are hunched up against my neck as I scooch into the back seat. I can feel the thud in my chest when the police officer slams the door closed. I'm trapped. There are literal bars separating us from the driver, which doesn't help with that cagey feeling.

I'm fidgeting so much that I sit on my hands.

Luis and Shoshana, though, look completely unbothered—as if this is not at all scary, but instead, the most annoying thing to happen. But they aren't vampires. Maybe they don't feel the same way about being trapped by mortals.

"You shouldn't be out," the police officer says once he's in the driver's seat. He pulls the rearview mirror down to look at the three of us in the back. "There's a serial killer out there."

"I know," Luis mumbles.

The police officer keeps looking at him in the rearview mirror, but Luis doesn't lift his head.

"Who's your friend?" the police officer asks.

Luis looks up at me and then back down again. "Adam. Just a kid from school."

"Ah," the police officer says. "Adam. Officer Espinosa."

"Hi," I say. My voice comes out as a squeak.

Luis finally mumbles to me, "It's my dad."

I pick up my head.

Oh… oh, so that's why they find this annoying instead of horrifically terrifying. But wait, duh! That's why Shoshana asked Luis to get details from his dad! Luis's dad is a police officer. He's probably working on the murder case!

Though I guess it's no wonder why Officer Espinosa wasn't sharing those secrets. I'd been to one of those murders! And sure, I was on top of a building, but I could smell a lot of blood. And if I know one thing about mortals, it's that they absolutely hate blood. There are movies rated R just for blood in them. It's like, their life force, I guess? And they don't like seeing it outside of their bodies.

The murder I'd seen was bloody, but we needed those details. Luis was *just* saying how impossible it was going to be to even start to find this murderer without knowing the stuff the police know.

I clench my hands into fists.

I was going to need to concentrate.

Only yesterday, I was running through the trees, using vampire abilities I never knew I had. Does that mean I have others too? Like charisma? I'd drank a lot of blood—powerful, young blood. Would that be enough? Could I compel the details of the murder case out of Officer Espinosa?

Think, Rossi. Why would a police officer want to talk about the details of a murder case? *Think,* I tell myself. *Think like a grown-up. What would Mom say?*

Officer Espinosa is driving us all home. He says he's doing it because there is a murderer out there. I focus on that idea. *Drive the kids home. Keep the kids safe. Tell them the details to scare them. That will keep them home. They'll stay safe inside if you scare them with the murder.*

I take a deep breath.

"Officer Espinosa?" I ask. I don't recognize my voice. I sound so serious. "What did you mean 'there's a murderer out there'?"

"Dude," Luis says. "We were just talking about it! Though I don't know why I need to be driven home," he says, turning to his dad. "I thought you said kids were safe."

"Why are kids safe?" I try, stomping on Luis's foot to get to him shut up.

"Ow," Luis says. I struggle to ignore him and stay focused on the task at hand.

"It's a theory," Officer Espinosa says. Did it work? Did I do it? He checks us out once again in the rearview mirror. He doesn't look like he is being mind-controlled. I don't even know what mind-controlled people look like. I scrunch up my face and try harder.

"Tell us," I say.

"I think someone is out to get a vampire."

I lose all concentration. *What?* Did I hear him right? A *vampire hunter?* In Lacey? Right here? Right by our house?

Luis, sitting next to me, groans.

"Dad, you're not serious, are you?" he asks, as if Officer Espinosa's theory was too embarrassing to handle, even if it gives us all the evidence we are looking for.

I close my eyes and focus. *Calm down.* I'm trapped, sure. But I can learn something, right? Something that can help my family, help everyone. It's hard to focus again, to get my nerves to calm down, to put my thoughts on getting information rather than running away. I think about my moms. Sung. Victor.

"Wh-why do you think it's a vampire hunter?" I ask. I am pretty sure the warble in my voice means I've lost my charisma.

"There's something different about these murders," Officer Espinosa says. I wonder what mortals consider to be "normal" murders. "Bodies slashed up in the same ways, so the victims bleed out slow. Victims are all young, right? Youngest one was fifteen. Oldest one was thirty-nine. Even though there are a lot of older folks out. Homeless folks. Vulnerable folks. But he's not interested in them.

"*Young blood.* That's the blood vampires like. Healthy, young blood. Not too old. And it can't be kids, right? They say the blood doesn't taste good until their victims hit puberty."

I am feeling very sick to my stomach. How does he know so much?

"The murders are only happening on days when it's not raining," Officer Espinosa goes on. "Rain washes away blood, so the murderer wants the blood to stay in one place. And it started two weeks ago, in January. The air is humid. Smell carries a long way on humid air. And the nights are long—that's a lot of time for searching.

"And if you're hunting something that drinks blood, you need to draw it out."

"The murder victims are *bait*?" I ask.

"Exactly," Officer Espinosa says. "You do the same thing if you're fishing for sharks. Blood in the water draws them in."

I think back to that night when Victor and I smelled blood and went running to the crime scene. Victor kept peeking to see what was going on.

Had there been someone watching us? Once the police showed up and the hunter couldn't catch a vampire anymore, did he start scanning the area to see if he had drawn any? And when Victor and I ran off, jumping from building to building, did the vampire hunter see us? Did we give ourselves away? Did he notice that we were headed toward Lacey . . .

Were we responsible for the murder that happened last night? The young blood we drank? I am so sick to my stomach it's like I ate another of Luis's M&M's.

"Knock it off, Dad," Luis scoffs, and it's grating how much his laugh is at odds with how I feel. "Everyone knows vampires have been wiped out for like, five hundred years. We have a discount serial-killer here thinking that 'hunting vampires' will actually work as an excuse."

"Who says they're wiped out?" Shoshana asks.

"Uhh . . . we were both in the same history class?" Luis answers.

"Were they wiped out, or did they hide?"

I sink farther down in my seat, and I really hope it comes off as try-to-escape-being-in-the-middle-of-two-friends-fighting and not, like, hoping they both don't get light-bulb moments and turn on me.

"Oh . . . *man*," Luis says, instantly panicking. "Maybe they did? They look just like us! Except the fangs." My hands instinctively fly up to my scarf to make sure it's hiding that dead giveaway. "Didn't Mr. Fornoff say they could put people under trances too? Maybe they mind-controlled people into hiding them and—"

"Oy, so that's the only possible explanation?" Shoshana asks. "You have to admit it's weird that through all of human history, we're totally chill with them, then suddenly . . . bam! We've got Purification."

"Look, you're only upset about it because—"

"Because I'm Jewish?" Shoshana asks. "And after all the werewolves and the vampires were killed or driven into hiding, then what happened? Then they started to worry about the humans that weren't the right kind, didn't they? It was easy to get everyone on board with driving out difference when you started with something like vampires. Easy to dehumanize them, right? That's the stuff *I* grew up being taught—that it doesn't matter who it starts with, hate is hungry, and if you don't do something to stop it, it eats everyone."

I don't need details of that. My mothers had told me all about it, partly because we're still living through it. The first real effort of "normal" humans to get rid of everything in the world that wasn't like them. It isn't a coincidence they named it Purification.

"She's right, Lucho," Officer Espinosa says. "You have to pay attention when people start blaming all their problems on one single group, especially if it's a small group without a lot of protection or power. Someone a long time ago decided they'd solve their problems by taking care of the vampires, but here we are now. Vampires were supposed to be the ones causing all our problems, but there's a serial killer out there right now killing folks."

"Exactly," Shoshana says smugly to Luis.

"Yeah, well, it's not like vampires are going to be missed," Luis says. "What good can they do? Like, is the world really that much worse off without blood-suckers in it?"

I'm screaming internally. The desire to reach down and test that vampire strength by punching a hole in the window and running away seems like a really good idea.

"We'll never know, will we?" Shoshana says. "If the world is better or not. They're gone."

"Definitely better," Luis says. "It's not like they could live with us, right? How do they get blood if they don't kill people? It's not like they could do the 'swim with the sea monsters' thing. I mean, I know a lot of people who don't want to get their necks chewed, but who doesn't want to get their picture taken swimming with mermaids?"

I bite my lip to keep from saying anything. Mama's told me how vampires used to work as healers. We could do blood magic and pull sicknesses out of mortal bodies. We'd make a cut (biting would infect them with our vampire venom, after all), collect the blood, and drink. Everyone would be happy. What mortal would say no to that?

But I say nothing.

"They should shut that down," Officer Espinosa says. "No one should have to turn themselves into an attraction so they can keep living where they've always lived. Those sea people keep getting chased off their own beaches because we want to have nice, human-only vacations there."

I clear my throat nervously. I'm not sure if I can recapture my charisma at this point, but I still need to know. "Uhh, aren't we getting off track? Why would anyone think there are vampires here?"

"Why wouldn't there be?" Luis says. "It's Thurston County . . . you know. Vampires came here . . . to get their 'thirst on.'"

The silence in the car lingers for an embarrassingly long time.

"But . . ." I try again. I had no idea that keeping my family safe was going to fall so much on me. "There was no one getting murdered here before the serial killer showed up though, right? I mean . . . if there were vampires here, there'd be a lot of murders. L-like you said, lots of vulnerable people, and none of them were found dead, right? Drained of blood?"

"That's a good point," Officer Espinosa says. "But there are ways vampires can get blood other than killing."

The police car jolts to a halt and Officer Espinosa gets out. I bolt upright, ready to fight, wondering if this is when everyone will spring a "gotcha" on me and tackle me and—

The backseat door opens.

"But the big-picture point is, it doesn't matter if there are vampires here or not," Officer Espinosa says. "What matters is there's a murderer out there who thinks there are, and who's willing to kill to prove his point. So don't let me catch you out in that cemetery again."

Shoshana and Luis pile out of the car, as if everything is normal, but everything *is* normal to them. We're at the end of the street in a cozy little subdivision—the kind with beige, two-story houses lined up in rows, golden light glowing around cast-iron street lights. They don't know what it's like, sitting in a car while their supposed friends casually discuss how they don't deserve to live.

I try to copy their casualness, but my head is firmly in there's-really-a-vampire-hunter-here territory. I don't even wave when Shoshana says goodbye and runs to the house next door, which must be her house.

"Where do you live?" Officer Espinosa asks, and his sudden appearance by my side makes me jump.

"Uhhh." *Charisma, don't fail me now.* I tighten all my muscles. *You really don't want to drive another kid home. You have more important stuff to do. You have to get back to looking for the vampire hunter, not babysitting kids.* "I don't need a ride."

Officer Espinosa gives me a look, but he gets back into the patrol car without questioning me. Phew.

"Sorry about that," Luis says.

"About w-what?" I ask, jumping again.

"My dad," Luis says, as if it's obvious. "He's majorly embarrassing, believing in kiddie stuff like vampires and monsters and things."

"Oh," I say awkwardly. "It's okay."

"Well, now you know my secret," Luis says with a sigh.

I shrug. I'm pretty sure the "secret" is something more than finding his dad embarrassing. I thought I'd been paying attention to the conversation, but I had been so concerned with how everything affected me, I didn't stop to think if anything that had been said would affect my new friends.

"Shoshana is the real deal," Luis says. "I saw her the other night in her room, summoning a ghost."

"What? Right in her bedroom?" I ask.

"Yeah! I know, right?" Luis says. "So like, duh, of course I thought . . . if I could convince her to summon a ghost for me . . . my dad really wants to find the murderer. He's always been like that, you know, wanting to be the hero? Did you see the patch on the dashboard? The wing with the sword? He was in the army. That's my earliest memory—talking to him on FaceTime because he wasn't there. And then he got hurt. So that's my next earliest memory—going to church and praying with my mom that he'd pull through. And when he got out? I thought he'd be safe forever and I wouldn't have to worry.

"But that's not going to happen. You heard him, right? He's following this case. He's always got to be the hero. He's going to try and find this murderer, and I know—I just know—it's only a matter of time before Dad's luck runs out. But we can do something about it. Kids can't be used as vampire bait. He said fifteen- to thirty-nine-year-olds were the victims, right?"

Luis has said that age range so many times. I realize he's clinging to it like it's a lifeline.

"I just thought . . . it's selfish, I guess," Luis says. "Dragging you and Shoshana into it, but I just thought if we caught the killer first, my dad would be okay."

"It's not selfish," I say. "I get that. Completely."

Of course, I understand. Protecting my family is on my mind too. My thoughts are already racing back home. Victor. Victor wanting more blood. What if it stops raining? What if Victor steps outside and smells blood on the air?

If that murderer really is out there hoping to catch a vampire? Victor is going to stumble right into the vampire hunter's trap.

"I—I have to get home," I say.

"You're not creeped out, are you?" Luis asks. "We need you! You still want to stop the murderer, right?"

"And . . . if there *are* vampires?"

Luis laughs. "You *are* creeped out. Look, if it makes you feel any better, we could get some holy water and stakes and stuff. So we're ready to do some *stab-stab*."

I cringe. That wasn't the answer I was hoping for.

"Same time tomorrow?" Luis asks before I can argue.

"Uhh . . . sure," I say.

I am sure I'm *not* going to be there tomorrow. How could I? I survived sitting in a car where everyone was talking about hunting vampires. How many conversations can I bank on getting through before Luis turns to me and asks why I have a scarf wrapped around my mouth? Or why I can run so fast, so quietly? What if I'm only good being alive as long as I'm helpful? Once the murderer gets caught, will they turn on me?

I have to face it. No matter how much I want friends, I'll never be mortal.

14

VICTOR

The rain falling on my head is definitely not helping me pretend to be a bat.

Okay, probably not the coolest thing I've ever done, but I have no one to practice with. The forest is full of animals, though, and they've got to be easier to fool than mortals. But admitting I can't even persuade a deer that I'm an animal too? Maybe it's better that no one's around to watch me fail that spectacularly anyway.

My ears pick up the sogging smush of footsteps sinking into the wet, leafy forest floor and the snap of holly branches snagging on cloth. I could recognize that awkward stumbling gait anywhere. I freeze. *I'm a bat I'm a bat I'm a bat, I'm a—*

Adam runs right up to me and gives me a great big hug. I'm not even bummed that he can see me.

"What's this for?" I ask, completely confused.

Adam just shakes his head. *Don't take it personally.* He's

still sneaking out without inviting me along and still not wanting to share what's going on, but he's here now.

"You okay? You hurt?" I ask.

"No, I'm fine," Adam says.

I can see the way his huge, wide eyes sparkle with something like fear. Something is definitely freaking him out. And if he's not going to talk about it? I pause another moment, giving him the widest, most open chance to share and . . . nope. But that's okay—time for a diversion.

"Hey, come on," I say, trying to put all my hurt feelings behind me. "We've still got a lot of young blood in us. Let me see if I can do charisma on you."

"Okay," he agrees quickly.

I take a step back and splay my fingers wide, as if trying to zap bat-like thoughts into his head.

"Nothing," Adam asks. "What are you trying to do, anyway?"

"Make you think I turned into a bat."

"What happened to big, burly guys?" he asks with a mischievous grin.

I grin back and put on a fake-defensive act. "Just trying to start small. I was thinking, maybe the first vampire to pull off charisma was like, cornered by mortals, so made the bunch of them think he transformed himself into a bat. That legend has to have started somewhere, right? So now I'm trying to do batification."

"Well, you can't try to *make* me think you're turning into a bat," Adam says, like he's some kind of charisma coach all of a sudden. "It's not pushing what you want the other person to think into their mind. You have to . . . figure out what they *want* to see or think or whatever, and then . . . think about *that*, really hard. Almost like you're whispering what they want to hear in their ear."

"Okay, you *want* to think I'm a bat," I say. I flick my fingers at Adam, as if I could fling my charisma right into his eyes.

"It's not about force," Adam says, with another shake of his head. "You have to get into my head. Know me. Maybe you're right, about a vampire using charisma to fool mortals, but . . . that mortal would have to already think vampires were able to do that, I think. Mortals don't even call us human, right? So turning into an animal is totally not human. But me? I don't believe that stuff, so you couldn't convince me to think it. If you don't want me to see you, you have to know that I don't want to run into anyone. I want to be alone."

"Well, vampires must not have charisma then," I say, letting my arms flop back to my sides. "You've been wanting nothing but to be alone and you still saw me."

Adam blushes and looks away. "You don't want to help anyway."

I start. "Help with what?"

"I-I think the murderer is a vampire hunter. And th-those murders? They're bait to draw us out."

"Is this what's been bothering you?" I ask.

Adam nods.

Oh, man, he's really gotten himself scared. Bad. Maybe I overdid it the other day when he ran off the first time, telling him how mortals would turn into vampire hunters if they saw him. He's growing up, and learning how scary the world could be for us, and that's probably turning into nightmares. And me... putting on all those vampire movies, which, while cool, also tend to end with the vampires getting slaughtered.

But I can rectify this. With charisma!

I put on my biggest grin and stand in my most protective stance. I think as hard as I can: *Let Adam think this is really cool, supportive stuff.*

"Hey, what're big brothers for?" I ask. "I'll stop him for you."

"Victor, wait, don't, you'll get caught!" Adam calls out after me, but I'm pouring everything I have into jumping from tree trunk to tree trunk.

"As if I'd let a mortal catch me!" I holler back.

I don't stop until I get to a road.

I squat on the bough of a fir tree—I like the concealment it gives me. No mortal ever bothers to look up anyway. I watch the world pass below me. There is a lot of traffic— cars rush by, flinging water onto the sidewalks. Taillights reflect red light all over the wet roads. All the little mortals with their temporary lives rush from here to there.

Now... where would a vampire hunter be?

I've seen movies about it. But in movies, vampire hunters always seemed to know where the vampire house is, and they go all bravado and storm it and stab the helpless vampires in the heart.

At least this guy doesn't know where we live.

He's trying to lure us out.

I sniff the air. No blood. This vampire hunter should probably look for a new job instead of a new victim. How can I be looking for this guy and this guy is looking for me and we can't find each other? Worst vampire hunter ever.

I lunge through the trees again. I need to find a new spot, a new vantage point to smell from. I stop again when the tree line stops. Another road. I crouch among the boughs of my new tree and watch the sidewalk. Car after car after car rushes by. What time is it? It's late, right? No one is walking. A road is probably too busy a place to stab someone anyway. I race silently through the trees, draped in shadows, excitement pulling me forward, and then . . .

A marquee with annoying flashing lights spelling out ridiculous messages tells me that I've found Timberland High School. And as luck would have it? I can smell it. *Blood!*

I see a girl. She has a ponytail and bangs, glasses, and she's wearing a huge backpack. It isn't raining anymore, but she's wearing a bright yellow rain jacket anyways. But most importantly? She's walking.

Walking? How can she be walking? It's like she hasn't been stabbed. And she *has* to have been stabbed, because I can smell blood coming off her. I am so confused. It's not like I've lost my sense of smell.

I drop out of the trees without a sound and start to sneak up to her. How do vampires do this? I've seen movies where vampires attack people. Just act . . . casual.

I fall into step behind the girl.

"Did you get stabbed?" I ask.

"Excuse me?" the girl asks back.

"Stabbed?" I try again.

"Wait right there," the girl says, slipping her backpack off one shoulder and reaching inside. I'm not exactly scared of whatever mortal instruments she might have—nothing she has in there could actually hurt me.

It's some kind of flat wand thing. She waves it around me, glaring at me the whole time.

She turns it off, slips it back into her backpack, and says a quick, "I guess you're okay."

"What was that?" I ask.

"You've never seen a metal detector?"

I honestly haven't, but the girl asks me as if every mortal has seen one, so I force a sarcastic laugh. "Of course I have. When I said 'what was that,' I meant, like, 'what was that for?'"

"There's a murderer out there," the girl says. "Some random dude running up to me asking if I've been stabbed seems like a perfect setup to actually getting stabbed."

I hold up my hands in mock surrender. "No knives."

"No *metal* knives," the girl says. "Who are you?"

"Victor."

I immediately frown. *Wait a second* ... I'm supposed to be eating. Slurping up delicious blood, and now I'm getting trapped in a conversation? How did that happen?

The girl sighs before answering, "Alejandra. And I meant, who are you, like, what are you doing?"

"You're bleeding," I say. I'm absolutely convinced of it. Maybe the vampire hunter put a spell on her that makes her think she's okay just to lure me in . . . can mortals even do that?

"I cut my hand in shop," Alejandra says. "How'd you know that? You're not in my class. And you don't go to my school."

"I don't?" I ask.

"No," Alejandra says. "I would recognize you."

I smirk. "Oh?"

"Don't look that far into it," Alejandra says, rolling her eyes but smiling.

"Why's your face getting warm?" I ask.

Alejandra answers by laughing and doubling over so far that her ponytail flips completely over her head, her hair cascading down toward the sidewalk.. "Oh my God, what is your deal?"

"Nothing big," I say. "I'm a vampire. I can tell." I point at her face. "Blood rushing to your face and all that."

"*Right*," Alejandra says. "And how often does that line work?"

"Work for what?"

"I'm embarrassed for you," Alejandra says.

"I'm serious," I say. I seriously do not know why this isn't working. Shouldn't she be screaming and running away? A person running away is a lot easier to try to eat than a girl just standing there talking to me. "I'm a vampire."

"Hmm," Alejandra says, absolutely not convinced in the slightest. "Can you prove it?"

"See my fangs?" I say. "My canine teeth are sharp for—"

"Yeah, and humans have genetic variability." Alejandra rattles off the fact as if she'd learned it solely to disprove someone trying to convince her they were a vampire. "Some of us have bigger, sharper canine teeth than others."

"If the sun comes up, I'll get burned."

Alejandra shrugs. "Yeah, big deal. I have a cousin who gets sunburnt really badly. Like, he had to go to the hospital one time, it was so bad. If you're a vampire, fly or something."

"I can't fly," I say, flatly.

"Turn into a bat?"

"No."

"Aww, too bad," Alejandra croons. "Probably for the best. You know, there's a vampire hunter looking for you."

"So I was told," I say, a cocky grin back on my face.

"Seems so unlike a vampire," Alejandra says. "To not care that he's being hunted."

"Why should I?" I say, mustering as much bravado as I can. "He kills them, and I eat them. He hasn't caught me yet."

The girl stops and glares at me. "That was my friend! How dare you joke about it!" She lunges forward. Whether to shove me or something worse, I don't wait to find out.

I jump backward. I really wish someone other than an angry girl was there to see me. It's *so cool.* I have my hands in my pockets, which helps me look like I can't be bothered, and I jump back a good ten feet without even looking like I have to try.

The girl freezes where she stands, awestruck by my awesomeness.

"You really *are* a vampire," she says.

"I said I was," I answer back.

"But . . . they're extinct. They're not . . ." Alejandra pauses, hatred welling up in her eyes. "You really drank Ashley's blood. I should slay you."

I laugh. "As if you could catch me."

I can see the heat rising to her cheeks again, see the pulse in her neck. Her heart is racing. She might actually be angry enough to try to slay me. I take another jump, this time landing lightly on a low branch of a bigleaf maple. Well out of her reach.

"You coward!" Alejandra screams, running up to the foot of the tree. "That was my friend, and you killed her!"

I sigh. I glance up and down the road to see when this vampire hunter is going to show up and do his stabby thing already.

"*I* didn't kill her," I say finally. "The vampire hunter killed her. I just . . . didn't want to let all that blood go to waste."

Inwardly, I cringe at the use of my mom's own explanation. From my own mouth! But I had to say something that wasn't "my mom works at the hospital and brings me blood." Not only would that give away the fact that there's a family of vampires living in Lacey, but it also sounds like the least cool thing ever.

"That murderer is only killing people to draw you out," Alejandra says, narrowing her eyes in pure disgust. "If I kill you first, if I bring your bloodthirsty vampire head to the police station, the vampire hunter gives up. I save all my friends."

"Yeah . . . I mean, I guess," I say. "Good luck trying to kill me, though."

Alejandra puts down her backpack. I lean forward, curious. Did mortals walk around with vampire-killing instruments all the time? My chest gets flighty, in case I have to run.

She stands back up . . . with a stick in her hand.

"Oh no, a pointed stick," I say.

"Funny, I made this in shop today," Alejandra says with a very tacked-on, dramatic sigh. "I thought I was going to have to stab a murderer. You can't carry a knife to school, but no one stopped me from carving a wooden knife. Ironic that I forgot it, and just my luck that there's a volleyball game tonight. If I wasn't out, I wouldn't have drawn you to me. And if I didn't get to school, I wouldn't have a stake. Because now I have a vampire to slay."

"Yes, well, I'm way up here and you're down there, so . . ." I shrug. "Maybe get into archery, and better luck tomorrow."

Alejandra pulls the bandage off of her hand and gives her wound a squeeze.

I inch forward a little.

The blood smell absolutely saturates the air. And it's *delicious*. Young blood. Sweet, salty, beautiful young blood. I want nothing more than to jump down and—

I clench my jaw and press my feet into the branch.

"Come on," Alejandra says. "Psspspspssspss."

I grind my teeth together. This isn't fair.

"Aw, what's wrong, boy?" Alejandra calls up to me. "Scared of a pointed stick? Come on! Yummy, delicious blood— come get it."

She waves her hand around and I stand up, scanning the road. The number of signs that the vampire hunter is coming are exactly zero. Maybe he isn't going to show up tonight? Maybe he's already been caught? Maybe Adam freaked himself out and there isn't a vampire hunter at all?

Another wave of beautiful metallic blood smell wafts on the air and I look back down. I'm pretty sure I whimper. That girl just goes and squeezes her hand again! I can see drops, delicious, wonderfully red, *wasted* drops of blood! Falling off her palm! Onto the ground!

"Nah, I'm going to go," I say.

"Aww, but you're not going," Alejandra says. "So come down and—"

I vanish into the trees, leaping from bough to bough, as far from the smell of blood as I can get. I don't know how it's possible, but my heart is racing just as fast as when I drank young blood. But no matter how fast I jump through the forest, I hear Alejandra's voice echoing through the night.

"I WILL SLAY YOU, VICTOR!"

I hope my laughs echo all the way back to her.

15

VICTOR

Adam and Sung are doing chores by the time I get home.

I try my best to sneak up on them, but I'm still kind of amped up from meeting Alejandra. I can't stop replaying her getting mad that she couldn't kill me because I'm so cool and vampire-y, and because of that, I botch the sneak-up on my siblings. Sung turns and throws a branch at me.

"Oh, about time," they say as I catch the branch. "You can help."

The branches are part of house decoy duty.

At least once a week, before we go to sleep, we have to go out and make sure mortals don't think to come investigate our house. We don't have a gate to block out outsiders. Gates are suspicious—they draw attention. But gather up a bunch of branches (or, in my case, small, fallen-over trees) and lay them all over the gravel driveway? Let weeds grow in? Well, now the path looks abandoned.

No one can see the house from the road anyway. The

house is painted a dark, matches-the-pines green. There are no porch lights. The windows were all shuttered closed during the rain, but we always keep the windows facing the road shuttered so light won't reflect off the glass and draw attention.

Mom and Mama even encouraged the tree boughs to grow over our roof, so even from the air (or space, in the case of Google Earth) mortals can't see our house.

In short? Taking care of the house is serious business.

It's not like I *don't* take it seriously. But I just met a mortal who wanted to slay me, which has got to be some kind of vampire rite of passage. It's like, I have *arrived*. And it makes chores feel like some really weird callback from an unimportant world.

Still, Sung gives me an evil glare. I dash into the forest and come back with a tree.

"That might be going overboard," Sung says.

I drop it in the driveway and shrug.

"Chores done."

"You're really going to make your parents move this every time they need to drive somewhere?" Sung asks.

"I thought my chore was to make the place look abandoned," I say. "And this? This is abandoned material."

Adam is strangely quiet. I don't so much as acknowledge my brother is there until Sung starts to drag the tree back into the forest.

"You're back," Adam says.

"Yeah," I say. "Don't worry about that vampire slayer. She's nothing I couldn't handle."

"Just wait . . . you found—you said *her*?" Adam asks. "The murderer?"

"Not *exactly*," I say. "I'm pretty sure she was upset about us drinking her friend's blood, so I think . . . well, now that I think about it, I probably created a new vampire hunter. To add to the first one. So we have two now."

Adam face-palms.

"But . . . that was a good test run," I say, swinging my arms over my chest like I've seen basketball players do when they're stretching. "And I think I've got the hang of it. Next time, I've got to have my charisma perfected, because I'm going to convince her she doesn't want to slay me—"

"Forget her, Victor," Adam says. "Focus. We need to stop the murders."

"Why would I want to do that?" I ask.

Adam glares. I have no idea what's gotten into him. I went out there to protect him from the vampire hunter he's so scared of! Why the sudden attitude?

Maybe I should try the less sarcastic approach.

"Adam, look . . . this is the first time in my life that I actually feel like the vampire I'm supposed to be. And I'm scared I'm never going to be able to feel like that again."

Adam scoffs. The sound of his little, sarcastic laugh sets off a pulse of anger in my chest. Why do I keep trying to tell him who I am and how I feel? Each time I expose a tiny bit of my soul, he thinks less of me.

"If you want to do something with all our vampire strengths," he says, "we could be stopping the murders."

"I thought you wanted me to stop the vampire hunter," I say. "And that really should be our priority here."

"They're the same person!" Adam says. "We stop the murderer, we won't have to worry about a vampire hunter catching us!"

I narrow my eyes. "Well, you know, we don't have to worry about vampire hunters. The house is pretty secure—"

"Just admit you care more about getting young blood than anything else! More than us! I get you don't care about mortals, but—"

I laugh right back at him. "Oh, right. The poor mortals. They're in *such* need of saving. Not like they'd repay the favor. You think a mortal would see you in trouble and try to save you?"

"You keep saying that!" Adam snaps back. "Why do they have to treat me well before I can do anything to help them? I already have power they don't have. Why is this so hard for you to understand?"

"You're talking about going out of your way, putting yourself in danger, even, to protect them," I say. "They don't deserve any of your goodness, Adam. They *hate* us. You tell them you're a vampire and they're going to try to kill you. Besides, they're our *food.*"

"Mom gets us our food," Adam says. "And she does it without needing to—"

"Murder?" I cut in. "You know, *I'm* not murdering any-one. If mortals want to kill each other, then that just goes to show they don't deserve the blood they have. And I'm not letting anything that precious go to waste. At least I'll do something with it."

"But . . . ," Adam starts. "The vampire hunter is killing innocent people. They didn't ask for this."

I shrug. "Sounds like a mortal problem."

"I'm telling the moms," Adam says.

"You went from zero to snitch in—" I start.

"Not on you. I'm telling them there's a vampire hunter," Adam says. "I bet they'll do something about it."

"Oh, and that's supposed to prove something?" I ask. "Other than you being selfish."

"What?" Adam is absolutely shaken.

"Yeah. You tell them there's a vampire hunter, they're going to call off work," I say. "Stay home. Stay safe. If this goes on too long, maybe they'll lose their jobs. You really thought they'd go out there and try to hunt the hunter? You know Mom says she's done doing that stuff."

"She used to hunt *vampires*," Adam says. "That's completely different."

"She never hunted vampires that ate people," I point out. "Only vampires that turned people without their permission. What does that tell you?"

"You're not going to get me to tell you that this is okay!" Adam growls. "Vampires can be more than whatever a useless movie told you that you needed to be!"

"At least they *get* to be vampires in *The Lost Boys*," I say.

"Maybe you should stop threatening to leave and just go to Santa Cruz already," Adam snaps. "I bet there's a vampire coven you can join there. You can go find the only vampires you want to be with."

Fire roars in my chest. I don't remember ever feeling angrier. What's gotten into Adam? It's like every chance he gets, he finds another way to make everything I'm feeling seem small and pointless.

I'm trying to protect you, I think. But I'm so confused, I can't say it out loud.

16

ADAM

Having mortal friends is the hardest thing in the world. Because when I really need to hang out with them, it's two in the morning and they are definitely asleep. And they probably don't want to be shaken awake only to hear me talk about how badly we need to find this vampire hunter, like this exact second.

How could Victor be so selfish? I groan as I replay the conversation again in my head. It's been on repeat since Victor stormed off. I said all the right things, didn't I? What could possibly be wrong with saying we need to stop the murderer? And help others? Of course, I didn't give Victor all the details and say I *know* mortals deserve our protection because I'd tried to make friends with some of them . . .

And now they're all I have left to turn to if I want help to stop the murderer.

I can't ask the moms. What if Victor is right and they stay home and then get in trouble at work? I can't ask Sung.

What if they never finish writing that paper and fail school and then they can never get blood the way Mom does? No, asking the family is definitely off the table. But maybe I *can* still get help from my family . . .

Mom was a vampire hunter before she met Mama. She has to have some kind of vampire hunter diary or something, right? Like, our house is *full* of books. One of those has to be helpful.

I run into the house. It's the first time I notice how cavernous and echo-y my home is. I wish it felt warmer. But like, the comfy-cozy warm, not the temperature warm. The house is oddly lonely without a movie playing.

I start pulling books off the shelves—not the normal books with words on the spines, filled with stories, but the big leather-bound tomes, hopefully filled with how-to-stop-a-murderer information. It takes me a few minutes to find what I'm looking for: a Mom-journal. *Il diario di Beatrice Rossi*. I flip through a few pages before realizing just how impossible this is going to be.

I forgot for a moment that Mom was born in 1703, in Italy. I pull another journal off the shelf and then another. I growl. They are *all* written in Italian. Or maybe Latin? Mom didn't even move to the United States until like, 1900.

I keep flipping through the journals. I'm desperate. I've gone through twelve of them before I decide I'm not finding anything in English. But . . . there *are* drawings. I go back to a journal dated 1720, the oldest one I can find. There's a sketch on the first page of a big cathedral-type thing on top of a hill. Written next to it is *Monte Berico*.

I flip through a few pages and find a drawing of a monk dude. Maybe he was also a vampire hunter? He's wearing a giant cross, and that's vampire hunter high-fashion. *Il mio famiglio, Fratello Gregorio* is written next to it. *Right.* When Mom used to travel around slaying evil vampires, she always had a mortal familiar whose blood she would drink without turning him.

But where's the stuff about what non-vampire vampire hunters did? I know Mom never murdered people as bait. Did she always work alone? If she drew where she lived, then she might have drawn pictures of other vampire hunters. And that could tell me something about how to find a vampire hunter now!

I turn another page. The journal is seriously lacking in vampire hunters. I grab another journal. This one says 1890. I turn another page. There's the classic wooden stake. So unhelpful. I turn another page. Flowers. I turn *another* page. Sketches of maps. Maybe I shouldn't have expected to find a step-by-step guide to stopping this murderer. It's nothing but page after page of writing I can't read and drawings that don't matter.

I'm flipping through the journal so fast that, suddenly, the floor is littered with pages.

I freeze. When I can get my eyes to unstick from the mess that's all around me, I glance down at the book in my lap. I can definitely see right down to the spine. An entire section of pages decided it had enough with me and jumped out of the book.

"What are you doing?" Mama asks.

"Nothing!" I shout the most guilty answer in the world, but Mama startled me. I hadn't heard her come home.

Mama steps closer, her eyes scanning the mess. "Must be a very big nothing."

"Uhhh . . ." How do I find the perfect middle ground between telling the truth and lying? "I was just . . . worried. About—"

I glance down and groan. Right in front of me is the picture I was looking for: a sketch of about eight dudes, all decked out in crosses and wooden stakes and pistols, looking exactly like—

"Vampire hunters . . . ?" Mama asks.

I shrug innocently.

Mama sits on the ground next to me and picks up the drawings.

"They were strange men," Mama says, the normally bouncy tone gone from her voice. "With strange ideas about what we were. They would not rest until all the vampires were gone. And the village that loved us? It had to be destroyed too. These men hated us so much they had to kill even the idea of us.

"I survived only because I wasn't there. I had visited with my great-great niece. My brothers and sisters were not so lucky. They burned them all."

"*Burned?*" I whisper, trembling.

No wonder Mama never wants to talk about her past or relive any moment of what she'd been through. Just hearing about it is terrifying; I can't imagine living through something that traumatic. I don't want to pretend to know what it might feel like: a group of vampire hunters finding out where we live, bursting into our home, dragging us all out into the sunshine while we were all sleepy and confused and helpless—

"I have scared you!" Mama says, somehow joyful and guilty at the same time. "Do not worry so much! Mortals don't think we exist anymore."

I struggle to swallow. The guilt feels as real as if a hand is actually squeezing my heart.

"But . . . mortals used to live with us. Happily?" I ask.

"Oh, definitely!" Mama says. "How would we have lived otherwise? We watched over our villages at night, and in turn they would bring us their sick. We would heal them with our blood magic and drink their infected blood.

"We didn't have to hide back then. We were like doctors. I volunteered to become part of my coven. In those days, you wouldn't dream of a vampire biting someone against their will. Becoming a vampire was a very honorable thing where I came from, to become one of the masas dima. And it was all I wanted."

"That is *so cool*," I say. "Why doesn't Mom do this?"

"Ah, not every vampire is good at every ability we might have," Mama says. "And besides, Beatrice is from Europe. By the time she was bitten, the old ways had already been destroyed there. She never learned how to do it."

"You can teach me, right?" I ask.

"I will," Mama laughs. "I will."

"Right now?" I ask, because "I will" definitely sounds like one of those things parents say when they want to put something off until later. And I don't have later.

"When the situation is right," Mama says.

"How is it not right?"

"We need a mortal, first of all," Mama says as my heart sinks.

"We do?"

"Absolutely!" Mama says, cheerfully unaware that my enthusiasm has all but evaporated. "Our blood is free from sickness like they have. If I am to teach you, it has to be under the best circumstances. We have to find a mortal who is sick . . . and who will not mind having magic done on them. And someone who will not tell our secrets."

I frown. "Someone unconscious?"

"We would have to bring them here," Mama says, and my frown goes even more frowny. "And unconscious people can't tell you whether or not they mind having magic done on them."

"Oh . . . ," I say. "So . . . no one."

"Maybe not!" Mama says. "But do not despair! Some-times unexpected things happen."

I can't even imagine perfect circumstances, let alone unexpectedly perfect ones.

"Maybe I can go with Mom to the hospital?" I suggest.

"Ah, habibi, they don't allow children in to see patients!" Mama says.

I shrug. "Don't they have a Bring Your Kid to Work Day?"

"We are our own school," Mama says, as if considering it. "We can make one up."

But that makes me think about something else.

"Why aren't you a doctor now, Mama?" I ask. "Or the person who draws blood, like Mom. You wouldn't even need to *just* draw blood, you could help people too."

"It is not meant to be," Mama says. "The way we used to live with mortals, side by side, has been forgotten. Just like my village. Destroyed. I could not be a doctor now. Even if I could help, the help would be too much. Too..." Mama searches for the right word. "*Spectacular*. The mortals would suspect something. And now, safety is all that matters."

Another pang of guilt squeezes my heart.

I'm risking that safety, aren't I? Trying to make mortal friends. But it's become something bigger than simply making friends, hasn't it? Now there's a murderer out there—a vampire hunter, even! Safety *had* to come in second place when there's a murderer to stop.

If only I didn't have to hide. I imagine what it might be like if vampires had never been made into monsters. I wouldn't have to worry about friends. I wouldn't even have to hide my abilities from them. Luis could make a better plan, knowing everything I can do. There wouldn't even be a vampire hunter murdering mortals to stop. Maybe Mom and Mama would be seen as heroes, with their own little vampire-run clinic, working blood magic and saving everyone.

Imagining only makes my heart hurt more. I don't want to live in darkness forever.

"This isn't fair," I say.

"What isn't?" Mama asks.

"Having to hide," I say. "When we didn't do anything to deserve this. Don't you wish it too? That we could go back to the old ways?"

"Shwaiya baas," Mama says. I can't believe Mama has gone with "only a little bit." "It's easier when you can never go home again. When home was taken from you. Those traditions are gone, and they will never return. That's a hurt no amount of magic can heal. But I have so much in front of me right now. You and Victor and Sung? You bring so much light into my life."

I cringe as I hear that.

That light won't mean much if we are all snuffed out.

17

ADAM

I set my alarm for 4:39 p.m.—the exact minute the sun sets. I don't have a second of nighttime to spare.

It's not raining.

The path I take through the woods is pretty well-worn by now. I'm glad, because it's so hard to see with it being twilight. There's so much light—the sky looks almost white. Mama says it's blue, but I guess that's with mortal eyes. I keep my head down and hope it gets dark fast.

I'm starting to see the trail forming, the branches broken off, the slim line in the leaves and pine needles on the forest floor. I run through the shadowy evergreens, my thoughts racing as fast as my feet slamming into the squishy earth.

It's worth the risk. I have to keep telling myself that going back to see Luis and Shoshana is worth the risk. Mama had said safety is the most important thing, but I can't believe that hiding and waiting for the police to catch a vampire hunter while he keeps killing mortal people is better.

I need to stop the murders before someone else gets

killed. Before Victor tries to get his drink of young blood and gets captured. Before anyone else in my family gets hurt. I can do this. Vampires are more than just bloodsuckers—we can be the good guys.

Stopping the vampire hunter is a win-win-win. So why do I feel so nervous?

I get to the edge of the cemetery. I wrap my scarf tightly around my mouth before I run up to meet Shoshana and Luis, and that's the proof right there of why I'm so nervous. Even if everything I'm doing is right, I still have to hide who I am from my two mortal friends.

"Hey, you guys!" I say.

Luis wasn't kidding when he mentioned getting some vampire hunter gear. *Relax*, I tell myself. *Play it cool.* What kind of mortal would panic at the sight of crucifixes and stuff? Luis has a pencil tucked behind his ear too. I point to it first.

"Let me guess . . . wooden stake?" I ask.

"Yeah," Luis says. "Going for subtle. Don't want to tip the vampires off, you know."

I laugh nervously. Maybe Luis doesn't realize how quickly vampires heal, or that a tiny little pencil isn't going to do the kind of damage to our hearts that might actually kill us. And it's not like wood itself is dangerous to vampires.

"I thought we were stopping the murderer?" I ask. "What's all this? Are you changing sides?"

"*Pffft*, no. The way I figure it," Luis says with a shrug, "if we're trying to stop a vampire hunter, we might as well look like we're vampire hunters too. You know, maybe that'll make him come up to us? Reveal himself? And, well, if there *are* vampires here, we'll have to defend ourselves."

"With a pencil," I say.

"Hey, the legends can't all be wrong," Luis says. "You just have to stab them in their undead heart—"

"But which one is it?" Shoshana interrupts. "If vampires are 'undead,' then their hearts aren't beating, and stabbing them in the heart isn't going to make much of a difference. *Or* they're alive and more like people with special abilities than—"

"Can you stop thinking about everything so much?" Luis asks. "You're seriously ruining my entire ensemble."

"What else you got?" I ask, hoping to get Shoshana from thinking too much about vampires. I'm so glad the scarf is around my mouth so they can't see how hard I'm trying not to laugh. Luis pulls out a crucifix necklace and a water pistol.

"Holy water," Luis says, shaking the pistol, as if I hadn't figured that one out. I can almost hear Victor shouting out something like, *Put down the water and grab a flashlight, dummies!*

"Classics," I say with a grin. It's not like the mere presence of a crucifix is going to somehow magically push me away. And seeing someone believe that in real life? It almost makes vampire hunters a hundred percent less scary. Maybe stopping this murderer won't be so hard after all.

"Where's the garlic?" I tease.

"Don't give him any more ideas," Shoshana says.

"Nah, I skipped the garlic," Luis says. "Pretty sure if we get cornered by a vampire, the last thing that's going to work is 'Hey, eat this.'"

"It's the smell, actually," I say. Both Shoshana and Luis give me a weird look, which makes me regret how confidently I blurted out my correction. "Garlic smells really strong ... and vampires ... well, vampires don't eat mortal food, or you know, *regular* people food, heh." I cringe. "And it all smells bad—to *them*. But garlic kind of gets that, uh, vampire-repelling myth to it because it smells so strong, and vampires ... stay away from you. Because. Of the smell."

"Makes sense," Shoshana says with a shrug. "Vampires not eating food."

"Who says they don't?" Luis challenges.

"Logic," Shoshana says. "Just think about it. Why would they even need to drink blood if they were perfectly fine eating food?"

Luis shrugs. "I don't know. They're evil?"

I bite my lip. Inwardly, I scream that we're not, but I can't give myself up, so I just stand there with my cringe hiding behind my scarf and my eyebrows all scrunched up.

"More evil than the guy out there murdering people in our town right now?" Shoshana asks.

"We can talk about how pointless all this stuff is later," I say, quickly needing to change the subject, and Luis scoffs. "We need to hurry. It's not raining, and your dad said when it's not raining—"

Luis gasps in sudden realization. "There's going to be a murder tonight!"

"Yeah, probably," I say.

"Sorry, guys," Luis says. "I got us off track."

"Hey, this is good info," I say. "We can use this. There's a guy out there who believes all this stuff, right? And is still acting like vampire hunting is a thing."

"How does that help?" Luis asks.

"He might be carrying around a wooden stake." Shoshana picks up what I'm getting at.

"Or a water pistol with holy water," I join in.

"Or be decked out in crucifixes," she adds.

"So he'll stand out!" Luis finishes.

"Exactly," I say.

"Okay, so . . . where do we start looking?" Luis asks. "For a guy decked out in vampire hunter stuff?"

"A church, obviously," Shoshana asks.

"For what?" Luis asks. "Refills?" He shakes his water pistol.

"Does holy water go bad?" I ask.

"If he needed refills, he would have done it during the day, right?" Luis says. "Nighttime is vampire-hunting time."

Shoshana frowns. "Yeah, I guess."

"So, where do we start?" Luis asks.

"With a decision," Shoshana says. "Do we look for the guy, or do we try to figure out where he's going to kill next and stop him?"

I raise my hand. "I'd like to avoid running into a vampire hunt—I mean, murderer."

"What do you have to worry about?" Luis asks. "We're in a group, a team! Plus, we're too young."

"I don't want to find out if this guy is asking everyone their ages before he kills them, thank you very much," Shoshana says.

"Okay, fine," Luis says, typing quickly on his phone. "According to Wikipedia, we have seventeen square miles of possible murder sites."

"We could go to all the hotels in town and ask if—" Shoshana starts.

"Please don't finish that with 'do you have any vampire hunters here?'" Luis says. "Hotels are a bust. He could totally be staying with someone local, or living in an RV or a tent or something. He could be living out of a van, and that could be parked anywhere."

"But a van with an out-of-state license plate?" Shoshana tries.

"There *is* a military base like, on the border of our town," Luis says. "Our car had a German license plate when we first moved here."

"Alright, point made," Shoshana says.

"But what does that mean?" I ask. "If we can't figure out who he is, how are we going to stop him?"

"We'll have better luck trying to figure out where he's going to strike next," Luis says.

"Your dad said there were four murders already, right?" I ask.

"We need to get you caught up," Luis says. "Me and Shoshana already did some of the research." He opens up the map app on his phone. He must have stopped caring about his phone being tracked (or maybe he found a way to turn it off). There are pins dropped all over the map.

"Each murder is only about a mile or two away from the last one," Shoshana explains. "They always happen in or around parks or forests. And it's only in the Olympia area."

"So . . . we wait in a forest?" I ask.

Luis types on his phone again. "Well, we have twenty-six municipal parks to pick from. No, we can take out the ones he's already been to. So . . . twenty-four."

I nod. Twenty-four wasn't good for mortals stuck to the ground. But for me? Vampire speed, running through the trees—I could put it all to good use! I could run all over town, check out each park for a vampire hunter, and figure out some way to keep him from killing anyone. Let the police know, and . . .

My heart flutters. I can do this. I just have to sneak away.

"Don't either of you ever watch detective shows?" Shoshana asks. "What we need to do is go to where the murders already happened! There might be clues."

"The first one was in Huntamer Park," I say.

"The first murder in *Lacey*," Luis specifies.

"And the one the other night—" Shoshana starts.

"Dad drove me and my sister past it today to scare us," Luis says. "I know exactly where it is. We can take the bus!"

Every excuse I come up with gets shot down. "We'll *all* get in trouble," when I say my moms will kill me for taking the bus. "It's free," when I say I don't have money. And when my excuse well runs dry (I really need to work on my excuses), I find myself standing at the bus stop, waiting.

The 66 bus pulls up before too long. There are only a handful of mortals riding it, but I pull my scarf tighter around my mouth, just in case. I try not to smell them. I want to tell the older mortals that I'm sorry, though for what, I don't know. For aging? For almost dying?

I sit in a seat and feel weird.

"Hey," Shoshana says quietly, sitting next to me and pushing something into my hands. "I brought you something."

"Huh?" I ask. It's a book. The title on its cover announces that it's *Anyone's Guide to Being Jewish*.

"You said you were adopted so you don't really know anything but . . . ," Shoshana explains, "I thought this would be a way you could start."

"Oh, thanks!" I say, and flip through it politely. My supersensitive vampire eyes skim through the chapter names in the table of contents and lock onto one that says *Kosher: Dietary Laws*. I flip right to that page.

A grin spreads over my face. This is great! It's literally a long list of things I don't have to worry about because I don't eat food anyway. Don't eat mammals unless they have split hooves and chew cud? Easy. Don't eat shellfish, super easy. Don't mix meat and dairy together? I got this.

"Why does it say you need to drain blood out of meat?" I ask.

"It's against kashrut to consume blood," Shoshana says, arching an eyebrow at what was probably the most random first question anyone would have come up with. I didn't know what kashrut meant, but I did hear "against" and "consume blood" in the same sentence.

"In the Torah, it says we can't consume meat with blood," Shoshana says, "since blood is like the life force of the animal we're eating. So, like, we literally drain out all the blood and salt the meat with special salt to draw out any blood that's in there, so we can't possibly eat it. That's very, very, against the rules."

"Oh . . . ," I say, my eyes dropping back down to the page and landing on a quote. *Whoever eats any blood, that person shall be cut off from his people.* Ouch. I want to push the not-so-helpful-anymore book back into Shoshana's hands, but I can't.

"So I guess . . ." I laugh nervously, hoping it hides how crushed I feel. "No such thing as a Jewish vampire."

"Huh?" Shoshana asks.

"The blood-drinking," I say, running my hand through my hair nervously. "I mean, we're out here looking for a vampire hunter, you know? And vampires on the brain, I just thought—"

The bus shudders to a stop before the conversation can get any more awkward. Luis says it's *our* stop, sparing me from having to explain why I care about Jewish vampires. I don't know what else to do with the book, so I tuck it into my back jeans pocket and jump off the bus before the others. I'm surprised to see a giant sign at the corner saying Luis has taken us to Saint Martin's University.

Sung's school!

The vampire hunter knows there's a vampire going to class here.

18

ADAM

h no oh no, oh no. The vampire hunter couldn't have tracked down our family!

Did Sung write something in a paper that sounded too vampy? Maybe they dropped in a "mortals" when they meant every-person-who-is-not-a-vampire. They only went to see their adviser when it was dark.

No, calm down, Rossi. Sung takes all of their classes online. Even if the vampire hunter thinks they're on campus, Sung is home. They're safe. I take a deep breath. *They're safe.*

"It's over here," Luis says, walking to the murder scene. We follow the sidewalk skirting the woods. Students with giant backpacks walk past us, hardly glancing up from their phones to give us a second look.

The trees break, opening to a giant field. I know immediately where the murder last night took place. It's not a smell, or a vibe, but a huge pile of stuff. I can see it from clear across the field.

Fake flowers. Real flowers. Flags. Toys. All the same kinds of stuff I noticed in the cemetery. This must be a mortal mourning practice, to give the dead presents when they die. Everyone must have really loved this girl who died, because as we step into the parking lot, I realize the murder scene is now buried.

Candles burn. Posterboard signs are propped up with messages to the girl who was killed. There are cards. Stuffed animals. And flowers. So many flowers. Her name was Ashley—it's written on so many of the messages. And it creeps me out. It makes this so much more real.

I look down at my hand. It's starting to tremble. Just under my skin, Ashley's blood is still pumping.

I step away as a wave of weird feelings I have no words to describe washes over me.

"It doesn't make sense," Shoshana says. "Murdering someone in a parking lot. It seems so . . . random."

"Might've been the only victim he could find," Luis says. "The vampire hunter did the murder in the middle of the night, so no witnesses, you know? Plus, vampires. Nighttime. Look, believe me, my dad is a professional. If he says it's a vampire hunter, it's a vampire hunter."

My chest deflates. "Your dad knows a lot about vampires?" I ask hesitantly.

"Obsessed," Luis moans. "You should see his horror movie collection that I'm 'not allowed to watch.'" He uses air quotes around that last part.

A shiver runs down my spine. All we know about the murders is that the victims were "young," they happen on rain-free nights, and the victims bleed a lot before they die. It seems really weird that Officer Espinosa would jump to "vampire hunter" as the explanation just based off that.

I'm not about to say anything, but I'm beginning to worry that maybe the guy obsessed with vampires is also obsessed with catching us?

Maybe the reason he's told Luis not to be outside is because he knows Luis might try to catch the killer on his own . . . and he doesn't want his kid to know it's him?

I glance at all the vampire hunting stuff Luis has with him and the thought tugs at my mind. For about the hundredth time, I debate running away. I could point to the woods, say I see something that looks like a clue, and vanish into the night. It would be easy. I could go back home. Safe. Before it's too late.

I look down at my hand. It's still shaking, but I tighten it into a fist. I swallow back my fear. No matter who is doing the killing, there are still innocent people dying. And I have two friends who want to stop that. I'm a vampire. I could lunge out of arm's reach at any moment. Might as well do the best I can until that moment arrives.

"What do we need to do?" I ask.

Luis and Shoshana glance at me, probably confused over where my sudden resolve came from.

"Look for clues," Shoshana says, like it's a no-brainer. "The only hunch we have is 'vampire hunter.' And what do detectives do about hunches? They keep working off their hunch until they get more data."

"Yeah, so, data," Luis says, swinging his arm wide to gesture at the parking lot.

I look around. "I don't think the police left any data behind for us. It looks pretty much combed over. But . . . if a vampire hunter is hunting, then he's going to need a spot . . . like a vantage point."

"Oooh, good hunch!" Luis says.

"Somewhere he could be out of sight but still watch for a vampire to show up," Shoshana adds. "Now . . . where would a vampire hunter wait?"

"Somewhere the vampire couldn't smell him," I say.

"They can smell people?" Luis asks.

"Uhh, of course," I stammer. "Your dad said so, right? About the blood smell and everything. If they can smell blood that well, they could probably smell someone's blood . . . under their skin? Skin isn't really that thick . . ."

I let my words trail off. When I risk glancing at Luis, he's shrugging and nodding. Okay, I'm safe.

Shoshana is slowly spinning around, looking everywhere. "Where would he hide, where would he hide? There has to be a way we can tell from here."

I'm looking at everything too, imagining what the vampire hunter saw that we can't. What made him pick this spot. I glance around: the forest, the cars in the parking lot. So many places he could have retreated.

I growl at my mind for not figuring anything out. I'm the vampire! I should know this stuff! For once, I agree with Victor—Mom should have taught us more vampire skills instead of insisting we have a "normal childhood." The longer this night goes on, the closer someone else gets to their death. I'm trying to make all of this right— can't something, I don't know, make sense?

"You need to stop spinning, or someone's going to think we're doing a séance," Luis whispers as he steps out of the way of a college student trying to take a picture of the memorial.

"Oooh, talking to the ghost! That's a good idea!" Shoshana says. She swings her book bag off of one shoulder, reaching back to unzip it and—

"NO!" Luis barks. "No, it's not a good idea, Shoshana! It would be better if we tried *not* to get noticed."

"Noticed by who?" I ask. "You think the murderer is still here?"

"No, but all these people are going to think we're weird," Luis whispers.

"Oh, oh no, the unbearable pain," Shoshana says sarcastically. "There are a million worse things in the world than strangers thinking you're weird."

Luis looks at me for backup, but I gesture toward the memorial. "I mean, we *are* at a murder scene. She has a point."

"You should try it sometime," Shoshana says. "Not care what other people think. It's so freeing."

"That's fine, you can keep it," Luis says. "I actually want friends."

Shoshana's expression changes in an instant.

"Until they didn't want to help you?" she asks. "Is that why you had to ask me? Because they didn't care? But what they think still matters, doesn't it? Don't think I didn't notice you ignoring me at school. If you're embarrassed by me, fine—I didn't decide to do this to gain whatever cool points you think I want. I did it because it's the right thing to do. You go on caring about looking cool for your friends."

"I don't just care about looking cool, Shoshana!" Luis argues.

"Yeah? Prove it," Shoshana argues back.

"I don't have to prove anything to you."

I sense both of their hearts racing, their temperatures raising. The blood vessels constricting in their bodies and adding to the pressure, the heat rushing to their faces. I need to say something.

"Uhh, well . . . Luis, if you cared about people staring at you, they . . . kind of are now," I say. My joke definitely doesn't do anything to defuse the situation, and I cringe at myself for saying the wrong thing.

"Come on," I say to Luis, and then turn to Shoshana. "Shoshana? If you want to do a séance, we'll . . . we'll be looking for more clues over here."

"You know . . . ," Shoshana says, wringing her hands. "I don't *actually* do séances."

Luis glowers at her. "Whatever. If you don't want to help anymore, just say you don't want to help."

Shoshana doesn't say anything. I gently tug at Luis's sleeve, and he follows me.

"What does she know," Luis whispers angrily to me when we are out of earshot.

"It's alright," I say. "Shoshana doesn't have to know anything you don't want to share with her, but she'll probably keep thinking the wrong thing about why you're doing this until you do."

"I'm not about to tell her I'm scared of losing my dad!" Luis says.

"You told *me*," I point out. "You're neighbors with Shoshana. I'm sure she'll get it."

"Let's look for clues," Luis says.

"Right." I wince. I said the wrong thing again.

Okay. Clues. There *has* to be a reason the vampire hunter picked this spot. Well . . . there definitely are teenagers here. They keep walking past us with backpacks, going to and from evening classes. I tighten the scarf around my face some more, just to keep myself from losing focus each time they walk by.

Is that all there is to it? A university has students? No . . . that murder I saw was in Huntamer Park, not around any college. Surrounded by office buildings.

"Let me see the map again," I say to Luis.

I glance at all the pins. Two in Olympia. First was Percival Landing Park. Okay . . . *think like a vampire hunter.* Maybe he thinks vampires like living in big, noisy cities. Or maybe he thinks we target the homeless. Then he kills in Lions Park, in the middle of houses. Huntamer Park? Office buildings. If I keep lining the murders up—

"He's going east," I say excitedly. Even if the vampire hunter saw Victor and me leave the first murder scene? He didn't keep up with us. He saw us heading east and that's it.

"Maybe he's going to keep going east?" I add hopefully.

"Which way is east?" Luis asks.

I point.

"Wait . . . just like that?" Luis asks. "You know which way east is off the top of your head?"

I bite my lip. That must not be something mortals drill into their kids' heads, which way east is. So they'll never be caught by sunrise.

"*Cool*," Luis says. "My dad can do that too. He says it's because he did land nav all the time in the army. Have you done land nav?"

I shake my head. I have no idea what "land nav" is, but I don't want to ask.

"Uhh . . . should we go east?" I say, pointing in the direction.

"Yeah, let's check it out," Luis says.

We walk east, across the parking lot. There's a lot of landscaping with nice plants and stuff, but we walk right through them. Luis is very set on the idea of going exactly straight east from the murder scene. No deviations.

There's another little stand of trees on the other side of the parking lot. My head snaps up, because I can smell it on the breeze.

Blood.

I can tell by the way it smells that it's dried blood. I don't even know how I know. But I can tell it's Ashley's blood.

"I think . . . " My words trail off.

I step into the trees, looking at the ground. I sniff the air—I'll tell Luis I have a cold if he asks me about it. I need to find this clue! I keep sniffing. There's a little path in the trees, so I start to follow it. How do I do this without looking weird? I kick the leaves on the path, but nothing turns up. The smell is close.

"This is legit," Luis whispers. He's come up beside me and I stop. He's looking up at something.

"Huh?" I ask, and follow his gaze.

There's a giant brick cross in the woods, randomly placed. Like, it's as tall as a grown-up, and just casually in the woods. I walk up to it slowly, not because I think it's got magic vampire-expulsion powers, but because the blood smell is definitely coming from there.

We stop in front of it.

There's a wood carving in the middle of it and a Roman numeral XII. But what I notice is the dried blood, and the way the ferns are broken and smushed, as if someone had been standing on them for a long time.

"Do you see this?" I ask Luis, pointing to the dried blood stuck in the tiny crevices of the brick.

"Is that blood?" Luis asks.

"Yeah," I say, hoping he doesn't ask me how I know.

"Dad's *right*," Luis says, with a little touch of awe on his voice. "I thought he was just being weird, but this murderer really thinks he's a vampire hunter."

"What do you mean?" I ask.

"This is one of the Stations of the Cross," Luis says, pointing to the cross excitedly. "No vampire is going to be able to come near this place, right? The cross would push them away. This would be a perfect place to wait!"

He's wrong, of course. I could reach out and touch the cross without being magically shoved away, but it's not like I'm going to correct him right here, to his face.

"He can see the whole parking lot too," I say, turning around and seeing Shoshana lighting a candle and reading something out of a book.

"But . . . that doesn't really give us a direction to head toward next," Luis says.

He looks at his map and scrunches up his face like he's thinking.

"You know . . . Huntamer Park is . . . it's not even a quarter of a mile away," Luis says.

"So?" I ask.

"All the other murders happened miles apart," Luis says. "But this time, he just moves across the street? Dad told me that in land navigation, if you can't find your point, you start going around in cloverleafs, because you know your point is somewhere nearby. Maybe that's what this guy is doing?"

"What do you mean?" I ask, swallowing against the way my throat starts to tighten.

"He's hunting, right?" Luis says. "Maybe he got a clue from the last murder that the vampire's close."

My stomach sinks with guilt. Luis is right. The vampire hunter *did* see me and Victor—he saw us running east. Maybe he thought we hid at the college? That means . . . Ashley's murder was our fault.

"If he's setting bait, he's going to start bringing it in," Luis keeps saying. "Narrowing it down."

"What does that mean?" I ask.

"Maybe tonight's murder is going to be here too?"

"I don't know," I say. "They have a curfew going on. There aren't going to be any college students out. And there's police everywhere. Is there another park more to the east?"

Luis looks at the map on his phone and gulps. "Lake Lois? That's a little too close to Luis, right? That's got bad luck written all over it. Hmmm . . . okay." He clears his throat. "*Cloverleaf . . .* what about this? He tried going east and that didn't work. His next move is going to be north or south, and if he's only hitting open spots close to forests? North he's going to run into I-5. No good. But south? There's Wonderwood Park. Hey, it's on the way home! We should go check it out—come on! Let's go back and tell Shoshana. We've got to stop the next murder!"

I swallow hard.

"I hope I'm right!" Luis says with a grin. "¡Vámonos!"

I hope he's wrong. Our house is hidden in the woods across the street from Wonderwood Park. If a vampire hunter is going to set up bait so close to home? Blood smell is going to waft right into the windows I know are open. And Victor. With his newfound appetite?

This is getting way too close.

19

VICTOR

Vampires get attached to mortals, don't we?

I've heard a myth saying something like that. It might have been from a movie, so maybe it isn't real. Alejandra really wanted to murder me yesterday . . . so why do I want to see if she's out tonight? Is she hunting for me? What kind of silly mortal trap is she going to try to make for me? *Is* she going to make a trap to catch me? Do I want her to catch me? Why? Doesn't that mean she's going to slay me?

I try not to overthink it.

I step out on the back porch and smell the air.

At first, I think it has to be a trick my mind is playing with me. Is there such a thing as like, smell memories?

I can smell blood. *Alejandra.* Oh yeah, it is definitely Alejandra. But how did I know that? I've never smelled the same blood twice before. The only mortal blood I've ever been around was stuff I gulped down as quickly as I could.

It's not like there was ever enough for seconds, and Mom never takes blood from the same person twice.

A shiver of anger ripples through my body. I had no idea I could do that—recognize someone from the way their blood smells. And the only reason I didn't know I could do that—that I still don't know all that I'm capable of—is because Mom never teaches us to do vampire stuff.

I follow my nose, running and jumping through the woods again. North. I run across Ruddell, thankful for the four lanes of traffic that aren't illuminated by street lights. Back into the darkness and the safety of the trees. A baby-blue painted wooden sign tells me the blood smell is leading me into Wonderwood Park.

I come to a stop on a mossy branch, squatting on a bough of a bigleaf maple, fifty feet up in the air. I hate that this little patch of forest is almost completely empty of pine trees—it's a circle of alder and bigleaf maples.

Trees that shake off their leaves in winter. Which means I'm exposed, out in the open. Hopefully mortals can't really see that well in the dark or else Alejandra will have no problem spotting me coming with all these naked trees. It's a perfect place to draw me in. And if she's thinking like that? She's really taking this slaying stuff seriously.

Stretching out before me is an open field, the grass floor heavy with rain. The blood smell is strong, so she has to be close.

A towering bigleaf maple tree stands alone in the middle of the sea of green grass. That *has* to be where the blood smell is coming from. The trunk is fat enough that, theo-retically, someone could be on the other side and I wouldn't be able to see them. I glance around the park, but every-thing is quiet. Everything is cold. Sound moves better in the cold.

I listen for another moment, trying to single out the sound of breathing, of a heart beating. I hear nothing.

I'm alone.

Oh man, is she dead already? How can I smell her blood but not hear any of the normal sounds of a mortal body doing what it does to live?

I jump down from the tree, not so much as making the leaves rustle as I hit the ground. I sprint to the tree in the middle of the field, too fast for a mortal to follow, just in case there actually *is* a vampire hunter tracking me.

I round the tree, expecting to see a slumped-over dead body.

Instead, I see a tiny, minuscule little fishing line as plain as day.

It's black and not shiny, so I'm sure I'm not meant to be able to see it. I look down at the ground. Oh yeah, there's more of it! Even though some leaves are thrown over the fishing line, the hiding job isn't perfect. Or maybe it's per-fect to mortal eyes. Yeah, there it goes, all around me in a big circle and the other end is tied to . . .

What is that? A *bandage*? Yeah . . . with some of the fish-ing line tied around it. The same bandage Alejandra had wrapped around her hand the other day. I remember the pattern that was on the gauze—the tiny little crisscrosses.

But what is it doing *here*? In the middle of the park? Stuck to the side of the tree?

It's . . . a trap.

A trap for me!

I almost burst out in giggles at how absolutely ridiculous this is. She *did* build a trap to catch me! And it's fishing line. As if that could hold me.

I should spring the trap. That would be hilarious—to make her think she caught me, and then when I break out of it, she's going to realize how awesome vampires are. Maybe she'll be so impressed she'll want to be a vampire too?

I grab the bandage.

I hear the whipping sound of the line snapping tight. I don't move, even though I can easily escape. I feel ridiculous standing still. The line cinches around my ankle and the bandage gets yanked out of my hand. Before I know it, I'm hanging upside down, twenty feet in the air, dangling by my foot.

"Ow!" I shout. Hmm, maybe that was too dramatic. I need to make this realistic. What would I say if I was in a trap, like the one I'm in, but like, by accident? What do I say when I'm surprised?

"What the?"

I think I say it pretty realistically too. What would I do, though? Wiggle around? I look up at my foot: yep, fishing line. I pull myself up so I can act like I'm trying to escape.

The fishing line's so tight around my ankle I can't wriggle my foot loose or pry my fingers underneath it. Where's Alejandra? I turn back to the line. I'm not selling this well enough. Trying to climb the line hand-over-hand is going to be out of the question too. I can't get a grip on the line—it's as skinny as thread but surprisingly strong. I go to snap it in half and my hands slip instead. The line is covered in grease or something.

Oh man. I might actually be trapped.

I sigh and let myself hang back down.

"Aww, what's wrong, boy? You stuck?" I hear Alejandra laugh.

She steps out from behind a tree. No wonder I couldn't hear her heartbeat. She looks like she's wearing every piece of winter gear known to humanity. All that cloth would muffle the sound of her heart, and the scarf around her face would silence the sound of her breathing.

"I am *not* stuck," I say. "I'm wriggling around to draw you out."

"Oh really?" Alejandra says. "That scared, helpless look on your face is very convincing. Well, here I am. You've drawn me out of my hiding place. What are you going to do now? Eat me?"

"Yeah," I say. "As soon as I get down."

"Mm-hmm," Alejandra says, stepping right to the bottom of the tree and putting her backpack down. "And how long is that going to take?"

I scowl.

"Looks like I guessed your weight perfectly," Alejandra says, sounding exactly like some supervillain monologuing her evil vampire slaying plan. I continue to glower at her, though I definitely know I'm not going to come off as threatening as I swing upside down.

"You looked skinny," Alejandra says. "Not a lot of calories in blood, is there?"

"What difference does that make?" I wrap my arms around my chest, because the last thing I want her doing is judging how skinny I am.

"It makes a difference because that's 120-pound-test fishing line wrapped around your foot," Alejandra says. "There are only so many ways someone can catch a vampire, and you know, I didn't think a snare trap was going to work. I figured putting leaves all over the fishing line wasn't going to trick you, but you were zoning in on the blood like a good little vampire, weren't you? Struggle all you want, *Victor*. You're not getting out."

I am *not* going to let her tease me like this. What does she know about catching vampires? Fishing line? Is she serious? I'm a vampire, not a shark! I'm supposed to be showing her how cool vampires are, and she's just laughing about how easy I was to catch.

"I got caught on purpose, just so you know," I say.

"Why?" Alejandra says.

I don't know how to answer. I don't want to say I wanted to get caught so I could impress her by escaping, because, well . . . that escaping part and the impressing part aren't happening.

I close my eyes and focus as hard as I can. Maybe being stuck in a life-or-death situation is enough to get me to use my charisma? I focus on Alejandra, my forehead stinging with how hard I'm concentrating.

"Let me down," I say.

"Uh, no," Alejandra says, shaking her head for extra "no" effect.

I try kicking my trapped foot again, hoping it will somehow send some kind of energy wave up the line and break the branch above me. All I manage to do is swing back and forth.

"Aww, you forgot about Newton's First Law of Physics," Alejandra says. "You're not going to be able to kick yourself free. You forget that force applied in one direction will keep going unless met with an opposing force. And you're hanging from a tree, so there's no opposing forces for you to use."

"Try this opposing force," I mutter, and kick some more.

"Oh, yes, very impressive."

I grind my teeth together. That's what she was supposed to say, but not sarcastically, and definitely not while I failed to get out of her trap. I have to get myself free—and maybe Alejandra gave me the answer. I need to find an opposing force. I wonder if I can swing myself toward the tree trunk. I'm only a few feet away from that. Solid plan—swing over to the tree trunk, grab onto it in a massive hug, and use it as an anchor as I yank my foot free.

"Oh, no, down boy," Alejandra says, the second I start moving again.

"Right, I'm going to—" I start, and then I scream. My eyes burn, like the sun has somehow come up and directed millions of volts of electricity right into my face. I fling my arms up over my head, hiding my eyes in the protective crook of my elbow, but the throbbing, dull ache doesn't go away.

Alejandra has a flashlight and is shining it right into my face.

"OW!" I shout. "TURN THAT OFF!"

"So you *are* sensitive to light," Alejandra says, clicking the flashlight off. "I thought you might be. Yesterday I noticed how dilated your eyes were. That must be so you can see in the dark? Imagine being so vulnerable to a *flashlight*."

"What do you *want*?" I growl. I blink my eyes, but I can hardly see anything—red blobs still dance in my vision. All of that awesome night vision? Lost. Everything just looks black, or more black. Ugh. Is this how mortals see?

"Like I said last night," Alejandra says. "I want to hand you over to this vampire hunter and keep my friends' blood out of your mouth."

"I'm not eating anyone right now, am I?" I say.

"Emphasis on 'right now,'" Alejandra points out. I groan to myself. Showing off was really coming back to bite me.

"What if I promise not to eat them?" I say.

"Yes, the promise of a blood-sucker to not suck blood. You know, forgive me for not believing you," Alejandra says.

"Well, not *everyone*," I say. "But hey, tell me who your friends are, and they're off the menu."

"No dice."

"You want me to not eat anyone ... *ever*?" I say. "I'll starve!"

"Poor baby," Alejandra says. "There are a billion other things you can eat."

"There is literally not," I argue back. "Vampires are obligate hemovores."

"You can only eat ... ," Alejandra thinks. "Blood. So? Eat animals or something."

"Are you serious?" I ask. "I can't drink animal blood! Do they put animal blood in people? What if ... you know, we make a deal? Let me drink some of your blood every now and then and I won't *have* to kill anyone."

"Absolutely *not*."

"What?" I ask. "It's a win-win! Mortals let us do it all the time. It's—"

"It's *gross*," Alejandra growls. "You're going to hold that over my head? If I don't let you turn my body into your personal blood tap, then *I'm* responsible for you killing my friends? No, you know what? I have a better way to get a blood-sucker to stop killing people."

She pulls the wooden knife/stake thing from yesterday out of her backpack.

"The pointed stick makes a comeback." I sigh with my whole body.

"So, tell me," Alejandra says. "Does that whole 'you can only come into a house if you're invited' thing really work?"

"Are you ... are you inviting me over?!" I ask. "At stick point?!"

"No!" Alejandra says angrily, blood rushing to her face again. "It's the principle. I need to know if you can only do things if you're given permission!"

"Uh, yeah," I lie. I would love to gloat that mortals have no power over vampires whatsoever, but at the same time, I don't want to tell her the truth. I really want to know where she is going with this.

"Then the opposite must be true," Alejandra says. "If I make you give me your word, to not hurt me, I can let you down."

"Oh, okay!" I'm surprised. Maybe she just trapped me to like, scare me. Kind of one of those "see how serious I am" threats that never actually go anywhere.

"And once you're on the ground, I stab you in the heart with my wooden stake," Alejandra finishes casually.

"*What?!*" I ask, and flail around again, but nothing gives. Not the line, or the branch, or Alejandra.

"What difference does it make to you?" Alejandra asks. I'm very creeped out by how she's still so casual about it. "It's not like you care if *we* live or die. If our lives don't matter to you, your life doesn't matter to me."

I groan.

"Do even know what it's like to have someone you care about die?" Alejandra asks softly, running her finger along the wooden blade.

I hate that, without wanting to, I can imagine how I'd feel if she'd caught someone else in my family. If she cornered Adam one night. There's no way Adam would be able to get away. She could slay him easily. I'd burn the entire world as badly as the sun burns me if anything ever happened to him. But it's not like I'm going to admit that to a *mortal*.

"Everyone I care about lives forever," I say.

"Truly, you're a monster," Alejandra says.

I roll my eyes. This is definitely not going the way I wanted it to.

There is no way I'm going to ask her nicely to let me go. What I really need is some young blood—get back my super-vampire-strength, get out of this pathetic trap, and run away. Without making it look like I'm running away, because mortals are not that great. I let myself get caught— I wouldn't be in this trap if I didn't want to.

I should've held on tighter to that bandage. There's at least one drop's worth of blood I could've squeezed out of it. But that doesn't do me any good right now. Where else is there blood? Alejandra has blood—well, duh. Obviously she has blood—that cut on her hand is oozing young blood smell all over the place . . . oozing all over the place because she used her bandage as part of the trap. I know how I'm going to—

The entire night lights up. I throw my arms around my eyes again as a bolt of lightning streaks across the sky, followed by an ear-splitting thunder clap.

I say a whole bunch of swears that would get me grounded for a week before I shout to Alejandra. "Get me down!"

"Oh, no way," she says. She's backing away from the tree, though. Her eyes squint as pellets of rain start to fall from the sky. "What's wrong, Victor? Vampires can't survive electrocution?"

"Not from a lightning strike!" I shout. "Come on, let me down!"

"Oh no, this is better!" she shouts. "I'll just let the lightning take care of you!"

"Look! If lightning strikes this tree," I say, "I'm going to burn to death. And . . ." I'm searching for a way out of this. "It'll be like if we get touched by sunlight. I'll burn up. You aren't going to have a dead vampire to give to this hunter. You'll have a chunk of charcoal! And your friends are still going to die!"

That has to do it. That's the only reason she's out here, right? Alejandra thinks about it for a long time. She's going to give in. She has to. She needs me.

"I'm only letting you down if you give me your word," Alejandra says. "You promise me you'll be my prisoner."

She . . . really won't budge? I'm not going to be able to get away by showing how cool vampires are? I grind my teeth together and growl. I have to admit a mortal beat me?

"Fine!" I say. "You let me down, and I won't hurt you. Okay? You win."

Alejandra smirks and walks over to where she's got the line for her trap secured. A second later, I fall to the ground. I at least flip around on the way down and land on my feet, so I don't look completely pathetic. Alejandra takes a step back, narrowing her eyes even more.

I should run away, right now, while I have the chance. She's tightening her hold on the wooden stake, but I'll see her move before she's able to hit me. I force my face to look sad. Beaten. I kneel on the ground like a prisoner.

The smirk on Alejandra's face is gone.

"I'm doing this to save my friends," she says. Like she feels bad that she's about to stab me in the heart? I don't react. I can't react.

She finally lunges forward, and I roll away. She tries to move so fast and deadly, but she might as well be moving in slow motion. In one move, I grab the stake from her hand, her bleeding hand, her hand that isn't wrapped up in bandages anymore. The stake is all glossy from where her blood was on it.

She realizes what I'm about to do, and I can see her face morph into utter rage. I grin ear to ear and laugh like a maniac. Because now I have a stake, with her blood all over it. I lick it. And instantly, that electric, popping, young blood energy snaps on my tongue and down my throat, and I am running away before Alejandra can tell me how much cooler than mortals vampires really are.

20

ADAM

The bus ride is going to take forever. I keep looking out the window, imagining how much faster I could get to Wonderwood Park if Victor had decided to help me stop the murders. I hate how much I miss him, and he's not even gone.

"How much time do you think it'll take us to sneak around all of Wonderwood?" Luis asks.

Shoshana, Luis, and I take up the entire back row of seats, going over our find-the-murderer plan. I raise my chin off my hand and turn back to them.

I shrug. "A few minutes? I'll go faster by myself."

"Really? You want to do it alone?" Luis asks.

"It'll be faster," I repeat.

"Alright, so when we get there, we'll hang back while you investigate," Luis says. "And then, if you—"

"We can't let Adam go in there by himself!" Shoshana says. "I thought you said only people who are alone are getting killed. We—"

"No, it's okay," I say quickly. I'm definitely not going to be able to move with all of my vampire speed if they're with me.

"First of all, we brought him into this plan specifically because he could sneak," Luis says. "Like, really well. Secondly, he's not going to be a target, even if he is alone. Remember what my dad said—you have to hit puberty for vampires to eat you, and Adam looks like he could be seven, so the vampire hunter won't kill him. And thirdly, the three of us together will draw a lot more attention than Mr. Black Clothes being stealthy all by himself. What excuse do three kids have for being in the park after it closes?"

"Hiding painted rocks?" I suggest.

"Okay, but where are we going to get rocks?" Luis says.

"Here," Shoshana says, thrusting a round, smooth river rock into each of our hands.

"Oh, wow, well that's convenient," I blurt out, but before I can laugh at how random it is, she hands both me and Luis some paint markers she has in her backpack.

"Fine, we can all go together," Luis says. "I just want to know at what point during packing your 'stop a murderer' backpack you decided that you definitely were going to need rocks."

"The defense stage," Shoshana says. "Seriously, have you never gone on a hike and had your parents tell you to pick up a rock because you're in mountain lion country? Rocks are the best secret defense."

"And the paint markers?" Luis asks.

"You should always have paint markers with you, Luis," Shoshana says.

"Okay, so that means we can only paint stuff that'll let this guy know exactly what we think of him."

"Not sure he's going to be reading the rocks as we're throwing them," Shoshana says. "But *we'll* know. I'm in."

I laugh. Even Shoshana doesn't look that upset. And though I want to argue that I could go by myself, the fact that I've made two friends who would back me up while I looked for the murderer? My chest fills with warmth.

I pick a marker and start to scribble. My mind wanders. I can't believe it—I'm sitting with friends. Hanging out together. I imagine what it's going to be like, sneaking around the park with them.

"What are we supposed to do if we find the guy?" I ask, my eyebrows scrunching together.

"You're going to be *fine*," Luis says. "Here." He reaches into his shirt and pulls out a wooden crucifix necklace and pushes it into my hand. "Now you're protected *and* under-cover." Shoshana waves him off when he offers another crucifix to her.

"If we're posing like vampire hunters as a front to let the murderer come up to us, fine," Shoshana says. "But if you're trying to *become* a vampire hunter? I hope you know that all of this is going to do zilch to save you."

"Really?" Luis asks, his voice full of doubt.

"I've been thinking about what Adam said, with the garlic?" Shoshana says, and I sink further into my seat. "Like, it doesn't work the way we think it does. And now

I'm thinking 'Why holy water? Why crucifixes?' Vampires lived all over the globe, didn't they? Why would very specifically Catholic things stop a vampire?"

Luis shrugs. "Maybe it's any religious stuff and like, Christian stuff just gets the attention because it's the biggest religion? You're Jewish, right? Have you heard of anyone ever throwing a yarmulke at a vampire?"

"Kippahs are not holy objects," Shoshana sighs, and goes on, "but that's not the point. Think about it. Maybe stuff like crucifixes became associated with the whole vampire hunting thing because of who started killing them all in the first place. Purification started in Spain, right? It's just weird that 1492 comes around and we're hunting vampires all over the globe with Catholic stuff as our weapons."

"You even remember the year?" Luis asks.

"The Jews were expelled from Spain in 1492," Shoshana says. "Right after Purification killed the werewolves and the vampires, they came for everyone else, remember? They used crosses to push us out, too."

"Can you seriously stop talking about the past like people aren't still getting hunted today?" Luis says.

"They are?" I ask, completely surprised. "You mean, regular mortals—er, people? Not vampires—?"

"Yeah, my mom," Luis says. "She came here on a student visa. Those things expire after you graduate, but she'd met my dad by then and even though they got married and had kids, it doesn't make her a citizen any faster. So there was like, this period where she was waiting. She didn't do anything wrong, but that didn't stop random people on the street literally threatening to call immigration on her and have her deported back to Honduras."

I swallow. That sounds a lot like having someone call a vampire hunter on me.

"While she was waiting for her green card, she was always afraid," Luis goes on. "It didn't even matter that she was married to Dad who, like, doesn't even know Spanish, or that Dad was in the army. She wouldn't leave the house sometimes, even when she got her citizenship. People just assumed she didn't belong."

"That's what I'm saying," Shoshana huffs. "We let them tell us vampires were the problem, and if we'd just get rid of them, the world would be totally better. But then they said wait, it's not really vampires, it's the Jews. And then it's not really the Jews, it's this group. Or that group. Or immigrants. Every time the world doesn't get better, they just draw a new line between who's good and an entire group of people who are suddenly 'monsters.' And we all get so scared that there's a new monster in our midst, don't we? So scared that we rush to join the side of those who would 'protect' us from the monsters that they themselves invented.

"I'm just saying the stuff that hurt your mom is the same stuff that hurt my people is the same stuff that wiped out vampires, and if you don't do anything about it, eventually that line's going to be drawn to keep you out."

"Are you trying to say people should've stuck up for vampires?" Luis asks. "They drink *human blood*, Shoshana. I'm pretty sure that's like, the most basic level of evil there is. And anyway, we know the crucifix works. We found where the murderer was hiding, remember? And he was only hiding by that giant cross because he knew it would protect him."

"Or he *thought* it would," Shoshana says.

"Okay," Luis says, in an annoyed forfeit. "But the stake will still work?"

"Only if you're saying vampires aren't undead and have beating hearts now."

They go back to painting their rocks and I sink further in my seat, tightening the scarf around my mouth. My eyes dart over to the pencil tucked behind Luis's ear more times than I'd like to admit. He has all the right gear and the attitude to become a vampire hunter . . . and I ask myself again—is his dad the one who's trying to catch us?

"So, Luis," I say. "You said your dad was obsessed with vampires, right? What do you think he'd do if he ever saw one?"

Luis groans. "Geek out."

I cringe, waiting for more. "Could you, like . . . elaborate on that?"

"I told you, he's got like, every horror movie ever made at home," Luis says. "He loves all that stuff. If there's really vampires in Lacey? I would know."

How could Luis say so much without giving me an answer? "How . . . would you know?"

"Because he'd be best friends with them," Luis says. "He's like a little kid with all that stuff. He thinks they're the coolest thing in the world. If he ever met a vampire? He'd probably go into fanboy levels of freaking out."

I laugh at the mental image.

"What would you do?" Luis asks me, and I sputter in surprise.

"Oh, I don't know. I think it would be . . . neat," I say, and laugh.

Luis turns to Shoshana. "What about you?"

Shoshana doesn't lift her head, but I can feel her tensing up a bit. "I think I'd like to know if I'm right about them."

I bite my lip. I want to tell her that she is, but there's no way I can pull that off without giving myself away.

"Well, you weren't right about the ghosts," Luis says.

"I don't think ghosts can get summoned like that," Shoshana says.

"I've seen you raise one before," Luis scoffs. "You can say you didn't, but I totally saw you."

Shoshana sighs and puts her rock down. "No, you didn't."

"Why are you so embarrassed by it?" Luis asks. "I literally watched you light a candle, chant a bunch of spells, and then you were talking to your grandpa."

Shoshana huffs. "It was a yahrzeit."

"Is that the Jewish word for séance?" Luis asks.

"No," Shoshana says, with another frustrated huff. "It was the anniversary of my grandfather's death—what we call a yahrzeit. And we light a memorial candle, say a prayer in Hebrew, and . . . think about their memory. I really miss talking to him. I wasn't *literally* raising his spirit, but I get why you'd think that, and it's ... well, I just want you to know."

"But it was at night?" Luis asks.

"All Jewish days start at sunset," Shoshana says. "I mean, I could go on about how a lot of what the church deems witchcraft is actually just Judaism."

"But ..." Luis's eyebrows arch, and he looks hurt. "Then why'd you let me think you were a witch?"

Shoshana doesn't meet his eyes. She shrugs. "You needed help. And I wanted to help. I ... totally understand if you don't want my help anymore—"

"Are you kidding?" Luis asks. "I didn't kick you out when you couldn't get a ghost baby to show up, did I? Dude, I didn't even kick you out when you wanted to raise up a dead ghost baby in the first place."

Shoshana still looks a little embarrassed, but smiles.

"We're in this together," Luis says, and glances over at me. "Okay? 'Til the end?"

"'Til the end," I agree.

"'Til the end," Shoshana adds.

Luis holds up his painted rock.

"Eat rocks," Shoshana reads, unimpressed. But she gives a little "eh" nod and even says, "Very on the nose."

"Yeah, and if we have to tangle with some murderers, I hope to land this 'on the nose.' What's yours?"

Shoshana's rock has צדק on it.

"It says 'tzedek,'" Shoshana says. "The Hebrew word for justice."

"I like it," Luis says, then turns to me. "What'd you do for yours, Adam?"

I curl my hand around my rock. "Not yet," I say. "This one's just for the murderer."

I'd painted I DON'T WANT TO BE YOUR MONSTER on it. I couldn't think of anything better to throw at a vampire hunter's face. But to explain it to my friends? There was no way.

I'd like to believe that I've proven myself too, that trying to stop the murderer would be solid evidence that vampires aren't monsters. That we can use our power to help others. But what if I'm wrong? I shake my head.

I just need to find the murderer before my friends find out what I am.

21

ADAM

The entire night sky turns bright white and I snap my head away from the window, wincing. A second later, my ears are the next part of me to be assaulted as a loud *boom* shakes the bus. I hate lightning. It rains a lot in Lacey, but storms like these are rare in the Pacific Northwest. There's a reason vampires don't live in places prone to thunderstorms. I grimace as my ears ring and red dots dance before my eyes.

Shoshana and Luis don't notice me, but instead scream in happy surprise as rain starts to pelt the windows. And I really do try my best to join in. Rain means no murders, and I *am* happy for that, but my senses are slow to return to normal.

The other passengers must think we're weird. And at least for now, Luis is totally okay with that.

"Keep it coming," Luis shouts up to the dark sky when we hop off the bus.

I smell the air—nice, clean, rainy, murder-free air. No

blood, no ... the smile drops off my face. *Blood.* I can smell blood. *No* ... there can't be blood. There can't be a murder. It's raining. Unless the rain came too late.

"Hey Shoshana ... let me see your watch," I say as I shove my painted rock into my hoodie pocket.

It's only 7 p.m. That's not the right time—the murders were happening later in the night, weren't they? No ... no, they weren't. *The Lost Boys* started at 7 p.m.—by the time Victor and I got back to Lacey, the murder had already happened.

I recognize the blood smell. But where have I smelled it? How many mortals have I smelled today? No, not today—it was ...

"Hey, is your sister okay?" I ask as I turn to Luis.

Luis only gives me a funny look.

"Can you just make sure?" I ask again. I can't go right out and say "I smell her blood in the air." Luis keeps looking at me like I'm being way too random, which I know I am.

"She was out the other night, remember?" I ask. "And ... maybe she went out again tonight? And maybe she, like, ran into the murderer before it started to rain, and maybe—"

"That is way too many maybes," Luis says.

"But—"

"Luis!"

I jump at the sound of the voice and turn around. I can't believe it—it's Luis's sister! And even better? She's alive enough to find us annoying! But the blood smell is strong coming off of her. I don't know how to ask about it because if I'm the mortal kid I'm pretending to be, I shouldn't be able to smell it. Neither Shoshana nor Luis smell it. And I'm taking all my mortal cues from them.

"What are you three doing out again?" Luis's sister asks once she catches up to us.

"You're also out?" Luis asks.

"I'm not going to get killed, if you're going all Dad on me," she says.

"Dad says you're the most likely to get killed if you're alone—"

"No, I'm not," she says. "No one's getting killed anymore."

"Sure, Alejandra."

I silently thank Luis for saying his sister's name so now I know what it is.

"No, I mean it," Alejandra says, in a way that tells us she's got secret knowledge she's not sharing with us. "I met a guy at the park and he's—"

"You're sneaking out for *guys*?" Luis asks, fully offended.

"It's not that kind of guy." Alejandra sighs. "I'm going to help him stop the murders."

That makes me pause. Luis stops completely.

"How?" he asks.

"None of your business," Alejandra says.

She makes to push past us, but she wobbles with her step. I don't know if the other two notice, but I can tell immediately she's not well. Her blood? It's not pumping as hard as it should. It's not filling her veins the way mortal blood does. I lunge forward to catch her because she's falling to the ground.

"Hey!" Luis says in surprise.

"I'm okay," Alejandra says, but her voice is not as strong as it was. She's trying to stand up, but she can't. The only way I'm holding her up is thanks to my vampire strength.

The smell of her blood. I figure it out—she has an infection. For a second, a wild idea crosses my mind. Mama said she would teach me blood magic, if only a mortal would drop into our laps who needed it. Well, I literally have a mortal in my arms who has an infection. And she looks like she could lose consciousness . . . so she wouldn't tell our secrets . . .

What am I doing? I push away my selfish thoughts.

"One of you needs to call 911," I say. "She needs to get to the hospital."

"If you call 911, Dad's going to find out," Alejandra says.

Luis sighs. It's a surrender sigh.

"Fine," Luis says. "No 911. What'd you do to your hand anyway?"

That's where the blood smell is coming from. She's got an open cut on her hand. And that's where the infection must have started too.

"Vampires," Alejandra mutters.

My stomach drops. There's no way mortals randomly mutter things about vampires when they're losing blood. She's not just out here trying to stop the murders, she's—

"Wait wait, hold up," Luis says. "Are you . . . out here hunting vampires?"

"And what are *you* doing out here?" Alejandra asks.

Luis grins and laughs. "Not baiting myself to catch a vampire, I can tell you that."

Alejandra rolls her eyes. "I almost slayed him, okay?"

My heart jumps into my throat. Luis's sister is the "second vampire hunter" Victor accidentally pushed into slaying?

"Look . . . help me walk home," Alejandra says. "I'll ask mom to drive me to the ER."

I don't think Luis is taking his sister very seriously. He keeps smiling and holding back laughter, even though he's helping her get to her feet and she's very obviously hurt. I motion to Shoshana to help, and we each stand under one of Alejandra's arms. I picked the arm that doesn't have a bleeding hand, though I wonder if I should have—mortals get freaked out by blood, don't they?

We start walking forward. Luis leads the way but he keeps laughing like this is the funniest thing to happen.

"A vampire," Luis says, when he finally stops laughing. "Did he have fangs? What'd he look like? Must've been quite a guy for you to want to catch him. Did he try to woo you?"

"Don't *even* dare," Alejandra says through gritted teeth.

"But how'd you know it was a vampire, and not just a guy?" Luis asks. "I want to know. What do vampires look like?"

And then? Alejandra goes and describes Victor. Down to his hair style and the way he rolls up his sleeves on his button-up shirt. My blood is boiling. It *is* Victor. He's going to get our entire family in trouble! What if she tells? She's going to the emergency room! What if someone else believes her? And then *they* tell? And now, suddenly, everyone in town is talking about Victor, and then? Then the vampire hunter knows!

He'll know what Victor looks like, but worse? What if Alejandra watched Victor leave? And she remembers which way he went? And she talks about that at the hospital! Our house is not that far away! Anyone could stand where Alejandra saw Victor last. And if he ran straight home? Not going way out of his way as a diversion like Mom and Mama taught us? All a mortal had to do was walk into the woods and they'd find our house!

A tremble shakes my body as I picture what it would feel like if vampire hunters came in the middle of the day and dragged everyone outside and—

I need to get home. I need to fix this somehow. But I'm stronger than Shoshana and Luis—they need my help. So I stay and give them my strength. But inside? My heart is running for me.

Luis laughs again. "Wow, Alejandra, you described your vampire better than your date to homecoming."

"Shut it, Luis," Alejandra says.

It takes us forever to walk back to Luis's house. I thought it was bad enough walking down Ruddell, where the sidewalk is terrifyingly close to the road where cars zoom by at fifty miles an hour and their headlights burn into my retinas each time they pass.

But we turn onto Arcarro and it gets worse. All those houses, huddled closely together? There are so many mortals, and any one of them could peek out of their window and see me. I don't belong here... I shiver as a mortal waves at Luis on his way to the mailbox. I can't shake the feeling that I'm surrounded.

We pass by about twenty houses before we reach Luis and Alejandra's. It's near the end of the street, right before it turns into a cul-de-sac. I look at the forest looming over the roofs and feel a twinge of comfort. Through that forest, I'd find my house.

We walk up the steps to their front door. This is the closest I've been to a mortal house. Okay, well, technically I've run across a thousand mortal house roofs, but I'm not sure that counts.

"I better stand," Alejandra says. She reaches out an arm to brace herself against the side of the house as Luis digs in his pockets for the keys. "If my mom sees me getting carried, she's going to straight-up panic. Thanks, you three."

"No thanks for a duty," I say shakily as I duck out from under Alejandra's arm.

"What?" Luis asks.

"No... need to thank me for doing the right thing." I reword the phrase Mama always says, which I guess does sound strange when you translate it directly from Arabic. "It's... just something my Mama says. Speaking of, I've got to get home too," I say. "Before *my* moms panic."

"Oh, yeah, definitely don't want double-mom panic," Luis says.

"Same time tomorrow?" I ask.

"Yeah," Luis says. "Forecast says snow. Not sure if that's 'raining' or 'not raining.'"

"Either way, there's still a murderer out there," I point out.

Shoshana doesn't say bye. She hasn't said almost anything since we got off the bus. I wave bye to her—I don't want to make her feel like she has to say something if she's not in a talking mood. She beckons for me to walk with her, and after waving again to Luis, I join Shoshana on the sidewalk leading to her house.

She takes a deep breath, takes a step closer to me, and whispers so softly even I, with vampire-level hearing, can barely hear her.

"I know who you are," she says.

"Huh?"

"You said you got adopted after the Temple Beth Hatfiloh explosion, right?" she asks. I clench my jaw tightly and nod stiffly. I have a horrible feeling where this is going. "I asked my parents about it, and they said, yeah, totally—there *was* a baby who vanished that night. So I thought, like, maybe in the mayhem that baby got kidnapped. Thing is, that baby's mom died in the explosion still holding onto swaddling blankets and stuff, so she *was* holding her baby when she died. He would have been in the explosion too. That baby's name was Adam Schechter."

I stop. My blood runs cold.

"Where are you going with this?" I ask.

"I seriously thought you were his ghost at first," Shoshana goes on. "The way you moved so quietly. But like, where would you have come from? Pioneer Cemetery doesn't have a Jewish section. Plus, they never found a body.

"And then you got super sick eating that chocolate, which I thought was weird. And you kept that scarf tied around your mouth. You brought up that stuff with the blood. And I saw what you painted on your rock. Why else would you write that? I get it now."

"Get what?"

"You're him, aren't you?" Shoshana asks. "Someone turned you into a vampire."

22

ADAM

I do everything I can to not react.

I can't believe I messed up this badly. Shoshana *knows* . . .

What do I do?

I turn around quickly and walk away, though I probably look like a robot because my arms are glued to my sides and my shoulders are hunched up. I walk away as fast as I can, too afraid to look back, ignoring Shoshana as she calls after me, even breaking into a run when she begs me to come back. My thoughts race a thousand miles an hour.

Shoshana knows what I am.

I round the corner, out of her line of sight, and reach up to grab my hair in anger.

This is bad. This is so bad. Here I was, angry at Victor, but *I* put everyone in danger too! Mom said we needed to keep our secrets. Mama told me *why* we have to stay hidden.

I need to get somewhere safe. I lunge through the trees, vanishing into the shadows.

I reach home, but it's weird the things I notice now: the paint that camouflages the house so perfectly, all the work we did to make it look deserted, the house's wonderful shuttered-up windows.

The first floor is empty. Empty . . . ?

"Victor?!" I call out, my voice in a panic. Did he not actually escape? Is he okay, is he—

"Adam?" Victor calls to me from our room. "Is that you? Get up here!"

A wave of relief washes over me. I climb up the stairs in two bounds and step into our room. But my relief is short-lived. All the anger I had at Victor comes rushing back.

"You drank blood!" I shout.

He did! His eyes are all red and glowy and he's pacing around our room frantically. He didn't *only* almost get slayed . . . he didn't *just* put our whole family in danger. *He drank Alejandra's blood?!*

"Adam, shh, keep it down, will you?" Victor says. "I don't know how long this is supposed to last! It was like, *one* lick. Maybe I should try burning it off? Is that how this works? I can just run in circles around my room." And he literally starts doing that. "One of the moms is going to be home any second. You've got to cover for me. Help me hide this."

"No," I say.

"*What?*" Victor hisses in surprise. "I'm your brother!"

"No, I'm not helping you!" I say. "That's all you care about? Trying not to get in trouble? You seriously went out there and played like you were in Santa Cruz! You drank her blood—"

I think about how weak Alejandra had been, how I had to help carry her to her house. And to find out that Victor had a part to play in that? I had to sit next to Luis on the bus after he said drinking blood was the definition of evil, and here Victor's been doing exactly what makes vampires look like monsters to him.

"You're acting like I sucked her dry," Victor scoffs. "I literally licked the stake she'd been trying to slay me with. It was blood she'd already bled. I needed it—just like, a boost to help me get away. But that doesn't matter, I need your—"

"It *does* matter," I say. "She's going to the emergency room to fix her hand and she's going to tell them who you are and *what* you are and any second vampire hunters are going to—"

"Whoa, whoa, wait," Victor holds his hands up. "How do you know that?"

I tense up immediately. It's the second time in thirty minutes that I've accidentally given myself away. I take a step forward, pulling my shoulders back and standing up straighter.

"I'm trying to stop the murderer," I say, and take another deep breath. "I've made friends with some mortals and I could really use your—"

"You're doing *what*?" Victor asks, his eyes narrowing. "That's what you're sneaking out for? I thought you wanted me to protect you from vampire slayers. I didn't know you were trying to be friends with them!"

"You never listen to me!" I shout back. "I said I wanted to stop the murders—"

"And you'll pick the side of a slayer over your own brother?" Victor growls. "I just told you a mortal tried to *kill* me. I'll never—"

"Adam?" Mama calls out into the house. "Victor? Sung?"

Victor and I freeze. The panic on Mama's voice is *strong*! That can only mean one thing—the vampire hunters are here! Already?

"Come down here!" Mama shouts again.

I turn to Victor, but there's no way he's going to be able to come downstairs without everyone knowing he drank young blood. So what does he do? Help us defend our house?

He thinks about it one minute longer and then dives into his bed, hiding under his covers.

I growl and run out of the room. I bang on Sung's door and run down the stairs. Sung is on my heels.

"What's going on?" Sung shouts, with their headphones still around their neck.

"I need your help!" Mama says.

"Is it vampire hunters?!" I shout.

Mama turns to look at me, with a puzzled look on her face. And that's when I notice she has something small and fluffy and tan in her arms. It's a *coyote*.

"She's eaten poison!" Mama explains as she settles the animal on our dining room table. "Come here, both of you."

I stand next to Mama's left side as Sung steps up to Mama's right. We are both looking at her with a lot of confusion . . . until, suddenly, it clicks, and the fear of vampire hunters storming our house fades away. I smile.

"You're teaching us blood magic!" I say.

"Yes, here." Mama guides both Sung's and my hands on top of the coyote's chest. It's lying on its side and breathing quickly. Mama closes her eyes and I do the same. "Remember how we connected during our puzzle? Reach out for that same connection. Concentrate on how it feels."

I can sense the way blood fills the arteries and veins, the same way I could sense that Alejandra's blood pressure changed. I can feel its warmth, even if I can't touch it.

"Feel its life," Mama whispers. Maybe it's the slow, rhythmic way the coyote's blood pumps in its body, but my ears hear Mama like she's talking underwater—all garbled and hard to understand.

I concentrate, and . . . yeah. I can feel it, the blood pumping through the coyote's body. The expanding and contracting of its heart, pumping and pulling blood through its body. The veins and arteries, expanding and squishing and—

I stand up straighter.

"I feel something!" I call out. "There's something that doesn't belong!"

"I feel it too," Sung adds. "It's like . . . grains of sand."

"Yes, you both got it! Excellent!" Mama says. "Focus on how that feels, how sharply it stands against the warm, soft blood."

I feel Mama place her hand on top of Sung's and my hand. Her fingers curl, and we copy her, making a combing motion with our fingers. And I can feel it—inside the coyote's body, the grains of sand stop moving. I can feel the rest of the blood pumping along its arterial path. But I was able to hold onto the poison.

"We must gather it all," Mama says. "This poison has started working, so you must find it, where it's attaching in the body, doing harm. Sung, you have the right side of the body. Adam, take the left. I'll work on this poor creature's head. Hurry."

I comb my hands through the coyote's fur, but I'm searching for any loose grains of sand in its blood. There are lots, but I can grab them and pull them along. In a few minutes, I've worked the little grains through all the veins and arteries until I have a clump of them. Sung's hands pause close to mine.

Mama keeps waving her arms, curling her fingers, grimacing and pulling, until her own clump of grains meets with mine.

"I think . . . I think we've got it," Mama whispers. Her voice is strained.

"A cut needs to be made," she says. "Here, to drain the poison. Whenever we do blood magic, you must always use a knife, or, if you're like Mom, a syringe. Never bite, no matter what. You'll turn a mortal with your bite. We can't hold back our venom."

Sung pushes their clump of sand into mine and leaves to go get a knife. I'm not sure if I'm supposed to open my eyes, so I keep them clamped shut. I don't know who makes the cut, but I can sense the way the skin parts . . . the blood that wants to rush out.

Instinct tells me not to let it, but I move my fingers and let the poison sand stuff go.

"There . . . ," Mama whispers again. She nudges me and I open my eyes. She waves her arms around the coyote again and nods. "You two did it!"

But it also means we now have a wild coyote in our house that suddenly got better. We laugh as we spend the next few minutes trying to convince it to run out the open doors. A vampire house is anything but normal.

"You can do it, come on," I say. Maybe I say the magic words, because the coyote believes me and finally runs out of our house.

"Okay, but seriously?" Sung says. "I had no clue we could do that. What did you call it? Blood magic?"

"This is what vampires used to do, Sung," Mama says. "For thousands upon thousands of years. Before attitudes changed and we had to go into hiding. Practicing this part of who we are would have put us in danger, and for the longest time, the knowledge wasn't shared. Doing blood magic would have been too risky! And it wasn't passed down. I should have taught you sooner, but to be honest? I didn't want to remember the past, to remember what we lost. I have enough nightmares as it is. And maybe I thought doing blood magic again would only make it worse. But sometimes all it takes is some 'young blood' who dream of a different world."

Mama gives me a small nod, and pride swells up in my chest.

"Ooh, good pun," Sung says.

"Too bad we still can't let mortals know who we are," I say.

"Ah, do not be so sure," Mama says. "The future may yet change! The time may come when we help mortals once again. But no matter which way the future goes, if we let this knowledge die, that only means we let those possibilities die."

Sung smiles. "You don't have to worry about me. This is going to be the first thing I do when I go back to Korea. I'm going to teach everyone I meet. Everyone needs to know this."

"Not even everyone in the house knows this," I grumble, lifting my chin in the direction of the second floor, to where Victor is probably still hiding under his comforter.

"He doesn't know what he's missing out on," Sung says. "Doing cool vampire stuff is kind of his thing." And Sung rushes up the stairs, like they are going to get through to him. They don't realize the only vampire stuff Victor cares about doing is drinking blood.

I hope they have better luck with Victor than I do. But if they do? It's going to hurt.

Mama is busy unpacking new coffee mugs she's brought home. I walk over to the bookshelf. Immediately, something catches my eye.

"Hey, Mama, what's this?" I ask, holding up a wooden crucifix necklace. For a wild moment, I think it's some kind of trophy thing. Like, Mom fought some vampire hunter and stole their good luck charm.

But Mama laughs and says, "That was your Mom's."

"*Mom?*" I ask.

"Oh, yes," Mama says. "Long ago, when your Mom was still mortal, she was a nun!"

I remember the drawings in her journal.

I make a face. "A nun vampire hunter?"

"Oh, yes!" Mama says with a laugh. "She did not start hunting vampires until after she had been turned! She was bitten without her permission. She thought all vampires were like that, so she made a bargain with her order. She would hunt vampires for them in exchange for her life. And she did, for many, many years."

"So *that's* why she was a vampire hunter?" I choke. "Just so they wouldn't slay her?" I tremble at the thought. I would hate to have something like that over my head. But still, even if she was trapped, she was also killing to stay alive. "She must have really hated vampires."

"She did not know anything differently," Mama says. "What vampires used to be."

"Like blood magic stuff?"

"Yes, exactly! Beatrice knew of none of it," Mama says. "Only the idea mortals have now, that vampires are evil. Like a parasite: only taking from mortals, giving nothing back. Until by accident, she told me she found something. Some kind of ... notes? From a meeting long ago. Something that explained why mortals started to hate us. She escaped, which is always hard for a vampire—to be on their own. Not knowing where it will be safe to rest. Not knowing where to hide from the sun. But that's how we met. In an undercover network, she—"

The front door slams open right then, and Mama and I both jump.

It's not vampire hunters. Well, not really. Mom barges into the house, a wave of anger rolling in with her. It's the angriest I've ever seen my mom. For a wild second, I really can see the vampire hunter she used to be, and I'm just glad she's not after me. She mutters only one word.

"*Victor*."

23

VICTOR

"Knock, knock," I hear Sung's voice.

I'm wrapped up in my blankets, and I'm not coming out.

"Go away," I say.

But Sung doesn't. The vampire with a sign on their door saying they'll take off someone's hand for interrupting them is coming in here after I told them not to? I wish that whole "vampires can't go into your room without permission" myth was an actual thing.

"You didn't come down," Sung says. "Mama taught us how to do some cool vampire stuff. And you know, being a cool dude is kind of your thing. You missed out on blood magic lessons."

Sung says "blood magic" like the words are surrounded in sparkles. I let them think I'm interested.

"What is it? Like, charisma?" I ask.

"Nah, healing stuff," Sung says.

"We already heal fast."

"Healing mortals," Sung clarifies.

"Boring," I answer, but I lift my head. "Does that mean there's blood downstairs?"

"Eo-hyu." Sung sighs with annoyance. "You don't need to drink blood to do vampire things, Victor. Especially not you. Mom told you who you were bit by, right? An ancient vampire. There's a lot of power in vampire venom. And the older a vampire gets, the more powerful they get, which means you definitely don't need to drink blood to do vampire stuff."

I remember that time I tried to charisma the ticket guy at the *Lost Boys* showing. I thought about trying to use charisma on Adam to make him appreciate how much I wanted to look after him. Sung doesn't know what they're talking about, but whatever.

"Then I didn't really miss out on anything, did I?" I ask.

"We missed you," Sung says.

"No one did," I mutter under my breath.

"You say that," Sung says. "Except that I'm here. Specifically because I noticed you weren't with us. So yeah, I'm checking in on you."

"I'm *fine*," I say.

"I am very skeptical of your self-assessment," Sung says. "You've been gone all night. A day doesn't go by when I don't hear you and Adam arguing. I know it's getting to you. If you don't want to talk, it's okay—no presh. But you don't have to do everything alone. You don't even have to feel your emotions alone. You can vent. You can share."

"Like you can relate," I finally say. "You got to be a normal kid."

"Stuff is tough even if you're a mortal kid," Sung says. "But hey, no one needs credentials to listen."

I don't say anything. Like, okay, I get it. Sung is really trying. I don't doubt that they care. Words come so much easier to me when I'm trying to be funny, but this is serious. And sometimes, even if I know something's bothering me, I don't know how to say why. Or what it even is, exactly. Maybe Sung gets that.

"You know that night we drank young blood?" I ask.

I wait to see if Sung says something like they did last time I talked about young blood, like lecturing me on how much blood I need to survive. But they don't.

"It wasn't like old times," I say, "because it was something completely new, but it felt like how things used to be. But with this promise of something better. And I wanted to find out what 'something better' was. And now? That might have been all I get.

"And I don't mean just drinking the blood, Sung," I say quickly. "But like . . . it was such a fun night."

"Did you tell Adam that's how you felt about it?" Sung asks.

"How can I?" I say. I stop myself before I point out that Adam's been gone, off doing his own brother-free thing. Not that I think Sung would snitch on us, but even when Adam's around? He's not really here.

"You know," Sung says. "I remember when Mom brought Adam home. You were so excited—you talked nonstop about having a little brother. You'd stand by his crib and watch over him, and even though he couldn't play yet, you'd pretend to read to him, or shake toys at him."

I force myself to smile. "I forgot about that."

"I didn't," Sung says. "It was the first time I realized I had found a family. A real one. That would accept us all as we are."

"Tell that to Mom," I mutter.

"Actually, I think you should," Sung says. "She can't keep you from being what you are. Even if she's trying to give you a 'normal' childhood, you're anything but normal, Victor. You're a vampire, and I think you should be learning vampire stuff. And if you want? I can be there with you when you talk to Mom."

I smile an actual smile this time.

"I know this feels like you're in way over your head," Sung says. "But don't forget, we've got your back, dude. You're never alone. We're family."

"And here I thought you were just a dork who lived in front of the computer," I say.

"Maybe I do spend a bit too much time in there," Sung says.

"You've got that sign on your door."

"I would be so many hands in debt right now if I carried through with that," Sung says. "But you have a point. And if you didn't ask me for help earlier because I've been so very loud about how busy I am with school? If you thought I wasn't available for you? If I made you feel more alone? I didn't mean to, and I'm sorry."

I'm glad I'm still hiding under my covers so my sibling can't see what those words do to me. I could cry. I didn't realize that was all I wanted to hear: someone simply acknowledging that I feel alone.

I whisper a soft "Thanks."

"Hey, maybe it doesn't fix everything, but I'm here now," Sung says. "Not everyone understands what it's like to be lonely, to feel cut off from everyone. Or why you'd want to stay in your room when you would rather be with everyone. That sometimes, being with people hurts, but being alone hurts too, and life gets completely messy."

"Oh, man, you *can* relate then, huh," I say. It was my bad attempt at a joke, but Sung laughs.

"Maybe just a little bit," Sung says. "It's how I got bitten."

"Really?"

"Yeah," Sung says. "Believe it or not, for the longest time my entire personality was all about fitting in. Everyone in my life told me it was the only way I could be happy. I shushed up all the parts of me that weren't just like everyone else, but it never made me feel better, because . . . well, it was a part of me, so I always carried that with me, you know? And being *asked* to be a part of a vampire coven? I fell for it hard. It was so foolish, but—"

"Why would you call that foolish?" I ask. "It's not your fault you got bit. Some jerk vampire saw you feeling lonely and decided to trick you!"

"Yeah, it's hard to think right when you're lonely," Sung says. "You can get so desperate for any way out. I know it's hard being here sometimes, but you're really lucky to have Mom and Mama. Being in a 'real vampire coven' is not really all that glamorous."

"Like having to eat people?" I ask.

"Oh . . . *yeah*," Sung says. "My old head vampire didn't bring us blood. He didn't believe in using familiars either. I tried not to eat until I absolutely had to, and then, I decided I'd only eat bad people. But that's really hard to figure out if you're following someone. And one time, I picked the wrong person. After that, I just picked people at random. I tried not to listen when they pleaded with me. It's not pretty."

"Did you ever . . . ," I think about Alejandra, "get one that fought back? And, like, you needed just a little bit of their blood. Like, literally just enough to get away? And . . . how long did that last, exactly?"

Sung is quiet for a long time again.

"Why are you hiding under the blanket?" they finally ask.

My heart clenches in my chest. I don't know what to say, but I kick myself for asking them about mortals. I'm struggling to think of a valid excuse to be hiding my eyes when I'm saved by Mom calling for me.

Of course, the way Mom booms *"Victor"* so loud the windows rattle, I'm not sure I'd really call it a save.

"What'd you do?" Sung whispers.

Please let my eyes be normal, please let my eyes be normal.

I throw the blankets back and Sung immediately gets to their feet. I'm going to take that as a sign that my eyes are still red and glowy and definitely giving away the fact that

I drank young blood. I should have tried to swipe Mom's sunglasses or something.

"What. Did. You. Do?" Sung repeats themself. I hate the way their words sound. Accusatory, like I'm some kind of monster caught doing something disgusting. As if no one in this house is a vampire. I ignore them, because Mom calls for me again.

I jump down from my bunk. I should be angry—there's no way Mom could possibly have found out I drank Alejandra's blood unless Adam told on me. But I don't feel anything except . . . I don't know. There's a heaviness in my chest that I guess might be sadness, or maybe disappointment. I'm going to get in trouble for literally doing what vampires do. Drinking blood. And not just that! I drank blood to save myself. And somehow I'm going to be the bad guy.

I take the stairs slowly, one annoyed step at a time. I don't make eye contact with anyone. Sung follows me downstairs. Their jaw is hanging open, like they still can't get over their shock.

They can all tell, but Mom still says it.

"You drank a mortal's blood."

I shrug. "She was trying to kill me."

"Do *not* tell me you tried to bite her—"

"God, no, Mom. She was already bleeding. She was . . . it was a trap." My voice shakes as I realize my own mom doesn't care that I'd almost gotten slayed. "I was hungry."

"Why is there a mortal hunting for vampires within a mile of this house?" Mom asks. She says each word and takes a pause, as if she's trying everything she can to not get angry. But it's not working very well.

I don't answer. What am I going to say? Admit I snuck out, met a girl, and tried to impress her by revealing that I'm a vampire?

"Thankfully, for the rest of us, I worked tonight," Mom starts, not sounding thankful whatsoever. "Thankfully, I was the one to draw blood for this girl with an infection who came in muttering to her parents about slaying vampires, because according to Adam, you were just hiding in your room hoping all of this would blow over."

I glare daggers at Adam, who of course is suddenly very interested in the floor.

"Victor," Mom snaps to get my attention back on her before she goes on with her lecture. "Sneaking out, I could have forgiven. But telling a mortal that you're a vampire? I hope I don't have to spell out what kind of danger you've put us all in."

I still don't say anything. I keep my face blank. Numb.

"I forbid you from leaving our home," Mom says, her voice firm with all the authority of a head vampire. As if she turned me herself. As if she has any power over me.

"Good thing that doesn't work," I snap back before I storm upstairs.

I've already made up my mind by the time I slam my bedroom door closed. If Mom's so certain I'm going to destroy our family, then it's better for everyone if I'm not in this family anymore.

24

ADAM

I should take some of the heat off Victor.

I know I should. It's the right thing to do: admit that I also went out, tell Mom I tried to make friends with mortals, let her know that I put our family in danger too.

But I don't.

By now, I'm sure Shoshana has already told Luis that I'm a vampire. No way I'm going to risk hanging out with them again. And if I'm not going back out? Then no one needs to know that I was also doing the wrong thing by getting too close to mortals.

I wander back to the bookshelf as the moms talk. Sung goes back to their room. And everything just . . . goes back to normal—a really weird, silent, heavy, uncomfortable normal. Is Mom right? Is Victor being grounded enough to make everything go back to the way it once was?

I have Mom's crucifix in my hands before I realize I've picked it up. But it reminds me not of Mom, or vampires, but of Luis. Of Shoshana. Of us trying to help. Would they still try to stop the murderer if I don't show up tomorrow night? And if they do, would they be safe?

I groan.

If I know they'll try to slay me, why am I still worried about their safety? I close my eyes. It's just because I had fun. I thought I had friends. That's it. It'll pass.

It's the most boring night of my life. I listen to music that isn't loud enough to distract me from all my thoughts. I read books that aren't crazier than what's going on in my real life. And when it's finally time for dawn and I try to sleep? I don't have any dreams I'd want to have come true.

I don't pop out of bed at 4:40 p.m., right at sunset, like I have every other night. What's the point? I have no adventure to rush off to, no day to save.

I drag my feet downstairs and sit at the table. Alone.

I should see if Victor's awake and try to talk to him. Maybe he went looking for Alejandra for the same reason I went looking for Luis and Shoshana. I should swallow my pride and admit that the mortals acted exactly the way Victor warned me they would.

Movement catches my eye. It's Mom. Standing at the bookshelf.

"The mortals aren't coming to get us, are they?" I'm in a rush to ask. "Before Alejandra left, you convinced her that Victor wasn't actually a vampire, right?"

"Alejandra, is it?" Mom asks.

I wince at what I gave away.

Mom takes a deep breath before going on. "I almost wish that girl's infection was worse. Even mild sepsis will keep a mortal in their bed for a few days . . . but Alejandra? A little rest and a few antibiotics and she'll be fine."

"Like . . . tomorrow night fine?"

"She specifically asked if she would be feeling better by tomorrow night," Mom says, and smiles. "But I think we're in the clear. It's a date. She said something about 'he' wouldn't wait."

"Are *we* going to be fine?" I'm almost afraid to ask. "You told Victor he put us all in danger."

She doesn't answer, and I join her at her side. The matryoshka doll is disassembled into all of its smaller dolls, and she's holding the tiniest one in her hand. "I'm wondering," Mom starts off slowly, "if maybe not having a mortal life to look back on . . ."

Her words trail off. I'm not exactly sure what she's trying to say.

"You mean, why Victor's so obsessed with being a 'cool' vampire?"

Mom winces at my words.

"Me and Samira . . . we couldn't always be open," Mom goes on. "And I hated that, but what I hated more was how others interpreted that. They create a world where you're forced to live your lives in secret, then they get angry that you've kept that part of yourself secret from them, like you've done something to trick them."

Mom sighs. "But I've been making him do the same thing, in my own way."

"He's always hated school," Mom adds. "Maybe I should have indulged him more, done more to develop your

213

vampire powers. I just . . . allora, I wanted to give you both as close to a normal childhood as I could."

"Isn't it a part of growing up?" I ask, remembering the conversation I had with her the other day. "Victor finding his place in the world?"

Mom smiles sadly. "And he has one. This house. Lacey. Washington. Pacific Northwest." She repeats my answer back to me, but it sounds so wrong now.

Yeah, except that he's too busy pretending he's in Santa Cruz, daydreaming like he's a part of The Lost Boys *coven—*

I freeze.

I've been telling Victor that, haven't I? That he should just run away. Go find the vampires he wishes he could live like.

His bunk. He's been silent. All day.

I run up the stairs without explaining a thing to Mom.

25

ADAM

Good news? I'm not too late. But the bad news is definitely worse. I was right—Victor's turned our room into a mess. A duffel bag sits in the middle of the floor. He doesn't even turn to look at me.

"What are you *doing*?" I ask.

I know what he's doing. He's packing. He's leaving. But I want him to say it. Maybe if he has to say it, he'll hear what a ridiculous idea it is.

"Does it matter?" Victor asks.

"I didn't tell on you."

"At least have the guts to admit it," Victor says.

I glare at him. He doesn't trust me anymore either?

"You're going to get killed!" I say. "There's a vampire hunter out there, and if you're not going to stay in your room on your own? Then *good*. Good that Mom's grounding you. At least I still care about you enough to—"

Victor cuts me off with a sharp laugh. I clench my jaw so hard I'm surprised I don't shatter my teeth. He's making fun of me now?! He's about to run away, never to return, and he's laughing at how much this is hurting me?

"You're my brother, Victor," I say, my voice warbling a little.

He doesn't react. I don't know how else to break down the walls he's got around himself. The emotion in my voice isn't enough to get through to him. He can't feel it. He doesn't care. He doesn't come over and give me a hug and tell me everything's going to be okay. Fine. I'll say it. I don't want to say it. I don't want to find out if it's true, but I have to say it.

"Is this the way you wanted it?" I ask. "That's why you're packing? You've got an excuse now? You've been talking about how much you hate this family and . . . if you leave? You're going to turn into one of them. The monsters in movies. The ones you look up to? You're going to go out there . . ." I have to say it. I can see it, but maybe he doesn't yet. "You're going to kill someone."

Victor doesn't react. He doesn't say anything. He does nothing except shove more clothes into his bag. I might as well not have tried. I wipe my wet cheeks with my sleeve. My eyes sting, but it doesn't compare to the way my heart aches.

"They're all going to get wrinkly," I say.

Victor doesn't speak.

"I'm telling you since your clothes are the only thing you care about," I say. Why I really want to hurt Victor now, I don't know, but I do. Or at least make him think about how selfish he is. Or maybe goad him into talking to me.

"Don't forget your comb too."

I must have actually reminded Victor about it because he snatches his comb off his nightstand.

"So that's it?" Anger swells, replacing the ache in my chest. "You're going to run away? And leave all of us, leave *me*, without even saying anything?"

He smirks.

"The kid who's never around finally cares about having a conversation."

"*What?*" I ask.

Victor folds a shirt as he talks, not taking his eyes off it.

"You've been sneaking out," he says. "All week. And you've been gone for hours. Everyone asks where you are, and every morning I cover for you. And I did it, even though you were avoiding me. And you were calling me a jerk. You kept me out of whatever you've been up to, and I covered for you, because you needed space or whatever it was. It was important to you, whatever this is. If you didn't want me to be a part of it, okay, but . . . What'd I ever do to you? I've only been trying to help you and you really come up here and tell me I'm going to be a murderer, and you think you're doing me a favor?"

"Maybe you don't see it, but I do," I say. "Like going to see that movie? You wanted to scare those mortals, make them think they were going to get eaten. Yeah, because that's good practice for when you actually get to hunt people!"

"Is that all you think I care about?" Victor says.

I take a deep breath. "Yeah."

"Whatever," Victor says. "I'm out of here."

"Good luck with that," I say. Victor seems to really want to test head-vampire powers, because he's opening his window and pushing on the shutters. "What are you going to do? Mom said you can't leave the house. And you're not going to."

"She said I couldn't leave my *home*," Victor says. "This isn't my home anymore."

"*What?*" I ask.

But Victor smirks. It's the saddest smile I've ever seen.

"You know," he starts. "The mortals wanted to get scared. It was on the poster for the theater. 'Scream the night away with Olympia's first fright night of the year.' Didn't you hear them? When they were all waiting outside? There was one group teasing each other about what part they were going to scream at."

I growl. "It wasn't a haunted house, Victor! Those people wanted to get scared at a *movie*. Something that wasn't real. Not from an actual vampire chasing them down the streets. They'd think they were going to die—that's not fun, Victor."

"But then . . . you'd know they weren't anything to be scared of," Victor says.

"What's that supposed to mean?" I ask.

"You're scared of them. It's okay to admit it," Victor says. "You had that nightmare and you kept talking about vampire hunters and . . . well, if I got you to see that mortals weren't that scary . . . then you wouldn't have to have nightmares again."

I balk. He remembered that? And it made such an impact on him that he wanted to take me to scare mortals . . . just so

I wouldn't have another nightmare about getting hunted?

"And I was hoping I could get us to practice charisma together," Victor goes on. "So even if we did meet mortals who weren't afraid of us, maybe we could trick them into thinking we were both these big, huge, scary guys."

My mind flickers back to when we were trying to sneak into the theater. How Victor wanted to make me appear all big and burly . . . he was doing that to protect me? To build me up? Make me more confident?

Shame burns my cheeks and I look away, thinking of what to say. Something catches my eye. I'm sure it's not real at first, and my stomach drops. There's my mug! The beaches and smiling dolphins and everything. It's all glued together and fragile, but I walk over to it and cradle it gently in my hands. It's whole again. Complete.

"You did this?" I ask in a shaky voice. I had no idea he even realized how much it'd meant to me. "But . . . when?"

He meets my eyes. "Exactly."

I open my mouth to speak but I gulp back my words. I had no idea when he'd tried to glue my mug back together because I hadn't been around to see him. To be with him.

My chest is caving in. A chill fills my body and I tremble.

All this time, I was afraid I'd lose Victor—to the vampire hunter, maybe, but honestly, I was just as afraid I was going to lose him to growing up. I didn't want to accept that he was going to change and that I had to meet him where he was, to stick with him while he found his place in the world.

I can't even hide behind wanting to protect him from the vampire hunter, though, can I? Who treats someone badly and tells them they're going to become a murderer and says it's worth it as long as you want something good for them?

I look up: to apologize, to talk, to tell him how badly I messed up. But the space in front of the window is empty.

"Victor, wait!" I call out into the night, but he's already gone.

26

VICTOR

I step outside with every intention of running south. Except I smell blood. Alejandra's at it again with her traps.

Of course she still wants to slay me.

Who doesn't? No matter where I turn, someone is out to get me. Mortals think I'm a monster. My own family is disgusted with me. Fine. Screw it. If Alejandra wants to slay me so badly, two can play that game. I'm not getting caught this time. I'm going to eat her. Drink all her blood. Sung said that'd make me good for a month. There is a lot I can figure out in that time.

No one thinks I'm anything more than a monster anyway. No point in letting everyone down, right?

I follow the smell of her blood, running through the trees as quietly as I can. The excitement in my chest is gone . . . no thrill to figure out what trap she's made for me this time.

She's leading me into Wonderwood Park again.

Alejandra isn't playing around either. I can smell a *lot* of blood. How much blood can a mortal squeeze out of their hand anyway?

I stop on the same bough of the same bigleaf maple tree as last night. I look out across the dark field. No fishing lines. No other signs of a trap.

I know I should be cautious but . . . forget it. I drop out of the tree, drop my duffel bag, and follow the smell of blood. I see her feet sticking out from behind that same large tree in the middle of the field. She's lying on the ground.

I hesitate for a moment. What is this trap going to be? Whatever. Even if she jumps out at me or tries to stab me, she's still a mortal. She'll still be too slow.

I walk around to the other side of the tree.

Something heavy falls through my chest. Suddenly, the world gets very small, and everything I was thinking about vanishes. All I can do is stand there and stare, taking deep breaths. This isn't a trap. This isn't a trick.

There is so much blood. More than I have ever seen in my life. Fresh, almost sparkling blood. The smell fills the air, but I've lost my hunger.

Alejandra is curled up. Holding her stomach. Moaning.

I kneel down next to her and grab her shoulder.

"Are you okay?" I ask. It's a pointless question—duh, of course she's not. But I have no idea what else to say.

Her face is ghostly. The life is drained from it. Her lips are blue and trembling, and she looks awful.

She is going to die.

It's all my fault.

Okay, I know. Classic line. But it is. *I* teased her. *I* joked about drinking that blood Mom brought home. I made Alejandra mad. I made her think the only way she could help her friends was to catch me. I drew her out of her safe, mortal house. And I did it while knowing an actual murderer was out there killing mortals just like her.

And thanks to all that? Thanks to *me*? Her tricks, her laugh, her anger, her teasing . . . all that is going to die with her too. Adam was right—I had been a jerk. But I can still fix my mistakes.

"I'm going to get you to the hospital," I say. Even if Mom works there. She'll be angry that I broke her curfew.

"You're not going to eat me?" Alejandra's voice comes out with as much oomph as a breath.

I shake my head. How can I say I've lost my hunger?

"Bite me?" she asks. She doesn't tell me to do it. She asks. I can tell the difference.

Again, I shake my head. "You don't want to be a vampire," I remind her.

I worm my arms underneath her and she grunts in pain.

"Hey, hey, shh," I say as gently as I can, lifting her up off the ground. "Hold on, I'm taking you to the hospital."

"You're a good guy," Alejandra whispers. Now it's my turn for my face to go red.

"Please don't say that," I say.

"Watch out," Alejandra whispers. "Glasses Man—"

"What?" I ask, but I ignore whatever it is she's trying to say. I only care about getting her out of here. "Shh, you're going to be okay, just hold—*ow*."

Something sharp bites into my neck.

I have to fight to lift my arm. It's suddenly so heavy. I put Alejandra down before I fall, because now my legs are getting heavy too.

I blink.

Everything's getting fuzzy. I shake my head, but I can't get rid of the feeling. The world is tilting. I shake my head again but it doesn't help me figure out which way is supposed to be up. I try to focus my eyes on one thing—the tree—but it keeps sliding across my vision. I tilt my head to follow it, but now everything's tilting and—

My legs give out. I don't realize I can't move them until I am crumpled on the ground, face-first. My hair falls down over my eyes, and I snort, hating the way it tickles my nose. I can't lift an arm to brush it away.

Get up.

But my hands aren't answering. They just lay there on the ground, not helping at all.

The ground shakes. Someone walks up to me and kneels down. I flinch as a stranger's hand brushes my bangs aside, revealing my eyes. I slam my eyelids shut. When was the last time I drank blood? *They are going to find out.*

"Ah ah," I hear a man's voice.

Leather touches my face. Gloved hands, which is absolutely revolting. I don't want to be touched. I can't move away, though. Not even something as simple as shaking my head. Fingers pry my eyelids open.

"Ah, you *are* hungry," the man says, and then tuts like he's disciplining a child. "Couldn't resist the bait, could we?"

Bait.

My breathing becomes sporadic. Unsteady. It's the only way I can be angry. *Bait.* I know who the man is referring to. *Alejandra.* He's the one who hurt her, who made her bleed, who killed all those other mortals. All to be vampire-catching "bait."

The man is studying me and I study him right back. He's definitely a vampire hunter. Boots. Big trench coat. The leather gloves are like gauntlets going up his arms. A big hat with a wide brim. The high collar of his tan trench coat is popped around his neck. Everything he's wearing is made out of leather. Leather is bite-proof—he's protecting himself. His boxy face is pale and stubbly, but the glasses are what I notice the most. They're huge circular things that reflect the light so much I can't see the man's eyes. But that's still the only bit of person I can see. A man wearing glasses. *Glasses Man.*

His hand moves to my jaw, and again I try to pull away. The hand pinches my cheeks, forcing my mouth open. I know what the glasses man is checking for ... my fangs.

My lips are all numb and giant and clumsy, and I mumble something incoherent. Go away? Leave me alone? The thing is, though, I don't even know what I'm trying to say. No parts of my body are talking to each other. My brain is screaming, but it sounds like it's far off in another room, and my eyes are so heavy.

Stay awake. Fight.

The thought comes from so far away it's hard to pay attention to it.

I concentrate on my legs, thinking about how badly I want to get to my feet, to get away, but when it comes to moving? All I can feel is a tightening in my chest.

Alejandra stands up, like she's not hurt. And she doesn't run away.

"A deal's a deal," Alejandra says all casually to the Glasses Man, wiping her lips on the back of her mittens. The color returns to her lips. She'd been wearing . . . blueish lipstick? "I got the vampire for you. You got what you wanted. Now, are you going to leave my friends alone?"

"Color me impressed," Glasses Man says. "I didn't think that would work, but your plan to draw out enough of your own blood to make it look like a massacre . . . well, it did the trick."

Blood draw? Is that all that was? It was another trap? It slowly dawns on me—Alejandra *helped* him! She helped the vampire hunter catch me!

"Don't flatter me, and answer the question," Alejandra says again, more firmly this time. "You're going to stop killing my friends, right?"

"I wouldn't have had to kill them if it weren't for this." Glasses Man grabs a handful of my hair. "Vampires don't come nicely when you call, do they? We had to spill so much blood to get one to finally answer. But we've stopped another one of these creatures, thanks to you."

"I stopped *the murders*," Alejandra mutters under her breath. "What are you going to do with him now?"

"The trick is to move fast," Glasses Man says. "The tranquilizer dart? That can put a full-grown bull elephant to sleep for hours. But did you see what it did to this one? Not even a blink. The virus in there? It's finding all the drugs and neutralizing them. This vampire will be back to its full strength soon."

Oh, well, that's good to know, I think to myself.

"You have to move fast."

Uhh, that doesn't sound quite as good. Is this the part where I get stabbed? Glasses Man reaches into a satchel . . . and pulls out a glass jar. It's the most threatening glass jar I've ever seen. Even if there's nothing in it.

Why is it empty? Unless he's going to fill it with something? I realize what he's planning to do too late. He pries my jaw open with one hand and forces the cup into my mouth, pushing it up against the roof, behind my fangs. There is nothing I can do. The moment my teeth touch the jar, venom starts to drip out.

It's cold at first. The roof of my mouth feels like it's freezing . . . like ice. I can feel the venom pulling through my body. My jaw feels like it's stuck in concrete, slowly drying up and locking in place.

"It's harmless now," Glasses Man says after a minute, standing up and sealing the jar. "Will be for a while. Takes vampires a long time to make more venom. And while it does? It goes into a form of hibernation to protect itself. Everything shuts down. Which is what we need for the next step."

I whimper.

"Next step?" Alejandra asks.

"Oh yes," Glasses Man says. "You and I are embarking on a most important crusade. Ridding the world of this virus."

"Virus?"

"It's easier to think of it that way," Glasses Man says. "Vampirism isn't a sickness in the conventional sense. It completely rewrites the victim's DNA. Like those fangs? I've seen humans get bitten. They regrow those. Things that aren't even in the human blueprint . . . vampirism goes in and rewrites it.

"The cells themselves are always regenerating. That's how the vampire seems to live forever, why it heals so fast. Why that tranquilizer dart wouldn't work. Except for sunlight. We don't know why this virus is so vulnerable to sunlight, but it does leave a mark. Which will tell us a lot about what we are dealing with."

Glasses Man kneels back down again, grabbing my hands and looking at them.

"This one hasn't been on its own," Glasses Man says. "No burns, no scars. Nothing. It's been living in a house, probably. And see the way it's dressed? Not at all prepared for the sun. Look, it's got its sleeves rolled up. Collar buttons undone. Nothing to cover the exposed skin with . . . the house must be nearby."

I tremble.

"Very few vampires can survive as lone wolves," Glasses Man says, then smiles. "My apologies, I'm used to werewolf puns. No, vampires don't tend to live rogue. And one as clean as this one? No scars? No, this one has companions."

"What does that mean?" Alejandra asks.

"We can coax out all the other ones in its clan," Glasses Man said. "They are very much in tune to one another.

Imagine, if you will, that the virus is one creature living between multiple bodies. All it takes is making the others believe this one is in danger."

"How are you going to do that?" Alejandra asks.

No lie, I'm expecting a wooden stake. When the Glasses Man holds up his fist, I'm preparing for a punch in the face. But what he does? He pushes one of his knuckles in the middle of my chest. And pushes *hard*.

The pain steals my breath away. It is engulfing. Awful. And gone the instant Glasses Man takes his hand away. Alejandra covers her mouth with her hands.

Glasses Man smiles. "The sternum rub," he explains to Alejandra. "It causes an incredible amount of pain with the most minimal of effort. No need to break skin and risk exposing yourself to the virus. But it is enough—the others will know. They'll suspect mortal danger . . . that's how bad the pain is. They will come. Now, to wait."

Is that true? I've never felt ghost vampire-sibling pain before. I close my eyes and think as hard as I can, *Please come rescue me, hurry.* Maybe if they can feel my pain, they can hear my thoughts too? They have to.

Glasses Man might think he's a professional, but I just know the moms would wreck his entire world.

Glasses Man drags me. I wish I could put up a fight. I wish I could do something. He slams my back into the trunk of the bigleaf maple.

Alejandra shifts her weight uncomfortably.

"Don't be fooled by its appearance," Glasses Man says. "What's on the outside is already dead. But inside? Inside is a disease. A very powerful disease. So powerful and so dangerous it can move this boy's body around like a puppet, make it sound convincingly human. Enough that you let your guard down. And then it strikes."

I am seriously freaked out. Alejandra can't believe this, can she? I had a chance to bite her and I didn't. I was trying to get her help. She has to remember that. Would a virus-controlled zombie be as funny as I am? I try my hardest to ask for help, but my lips still don't move when I want them to.

"And now we wait," Glasses Man says. "And see how many we get."

"How many are there?" Alejandra asks.

"Here? We'll have to see," Glasses Man says. "In the world? Some say it could be as many as ten thousand. Can you believe that? Disgusting. *Ten thousand*. They look just like us too. Infiltrating us. Infecting us. They'd get away with turning more if it weren't for hunters like us keeping them afraid, keeping them in check. It's a lonely job, but someone has to keep humanity safe."

Glasses Man stands up, turning to Alejandra again. "I could always use a partner."

"That's why you're explaining everything?" Alejandra asks.

"You have the makings of an excellent vampire slayer," Glasses Man says.

Alejandra's eyes dart back to me.

Please, I try to say. *Help.*

"I appreciate it," she says. "I'm sorry if, you know, I gave you the wrong impression. I can't kill h—" It's the first time I've ever heard her voice get shaky. "I only helped you because I don't want any more of my friends to die."

"But you know they're out there," Glasses Man says. "These things. You can't ignore them. If we leave them alone, they'll only make more of themselves. They'll only get more numerous, until they can take over, and then they'll keep us like cattle. We have a responsibility to protect everyone."

"I'm sorry," Alejandra stammers. "I-I'm still in high school."

"So that's a no," Glasses Man says. Alejandra shifts her weight again and nods.

"In that case, thank you for what you've done tonight," Glasses Man says, offering his hand. Alejandra takes it, and immediately jumps back with a sharp "Ow!"

"I *did* tell you to wear leather gloves," Glasses Man says.

"What'd you do?" Alejandra asks. I struggle again against my body, struggle to focus on the two mortals. Alejandra stumbles back, a look of shock and disgust on her face.

Glasses Man smiles. "Ah, something you didn't consider, relying on your little metal detector? You see, I don't just use tranquilizer darts to hunt vampires. The others in my bandolier? You didn't notice my sleight of hand, but what you got injected with? That was a dart of strychnine. I prefer it over poisons that are more immediate, more peaceful— these blood-suckers have earned a painful goodbye. A death from strychnine is long and drawn-out, and there is no antidote. Every muscle in your body will begin to spasm within a few minutes. Those spasms will get so bad you'll break your back. Or your heart might explode. It varies, which part of your body fails first, but you will be dead from a very painful death in the next five minutes or so."

"*What?!*" Alejandra says. "But I helped you!"

"And you've seen my face," Glasses Man says. "What's preventing you from telling the police who the murderer is?"

Alejandra takes a step back and shakily gets her phone out of her pocket.

"Oh, dear," Glasses Man says. "You'll find you're going to have trouble getting a signal."

"You're jamming my phone?" Alejandra asks.

Glasses Man just tilts his head like it's not the most illegal thing he's done.

Moms, hurry up. Please.

How far away is the house? It shouldn't have taken them more than a few minutes to come rescue me. To come rescue Alejandra. Mama can do that blood magic stuff Sung tried to tell me about. Mom can destroy Glasses Man.

Until it slowly dawns on me.

No one is coming to rescue me. If they wanted to, they'd be here by now. I'm alone.

I need to do something.

I can't scream. I can't fight. I have no energy, but—*yes!* Alejandra pretended to be hurt. There was blood all over her clothes, but that's not going to do me any good right now. The ground?

There's got to at least be a drop somewhere on the ground. I just need to get there. I try to lean, to fall over. It'll be just like last night. I only need the tiniest bit, enough to give me a jolt of energy, and I can scoop up Alejandra and I can get away—maybe far enough away that she can use her phone to call for help. I can get her to the hospital. Maybe he's wrong about the poison.

I fall over, one of the tree's roots jabbing me in the side, but it's not a victory. Glasses Man walks over. He says something about me trying to crawl away, and I struggle as hard as I can. It only comes out as tremors, but Glasses Man decides I'm remaking venom too fast or something. Because it's back with the jar. Out goes the venom, and I'm freezing cold and trembling again.

But something worked out.

Glasses Man stands up and suddenly realizes that Alejandra is missing. All she needs to do is get far enough away to make a phone call . . .

Maybe it'll be enough to bring the police. Maybe it'll be enough to stop Glasses Man. But she's going to die, and it's all my fault.

It starts to snow.

27

ADAM

I honestly expect a bigger reaction.

I go to Sung, and I confess everything to them. I admit that I made friends with mortals, that we were trying to find a vampire hunter, that there *is* a vampire hunter in Lacey (like, a very scary legit one that's *not* Alejandra). That I was so stuck on trying to stop the vampire hunter, I ignored Victor this whole time. And now, thanks to me being such a self-centered jerk that I didn't realize my own brother was trying to hang out with me, I'd pushed him so far away that he didn't even feel like this was home anymore.

"But where is he going to run off to?" Sung asks.

I bite my lip. "Santa Cruz." I'm sure of it.

"California? That is *so* random," Sung says. "Why Santa Cruz?"

"It's my fault," I say. "It's where they filmed *The Lost Boys*. He loves that movie, you know? Every time he talked about wanting to do more vampire stuff, I kept telling him to go there."

"We have to tell the moms," Sung says.

I cringe and nod. It's going to be awful. I'm going to be in so much trouble. But we have to find Victor. I have to apologize and make things right.

Mom isn't as angry as I thought she'd be. She doesn't say much of anything—no yelling, no blaming. She waits for me to finish and then she grabs her car keys. Mama wraps a hijab around her head and grabs her keys too.

"Keep an eye on him," Mom says to Sung.

And with that, we're standing in the driveway watching the taillights vanish into the forest, and then they're gone. Driving south, and looking for Victor. It happens so fast, so suddenly. And it weirdly feels like I'm still waiting for Mom to yell at me.

"Do you think they'll find him?" I ask Sung.

"If anyone's going to find him, it'll be the moms," Sung says, and takes a deep breath. "Sun'll be up in . . ." They glance at their watch. "Thirteen hours."

I cringe at the unlucky number.

"Great," I say.

"He packed some stuff to hide from the sun, right?" Sung asks. I shake my head. I'm pretty sure Victor wasn't really thinking that far ahead, and I don't remember seeing him throw a blanket or anything that would work as sun protection in his bag.

"The moms will check bridges then," Sung says. "Once he realizes how badly he planned, he's going to look for shelter."

"I should be looking for him too," I say.

I'm positive Sung will tell me no, the moms have it covered. But they say, "Mom told me to watch you, not make you stay here. But I don't think you're going to run any faster than a car."

"I know, I just—" I start, but I don't really know what I want. Just that I *want*. So terribly.

"Need to be doing something too?" Sung asks.

"Yeah," I admit.

"Come on," Sung says. "Let's go for a walk. I have my phone. If the moms find anything, we'll know and be home before they are."

I pull on my boots and Sung steps into their white sneakers, just like it was a normal day.

I haven't walked to the cemetery using sidewalks instead of forest paths. But my inner compass knows where it is. Sung doesn't steer our walk. At every corner, they slow down a step so I make the choice of where we go. My feet are braver than my heart.

I stop talking as we get closer. My heart flutters in my chest, like it wants to fly the rest of the way to the tombstones. I stretch my neck. My eyes open wide. My body tingles all over.

I can peer through the rungs of the cemetery's iron fence before we reach the gates. Fog hugs the ground, but it can't hide the disappointment from me. The cemetery is empty, silent. What I already should have known. Shoshana and Luis aren't waiting for me—not like they'd been doing the past two nights. My chest tightens.

I don't know what I was expecting. I'm not exactly friend material for mortals. Vampires don't belong in their world. I was a fool to think it could be any other way.

I'm alone, again. Just like the first time I came here. It was only a few days ago, but how much has changed since then. And I still ended up in the same spot, lost and confused and feeling lonelier than before.

Sung and I stop at the cemetery gate. That iron banner hangs over my head.

Until the day breaks and the shadows flee away.

I should have paid attention to those words. It was a warning, and I thought I could laugh in its face. I thought I'd tell the world how it should be. I thought I'd wake the dawn.

Sung shifts on the sidewalk next to me. They haven't said anything or asked to keep walking. They were so still that I forgot they were there as I got lost in my thoughts. But they're here. Which means I'm wrong. I haven't lost everything. I'm not alone.

I might be wrong about the gate's message too.

Mama's story comes rushing back to me. How she and the other vampires in her coven used to watch over her village. They kept it safe throughout the night until the sun came up again and the shadows and all the danger we vampires were keeping an eye out for ran away.

I take a step forward. My heart lifts, something filling it up and pushing against my rib cage. That banner isn't telling vampires to go away . . . it is a call to action. Something *I* also feel. Something I need to do. To watch over them, all the mortals, all throughout the night, until the sun comes up, and they're safe.

I can't give up on that.

"The gates are open," I say.

"They are," Sung says. "You want to go in?"

"Yeah." I want to make a joke about zombies or ghosts or something, but I can't. There's only one thing I'm interested in. One thing to check on.

And it's there.

Like a little tiny promise that things will be okay, that nothing is over yet, secured under a rock. It's there—a new note on the same little tombstone.

Hey Adam, head to Wonderwood if you're still in.

It wasn't the handwriting I'd seen on the first note, so this must be Luis. He must not realize I'm a vampire! I turn to my sibling, grinning.

"We need to—"

My breath catches in my throat. I double over, grabbing at my chest. An image flashes over my vision. I'm suddenly Victor. I'm in trouble. Two shiny circles. And then the very next second, it's gone.

Sung meets my eyes.

"*Victor!*" I say, coughing as I regain my breath.

"You got that too?" Sung asks.

I nod, though I really wish they didn't sound so surprised. I was kind of hoping they'd be able to tell me what just happened.

"What'd he get himself into already!?" Sung asks.

I shake my head. "That *hurt*. What's going on, Sung? What's happening to Victor?"

"I don't know," Sung says. "Whatever it is, it's not good."

"A stake . . . ?" I ask, rubbing my chest. It felt like getting stabbed. But who would stab Victor—

Oh . . . *oh no*.

It's the vampire hunter.

I don't want to ask the obvious. *Is Victor dead?* Is it too late? Will I never have a chance to apologize? Will he never have a chance to feel loved again?

"We need to help him," I say instead.

"He could be anywhere," Sung whispers.

No. Not anywhere.

I look down at the note in my hand. I didn't make friends for nothing. We didn't try to find this vampire hunter for nothing. We knew where the vampire hunter was going to strike next.

My head snaps up and I hold up the note.

"He's at Wonderwood Park."

28

ADAM

We run as fast as we can. We fling ourselves from tree to tree, a hundred feet in the air, high above the roofs of the mortal homes.

The pain in my chest is long gone. Whatever link we all had with Victor was way too short. I leap farther with each bound, hoping against hope that Victor isn't already dead. That this isn't a lost cause.

Snowflakes follow us on our way down.

Our feet don't touch the ground until we're well inside Wonderwood Park. There's a spot where all the paths come together, and that's where we start our search. There are giant logs laid all around, some carved into benches. No one's sitting on them. I jump up onto the tallest stump, the one right in the middle of all the paths, and look around. The first thing I notice is the smell. *Blood.* Fresh young blood. Sung smells it too.

"You weren't kidding," Sung says. "There really is a vampire hunter out here."

It's Alejandra's blood. My mind darts back to the other night. Victor drank her blood. She said she was using her own blood to draw him close. Did she manage to slay him?

I close my eyes, trying to remember that vision, searching my memories for any hints that she was the one who hurt Victor. The vision was just way too vague. Pain, and two bright circles. Were those street lights? I scan the park again, wondering if we should check out the parking lots first. Maybe there were two orbs because Victor had like, double vision or something?

"Hey, Adam!" I hear Luis call out.

I freeze. My eyes dart down at Sung, who froze too. They are so obviously a vampire. I mean, it's snowing and they're wearing shorts. Both Shoshana and Luis are bundled up and—

I grind my teeth together. I don't have my scarf!

"You made it!" Luis says happily, running up to me with a smile. A normal smile. He doesn't know what I am. Shoshana didn't tell him.

Shoshana, on the other hand, gives me an awkward wave and peers at me a good, searching moment before saying hi. What does that mean? Is she scared of me?

"Hey, Adam," Luis says again, glancing between me and Sung. "Who'd you bring?"

"Uhh . . . my sibling. Sung," I say, trying my best to keep my lips as smooshed together as I can while I speak. "They're, uh . . . here to—"

"We're looking for the vampire hunter," Sung says, getting right to the point. "He's got our brother."

I tense up again and shoot Sung a look of utter disbelief. Didn't I tell them that Luis said all those things about vampires being evil and blood-suckers and ... there's a vampire hunter in this park! Right now! All Luis has to do is scream and it'll be over for us too!

"Why would a vampire hunter have your—?" Luis starts.

"*Luis?*"

The voice is barely a whisper, but my vampire ears catch it. I snap my head in the other direction, because I definitely recognize that voice. It's Alejandra! I look her up and down real fast, searching for any vampire-slaying things, but what I notice is how weird she's walk-run-stumbling. I'm pretty sure she's trying to run, but it's like her body forgot how to do it. She's holding her phone out wildly in front of her, and her hand is shaking. Her eyes are wide. Her lips quiver.

"You're supposed to be grounded," Luis says with a laugh, but the smile drops from his face. "What's with you?"

Alejandra's lips are moving, but she doesn't talk. I glance over at Sung, trying to pick up a cue from them on what to do. The smell of blood is coming off of her, but she can't be bait if she's not dead. Did she kill Victor? She's panicking. Is this what a murderer looks like after they kill someone?

No. I've seen what mortals do after they've killed someone in movies. They act all cool, like they couldn't care less. Then why is she acting so weird?

"Is this what it looks like when someone gets bitten?" I whisper to Sung.

"No . . . no, getting bitten is like, you drift into la-la land," Sung says.

"Then what is—?" I start, but Alejandra suddenly collapses on the ground. She starts shaking.

"She's having a seizure!" Shoshana says.

We all rush forward. Luis is now the one panicking. I can't understand what he's saying. I can smell blood on Alejandra, but worse? I can see it. It's stained her jacket. Is she having a seizure because she's lost a bunch of blood again? Alejandra's arms are shaking so badly I'm afraid she's going to accidentally hit someone. I grab one of her wrists and that's when I can feel it.

"No, it's . . ." I look up at Sung.

Those little grains of sand. She's *full* of them. *Poison.*

I tighten my fists. I need to do blood magic. I meet Sung's wide eyes. They know it too. I glance at the others. Shoshana is trying to call 911 and saying that her phone doesn't have a signal. No ambulance. No doctor.

Alejandra's going to die.

Unless I . . .

I bite my lip. There'll be no stepping back from this.

"There's no stab wound!" Shoshana says, after pulling up enough of Alejandra's shirt to reveal her completely unstabbed abdomen.

"She's been poisoned," I say.

"How do you know that?" Luis asks.

I don't explain anything more. I close my eyes and block everything else out. I feel for those grains of sand, the little molecules of poison. I can feel it pushing out from her chest. There's a big artery there, right above her heart. The aorta. I put a hand above her chest, to strain the grains of sand out. There's so much. I can't do this alone.

A pair of hands joins mine.

"You sure about this?" Sung whispers.

I know what they mean—if I do this, there's no way I can ever pretend to not be a vampire. There's no going back.

But if we don't do this, there's no going back for Alejandra either.

"It's what we're supposed to do," I say. "Use our strength to help."

Sung gives my hand a squeeze.

We begin. I'm concentrating so much I've completely zoned my friends out. I have no idea what Shoshana and Luis think we're doing. Alejandra stops shaking so badly, and I hover my hand over her heart. It's still beating.

Sung has their hands up by Alejandra's head, the same as Mama did when we were learning on the coyote, while I start dragging my little pile of sand-poison down Alejandra's arm toward her hand. There's already a cut there. Too bad for the stitches.

I hear Shoshana and Luis both gasp as the poison drips out of the cut on Alejandra's hand. I'm not sure if they're putting two and two together, but I open my eyes. Sung drags out their own collection of poison.

There's blood all over the ground, and no lie—it makes me a little woozy with hunger. All that blood going to waste . . . but I've got to waste it. No way I'm going to drink blood right in front of everyone.

I hold myself up, my arms trembling, and I take a few deep breaths.

Alejandra props herself up on her elbows so she can look at me and Sung. She focuses on me—she's met me before. She's out of breath, and I can't blame her. She'd been poisoned. She knew she was dying. And now she's fine. She definitely looks a bit shocked.

"What'd you do?" Alejandra asks.

"We pulled the poison out of your blood," I say. "Which is ... uhh, something I can do. Something vampires can do."

Expectation sits heavy in the air, but I'm not going to wait for someone else to say it.

"Because I'm a vampire."

29

ADAM

That's it.

I let my secret go. Everyone knows who I am. Now to see if it's the biggest mistake of my life.

"You're . . . you're a *vampire*?" Luis laughs. He thinks it's a joke.

"Yeah," I say. "See? Fangs."

I open my mouth, touching the tip of one sharp canine with my tongue. Luis's scoff slowly melts off his face. He looks between me and his sister. Over and over again. I hold his gaze each time he looks at me. I'm not going to give off the impression that I'm ashamed. He opens his mouth to say something, thinks better of it, and closes his mouth. He glances down at the pool of blood on the concrete below us.

"Baruch atah Adonai, Eloheinu melech ha-olam, m'shaneh habriyot," Shoshana says under her breath.

"What?" Luis asks.

"Umm . . . that's the blessing for seeing an unusual creature," Shoshana says.

"You seriously have that memorized?" Luis asks. "Like, just in case you run into—"

"No, I learned it last night," Shoshana says.

"You did?" Luis asks. "I mean, you figured it out?"

"I mean, not many people's first question on being Jewish is whether or not they can consume blood," Shoshana says. "Which, I wanted to tell you, Adam. I looked into it, and centuries ago, the old rabbis ruled that vampires can totally be Jewish because of pikuach nefesh—that saving a life, even if it's your own life, takes precedence over any religious law. Vampires can't help that they have to drink blood. So as long as a vampire wasn't killing people, then it was totally kosher . . ." Shoshana's words trail off. "I just thought you'd like to know."

"Oh . . . thanks," I say. "That's actually . . . yeah, that's good to know. So, we're still friends, right?"

"Yeah," Shoshana says with a smile.

Luis doesn't meet my eyes again.

"Are you okay—" I start, but Luis cuts me off.

"No, I'm not okay," he says. "My sister was literally dying right in front of me and she's been saved by *vampires*." I don't know how to read the way he stresses that word. He takes a breath before continuing. "And of course you didn't tell me that's what you were. I was making jokes about killing you to your face. And you were still my friend. You still saved her. You could have laughed and said that's what we deserved, and you didn't. I'm sorry."

"Thanks," I say. "But, like, you still want to help us stop the murderer?"

"What?" Luis asks.

"That's why we're here," I say. "That murderer, the vampire hunter. He's got my brother."

"You know Victor?" A smile brightens Alejandra's face. "You're going to rescue him?"

"Unless it's too late," Sung says.

Alejandra shakes her head. "Glasses Man has him."

"Glasses *who*?" Shoshana asks.

"Glasses Man. The vampire hunter: look, he didn't say his name, and I had to call him something. It doesn't matter," Alejandra says. "You don't know what you're up against."

"We've got him figured out," Luis says. "Crucifixes, holy water, a bunch of stuff that doesn't work. Right, Shoshana?"

"Oh, he's beyond that," Alejandra says. "He's smart. Like, creepy-level smart. When I told him I didn't want to learn how to hunt vampires with him, he decided to kill me. He literally had a back-up plan ready for every contingency."

"How'd you get mixed up with a vampire hunter anyway?" Luis asks.

"You know, last night?" Alejandra says. "I was here, trying to . . ." She winces and turns to me and Sung. "Don't get mad, but last night before I caught up with you three, I was right here legit trying to slay your brother. And after Victor got away, Glasses Man showed up. I told him I'd nearly caught a vampire and he was impressed. We made a deal. I'd help him catch Victor, but . . . he's a good guy, you know? I was pretending to be dying, and the plan was that when he went to eat me, Glasses Man would knock him out, but Victor was trying to take me to the hospital. I misjudged him."

"You were the bait?" Luis asks.

"And now Victor is," Alejandra says.

"Vampires don't eat other vampires," Sung says.

"He said something about if you feel his pain, you'll come to help him." Alejandra stares at each of us, her eyebrows raised in concern, like she's remembering something terrible.

"What happened to him?" I ask sharply.

"Nothing serious!" Alejandra says, holding up her hands in defense. "He just rubbed Victor's chest. He said it was supposed to hurt a lot."

So that's what that pain in my chest was? A shiver shakes my shoulders. Glasses Man knows more about vampires than I do, and that is seriously creepy.

"Alright," Sung says. They take a big breath and push their sleeves up their arms. "Tell us where he's got Victor. We'll take care of the rest."

"He's expecting you," Alejandra says. "We *need* to call 911. Call Dad—"

"We can't call Dad!" Luis says.

"He's the *police*," Alejandra says. "He's, like, the one person out of all of us who's actually meant to stop murderers!"

"We can't!" Luis says, his voice trembling.

"Luis . . . ?" Shoshana starts.

"That's why I started this," he says. "I shouldn't have dragged you into it without telling you, but kids can't be used for bait, remember? I thought we'd find the killer and . . . I'm scared I'm going to see my dad get hurt again."

Alejandra sighs. "Luis . . ." Her tone is a mix of sympathy and regret.

"No one needs to get hurt," Sung says. "We can handle this."

"You can't do it by yourselves," Alejandra says. "Believe me. This guy is expecting vampires to show up."

"Right," Sung says. "We need the moms."

Sung pulls their phone out of their pocket as Alejandra whispers, "Victor has parents?"

"There's no signal," Shoshana says.

"Glasses Man has a jammer and—" Alejandra starts.

"I'll find a signal," Sung says. Without warning, they jump straight up, probably forty feet into the trees towering over us.

Ultimately, leaving me behind to awkwardly deal with it all.

"They'll find a signal," I repeat in a mumble.

Shoshana, Luis, and Alejandra are all looking up into the trees, awed by Sung's vampiness, and it reminds me just how vulnerable mortals really are. How scared Luis was that his dad could get hurt. How Alejandra nearly died. It doesn't matter how scary this vampire hunter is. Nothing he can do to me will ever hurt me as badly as it could hurt them.

"You guys . . . you don't need to get involved," I say.

"Of course we do!" Luis says. "The dude tried to kill my sister! And besides, we're the ones who were trying to stop him in the first place! We aren't backing out now. 'Til the end, remember?"

"He thinks vampires are going to show up," Shoshana says. "He can't imagine in a thousand years that kids like us would want to help you, right? It's not like we're going to fight him, but we can be a diversion."

"Alright, what's your plan?" I ask.

"Does he have a gun or anything?" Shoshana asks Alejandra.

"Just a rifle that shoots darts filled with strychnine," Alejandra says. "He says any other weapons won't do— knives rip open skin and bullets fling infected blood everywhere, opening you up to the possibility of getting yourself infected."

"What difference does it make if he has weapons or not?" Luis asks.

"We're going to play hide-and-seek," Shoshana says with a smile.

"*What?*" I ask.

"Just like the first night we met," Shoshana says. "Me and Luis . . . we pretend to be normal kids. Alright, I know, Luis, we *are* normal kids. But I mean, not, like, not-vampire kids—I mean kids that aren't trying to stop a murderer. Look, we go and play hide-and-seek and he gets all angry at us. Because we'll be loud and annoying, and he's going to think we'll scare off the vampires or something. He won't kill us, right? He's already got a vampire, so he won't need to kill anyone anymore for bait.

"We won't have to let him get close to us, even if he *is* in a killing mood. As long as we're loud enough, we can stay on the path. We just have to be annoying enough that he'll come over like a cranky old man and tell us to beat it. Adam, that's when *you* can sneak up and grab your brother!"

"And while you're getting Victor out of there, I'll check out his van, see if the jamming device is in there, and disable it," Alejandra says. "Then we call the police once this park is vampire-free." She gives Luis a stern look. "They'll roll in deep. Dad'll be fine. He says the FBI are here investigating the serial killer now anyway."

"Alright," I say. That's really all I can say. We don't have time to make a better plan.

Sung lands back on the ground so silently that the mortals all jump.

"What?" Sung asks, then turns to me. "Okay, I got the moms. They're on their way back."

"Let me guess," I say, scowling. "Mom said don't do anything until she gets here."

Sung shrugs. "Couldn't say. I lost signal again for some weird reason."

"Sung, you're the best," I say, knowing they were sarcastically telling me they hung up before Mom could forbid us from doing anything. "Go with Luis and Shoshana. If Glasses Man gets murder-y, they'll need you close to protect them."

Sung nods.

"It's the open field thing next to the tennis courts," Alejandra tells them. "You three stay on the sidewalk and don't go into that field! If Glasses Man doesn't come out, we'll think of something else!"

"But really, really do your best to draw him out," I add. "He's got to leave before we can grab Victor."

Luis, Shoshana, and Sung run off. They act like they're chasing each other, but they're also arguing, which is still pretty much on-brand for them. I wait for a moment.

"Follow me," Alejandra whispers.

I creep in the dark, through the forest paths, toward the field where Alejandra said Glasses Man was keeping Victor. I hate that it's winter—all the bushes are bare, and it's harder to hide. And what's worse? The snow is sticking. Even if I can be silent, I'm going to leave footprints behind. I'm light on my feet, but not that light.

It's not like I can call it off now, and there's no way I'm going to wait for Mom. Who knows if the vampire hunter has a time limit for how long he's willing to wait for other vampires to show up? What if he gets bored and decides to kill Victor now?

Alejandra grabs my sleeve and points to the parking lot. There's a van there.

"What?" I ask.

"That's his van," she whispers back. "Right up ahead, the forest opens up to this circular meadow-field thing. Victor's leaned up against the tree in the middle. Glasses Man is behind a stump, a few feet back into the woods."

Alejandra holds out her hand and I shake my head. "Don't you need it to get stronger or whatever? It'll make my eyes get all red and glowy. Not good for sneaking."

Alejandra drops her hand. "Good luck. And thanks again."

She hurries away, and once again, I'm alone. I step off the forest path, walking as quietly as I can. My feet don't make a sound. I get on my hands and knees and creep under the fronds of a sword fern.

I wait. Luis and Shoshana run by only a few moments later, laughing loudly and chasing each other. Sung is doing their absolute best to contain their awesome vampire speed. They aren't going into the field, just like we planned, but running back and forth on the path that's just on the other side of the tree-ringed field. Being loud. And annoying.

I can't believe it—our plan is actually working! Shoshana and Luis are screaming and laughing and I can see Glasses Man. His big, round, creepy glasses are turned toward them. Watching them, not Victor. He doesn't see anything suspicious when he sees them. He's not looking around the bushes or the trees to see if a vampire is about to drop down and rescue anyone.

He waits. Why is he waiting? Why doesn't he get up and go over there and tell them to shut up and go home like we thought?

Oh wait! He stands up. I hold my breath. Even if he can't hear me breathing, I still hold my breath. I have to be quick. I have to be quiet.

I go.

I'm literally tiptoeing in the man's shadow and he doesn't turn or suspect a thing. He can't hear me. My feet fall quietly on the ground, using the footprints Glasses Man leaves in the dusting of snow. I creep as quietly as I can. I keep my eyes on Glasses Man's back, seeing if he'll turn around at the last minute.

But he doesn't, and instead keeps going toward Shoshana and Luis. I stop when I get to the tree.

Victor looks *bad*.

"Victor?" I whisper.

He doesn't seem to hear me at all. His eyes are open, but they're just blank, not really seeing anything. He's just sitting there. He's trembling. No. *Shivering*. How can he be cold? What did this guy do to him?

My chest burns with anger.

"I'm getting you out of here," I whisper.

I wrap my arms around Victor and pull, but he doesn't budge. My heart jumps into my throat. He's way more heavy that I can remember, and I have a lot of memories of Victor sitting on me to know.

I tug again but I can't move him. I'm starting to panic. I look down at my scrawny arms in terror. Victor wasn't joking—I really did need to work on my vampire strength! I can't pick him up! I glance back at the bushes, at least forty feet away, where concealment and safety are waiting for us. I don't know what to do.

I grit my teeth.

"Victor," I whisper, pleading. "You have to snap out of it! I can't pick you up on my own!"

The fear that slowly floods me is ice cold. I can't do this. Our plan was perfect—I found mortals that want to help us. That don't see us as monsters. How could none of that matter? How could everything go right up until everything depends on me?

I look up at the sky, as if desperate for an answer, and something bright catches my eye. It's Gemini, the constellation, lighting up the navy sky. *It represents dual natures.* I can hear Mama explaining to me. *Even if they have all the sky to move around in, they are walking the same path, and they do so together.*

"We're going to pretend we're invisible, okay?" I whisper. That's the only other option I have left. Except we've never done it before. And now? With Victor so weak and drained? I grab onto his hand. "I'll help you, okay? It's going to be like doing the puzzle—just reach out and connect with me. We're going to hide from the vampire hunter until you get better, or the moms get here, but I need you—"

A hand clamps down on the scruff of my neck as I yelp in surprise. The hand tightens around my hoodie and lifts me up. He pulls me clear off my feet, off of Victor.

I struggle to get out of Glasses Man's grip, but at the first sign of me fighting back, Glasses Man wraps an arm around my neck in a headlock. He's not choking me, but I can't get loose either. With his free hand, he pulls my lip up.

"Ah!" I struggle to get away, but it's too late. He's seen my fangs.

"Hey!" I hear Luis say. "What're you doing, grabbing a kid?"

Glasses Man tightens his hold around my neck and now I *am* choking. I claw at his arm, trying to pry it off, but he pulls back, and I'm barely on my tiptoes. I can't get any leverage. I really can't breathe now, but my vampire venom is at work at once, healing me over and over again.

It's more dizzying knowing that I can't help.

"Say something else," Glasses Man says, turning to face Luis, his eyes narrowing. "Open real wide."

A cold panic grips me. Victor's a teenager. I'm a kid. He's seen our fangs. He's thinks my friends are vampires too.

Do it! I need to tell them to show Glasses Man that they aren't vampires. Maybe if he realizes they're mortals, he'll leave them alone . . . but I can't get the words out. My vision keeps swimming with black blobs.

"Open your mouths." Glasses Man spits the command out at Luis and Shoshana. Neither of them moves. Sung has their mouth clamped shut.

Glasses Man doesn't ask a second time. He reaches into his jacket and pulls out a *rifle*. He hoists it up onto his shoulder with just the one hand holding onto the grip and points the bad end toward the others. I freeze. Luis and Shoshana freeze. I can see them shifting their weight, making to run away. But they don't. They stay.

Please don't run away. Show him you're mortal.

I try to grab for the weapon, but Glasses Man wrenches his body, keeping the rifle out of my reach without even loosening his grip. I can't knock the weapon away. I claw at the arm wrapped around my neck. I need to breathe.

I need to tell Luis and Shoshana how I can heal up super-fast if I get shot . . . and that they can't. Sung stands in front of them protectively, using their body to shield my mortal friends from harm.

"I will not ask a third time," Glasses Man says.

Sung darts forward, but it's like Glasses Man has vampire-level reflexes of his own. The rifle gives a jolt, and I cringe in a silent scream as a shattering crack pierces my ears, a sound so sharp it's like an actual shaft of lightning impaling my head. My ears are ringing, but I'm not so disoriented that I don't notice Sung slumped over on the ground. They've been shot! Luis and Shoshana jump forward to help and freeze again when Glasses Man levels the rifle on them.

Victor . . . help . . . we need you.

Ever so quietly, I can hear a voice in my head. Willing me to *connect. Victor!* I close my eyes, feeling for that thread of connection that will tie me to my brother and—

A voice booms suddenly in the night, cracking like thunder over the field. It's so loud all of us jump, even Glasses Man.

"PUT YOUR HANDS UP!"

30

VICTOR

Adam's voice reaches me. Even though everything is all fuzzy and unfocused, I can hear him.

I reach out and find Adam. He's burning bright and vivid in my mind, like this solid, unwavering rock. I reach out and hold on.

A thread of light splinters off of him and *there*! Sung is here too. They're heavy and motionless and full of tranquilizer, but once I focus on them, they coalesce into my mind as someone vibrant and powerful. Even further away, there's Mom. And Mama, racing this way. They feel me reaching out to them and they throw their whole selves into giving me all the strength I need.

I'm connected to all of them, and they're connected to me. I can feel each of their hearts beating, like ripples across space. I breathe out slowly, reaching out, concentrating on the link. And each heart, each in its own time, starts beating in time with mine. I can feel it. Like a pulse, echoing in my chest. Filling up what was hollow. Filling me up and making me whole.

I remember what Adam told me about pulling off charisma—how you have to know the person you're trying to influence. They'll only see what they want to see. But what about what they *don't* want to see? And Glasses Man? He opened himself up like a book. Those obsessive levels of control? I know exactly what he's scared of.

You're too late. They're here to stop you.

"Put your hands up!"

A shadowy figure appears in my mind. They hold a flashlight, shining it in Glasses Man's face. It's supposed to be bright, and it is. Glasses Man raises a hand up to block out the blinding beam—which, in my opinion, means I've nailed an absolutely perfect mirage. Scary, but not too heavy on the details. It's not like I can really do details right now.

My head pounds, but I hold onto the image with everything I have.

"Who is that?" Glasses Man calls to my mirage.

Adam squints. He can see the figure too? *Cool.*

"It's the police!"

But Glasses Man doesn't surrender.

"Dad, *no*," one of the kids whispers.

"Drop the kid!"

"It's not a kid!" Glasses Man shouts back. "It's a vampire. A monster!"

I clench my jaw in anger. Mistake—big mistake! I'm losing my focus and I scramble hard to find the connection again, but just making Glasses Man think he is surrounded

260

by the police for a single minute is making my head pound. I don't think I can go much harder.

"Put your weapons down!" Glasses Man yells at my mirages. "Come and inspect it for yourself. It's a vampire, and it's perfectly legal to hunt—"

Glasses Man never finishes.

He broke the illusion.

All the shadowy figures with the flashlights vanish. I moan and slump back against the tree. My arms are still numb, which is awful, because what I want more than anything is to rub my forehead. It feels like someone is slamming into the back of my brain with a hammer. I whimper involuntarily and Glasses Man turns to me.

"*You?*" Glasses Man says.

And worse than getting found out? He's *impressed*, in a really creepy, I-hate-you-even-more kind of way. "I must say, that was quite the illusion. And you managed to pull that off even without having fed? Without blood?"

I want to tell him exactly what's giving me strength: seeing Adam in danger and wanting to protect him. Knowing I'm connected to my family. But I can't push air out of my lungs with enough force to say anything.

"You're much too dangerous," Glasses Man says, and points his rifle right at my face. "And you've served your purpose."

I'm not going to survive this. I hold my breath and brace myself. The last thing I'm going to do is die afraid . . . though it stinks that the promise of an immortal life only ended up being fourteen years long.

Glasses Man never sees the attack coming.

Adam doesn't even catch what happens at first, and he isn't all venom-drained and tranqed up like I am. A blur rushes Glasses Man, shoving him over with such a force that he lets go of Adam. The rifle clatters onto the mossy ground.

"Don't you ever touch any of my children ever again!"

"Mom!" Adam coughs.

In any other scenario, I would be totally embarrassed to need rescuing from my moms, but not in a fight against this creep. Though Glasses Man still has an advantage—we can't fight him together in our current state. Mama kneels next to Sung. I'm guessing she's doing blood magic to pull the tranquilizer out of Sung's body. Adam is on all fours, coughing. I'm, well, still not moving much.

Glasses Man grins, like he realizes he's got an advantage too, as it's only Mom who squares off with him.

"Ah," he says. "Mom, is it? I suspected with all these vampire children, there was bound to be a parent nearby, coming to the rescue. What cruelty, murdering children and turning them to this virus. It's a good thing I'll be putting an end to you."

He very pointedly looks at the rifle on the ground—like, he turns his entire head to look at it, and I can pick up the feeling that it's a diversion. And yes . . . he flicks his wrist. It's such a small movement. I'm not sure if Mom saw it, but I remember what he did to Alejandra.

But my jaw still doesn't move when I will it to. I wince. What to do? I was able to make an entire mirage, so what else can I do?

I'd heard Adam's voice in my head, encouraging me and imploring me to help . . . was that because we were connected, like what Mama said about doing the puzzle? We could become one person, sharing one body. One mind. My parents really *had* been teaching me some cool vampire stuff all along, getting me ready for this moment.

Mom! I try think-talking to her. *He's got a dart in his hand. Victor?!*

It worked! *Be surprised another time—he's feinting about going for the rifle. He's got a killer-poison-dart in his hand. It's the same thing that's got Sung down for the count, and if you get too close to him, he's going to stab you with it.*

I sense Mom pausing, and I really hope she's not about to question how I know this or tell me I'm just a kid and I've got no right making battle plans. *What do you suggest we do?* she think-asks me instead.

My heart warms. *Stall him. He likes to talk a lot about how smart he is.*

Mom takes one step back, settling back and resting most of her weight on one foot—clear body language of not-ready-to-fight.

"Allora," Mom says in a tone that's part giving up and part pretend-impressed. "I've got to hand it to you. I've been hiding my family for more than a hundred years, and you're the first hunter to ever find us." I cringe. That safety was blown all because of me. "As a former vampire hunter myself, I thought I knew enough to keep my children safe. Only the best could have found us."

Glasses Man tilts his head.

"I notice you started what you were saying with 'allora,'" he says. "A very typical Italian filler word, I believe. Former vampire hunter, is it? Forgive me, but I believe I am in the presence of . . . Beatrice Rossi."

I can feel Mom's heart skip a beat.

Adam scrambles over and dives toward me the next second.

"Victor, are you okay?" he asks, his voice muffled as he smushes his face into my chest, crushing me in the biggest hug of all time. I think he's crying. "I'm sorry, Victor. I'm sorry, I—"

"Don't you know you wait to apologize until after battles?" I ask, my voice rough, but I'm finally able to talk again.

"I must say, I never planned to capture any legendary vampires," Glasses Man is saying. Hey, even though he must have a freakishly detailed knowledge of vampires to know who Mom is based on like, two bits of information . . . at the very least, our plan is still working and he's still just talking. "And yet here you are, surrounded by children. It must be that there is still a mothering instinct somewhere in there that the vampirism is encouraging. How wonderful for me that you chose to turn children instead of surrounding yourself with more capable vampires. So much easier to hunt children, as you can see."

"Hunt children? I thought *I* was supposed to be the cruel one," Mom croons back.

Adam pulls me up to my feet. I'm still wobbly, but I lean on Adam. He's got me. We lock eyes.

"We can still do this," I say. "We just have to give him some fake targets."

"Together," Adam says.

I nod. "Together."

And not a moment too soon, because Glasses Man makes a lunge for the rifle while he's mid-sentence.

I close my eyes and focus again. The connection comes faster this time, and like turning on a light, I can feel myself linked with Adam, all his strength pouring into me. I connect with Mom and Mama and Sung. But I reach out beyond that, beyond the park boundaries and the mountains and the long stretches of the sea.

I'm so glad Adam is here. I can't remember who all my siblings are, but he's thinking of them. He remembers where they are. He remembers their names, their faces—so clearly that I can picture them too.

I don't stop reaching until I can feel them all. One hundred and seventy-three siblings.

"Hey!" I shout at Glasses Man, thinking as hard as I can on the feeling of us all together, and pushing that out as hard as I can. "Hope you've got enough rounds for all of us!"

Shapes drop from the trees above and rush in from the forest, until Glasses Man is surrounded by mirages of the entire Rossi family. He wheels this way and that, growling in frustration, but he doesn't put his rifle down. He doesn't give up.

"Surrender!" Dozens of mirage vampires around me shout at the same time.

"Surrender to blood-suckers?" Glasses Man spits his words. "That's how you've managed to live here so long without murdering, is it? Do you have living victims stashed away in your cave? That's what you'll do to me—lock me up and keep me alive and bleed me when you're hungry?"

"We want you to stop hurting people," I urge the mirages to answer. "We just want to be left alone."

I guess Glasses Man would rather go down fighting. He lifts his rifle and shoots into the crowd. One of the mirages crumples. *Mason.* His name jumps into my mind. That's the guy who has a dragon-egg rock on our bookshelf. At least the real-life Mason is thousands of miles away, so the real-life dart sticks harmlessly in the snow.

A mirage of a girl with two long braids falls forward next. *Radha.* A dart passes through her and lands in the ferns.

A girl with long, blond, wind-swept hair slumps down from the trees above. *Michelle.*

A tall, bald man dashes forward. *Ifeanyi.*

A mirage swinging back on crutches. *Natan.*

And another. And another. And—

Glasses Man tosses down the bandolier he's been holding his darts in. That can only mean one thing—he's down to his last dart. I grin. As soon as he's shot that off, the moms can piledrive him to the ground and—

But I guess there's only one person he's saved the last dart for. Me.

He turns the rifle in my direction again and I freeze. It's too late to try miraging myself invisible.

BAM.

Glasses Man stumbles back as something hits him in the head. He shakes it off quickly, looking left and right to see where the attack came from. He must've thought it was a new super-fast vampire . . . but "together" doesn't end with just our family.

Those two mortal kids launch another rock at Glasses Man and he stumbles back again. And what's even better? He had his finger on the trigger, and when he got hit with that rock, he definitely pulled it. The dart went flying off in a totally harmless direction.

"Ooh, you wasted your last round," the boy mortal sneers.

Glasses Man freezes.

He's outnumbered. Mom and Mama, me and Adam and Sung . . . even those two mortal kids. We're all ready to fight. But who makes the finishing move, even I don't expect.

"DROP THE WEAPON!"

Glasses Man smirks, looking at me. "You tried that trick before."

But the very flesh-and-blood police officer takes another step forward into the clearing, his very real pistol pointed at Glasses Man. "I SAID, DROP THE WEAPON!"

Alejandra is standing super confidently next to him . . . wait, *Alejandra*? Definitely not dead? She's not dead! I had no idea I was going to care so much about her not being dead—this is incredible!

"Don't worry, Dad," she stage-whispers to the police officer. "Glasses Man doesn't believe in guns or knives, or any weapons that'll break the skin, and I think that dart gun's useless now."

Glasses Man very slowly raises his hands, and as my vampire-level hearing is coming back, I swear I can hear him grinding his teeth in frustration.

"We did it! We stopped him!" The mortal kids rush Adam. They're all hugging and celebrating.

"Masha'Allah, intum kwaiysiin," Mama gasps in relief, showing us just how happy she is that we're all okay with how tightly she squeezes me.

Sung grips me in astonishment. "Victor, I can't believe you! That was so cool!"

I smirk and try to brush it off. "I'll teach you if you like."

"You're on!" Sung says.

Mom doesn't shake out of vampire-hunter-hunter mode, not even when the most satisfying *clink* in the world fills the air and Glasses Man is finally in handcuffs. She glances at me, pride swelling in her eyes.

31

ADAM

Wonderwood Park is in absolute chaos.

Red and blue flashing lights bounce off of everything. There are at least a dozen police cars. Two ambulances. Three fire trucks. A bunch of black SUVs that I think have FBI guys in them. And for whatever reason, they *all* need to have their lights flashing.

"You'd think they would turn those off." Mama sighs, adjusting her leopard-print glasses. "They wouldn't have to tell everyone to stay away if they'd turn off the lights that are attracting all the attention. Look, there he goes again to tell those people to stay back."

Our family is huddled together on the opposite side of the park, watching through the bare branches of the forest and across the open baseball fields. The parking lot is full of very official vehicles.

Even across the distance, I can see Alejandra sitting in the back of an ambulance and Luis and Shoshana huddled under blankets talking excitedly to someone I'm guessing is an FBI agent.

The FBI guys did a quick sweep of the park when they first arrived, but they didn't see us. It's not like mortals tend to look up into the trees. They're probably too busy doing their investigation stuff. I mean, we *did* just catch a serial killer. Officially, Alejandra, Luis, and Shoshana will get the credit. The Rossi family? We were never here. No one talks about vampires. And I know I can count on Luis and Shoshana to spin a story that makes sense while leaving us out.

It's all super overwhelming, but I'm only really paying attention to one thing right now: Glasses Man. I don't relax until the black door of an FBI SUV shuts him in. The tinted windows might as well be a wall. And just like that, the guy is gone.

I hear a small group approaching, walking four across on the sidewalks through the forest, talking excitedly. I grin at the other Rossis and drop out of the trees.

"He doesn't believe us, by the way," Luis calls out to me as he runs up. "That you're vampires."

I glance up at the giant of a man towering over me and I grin. Victor drops down to the sidewalk next to me and copies my grin for just a second before giddily approaching Alejandra and asking if she's okay and what had happened.

"Hey, those are some pretty good teeth," Officer Espinosa says, and he smiles. "They almost look real." He winks. I guess this is as excited as he gets.

Mom and Mama and Sung have joined us—they were so quiet I didn't even hear them approach. But before Mom could go all parent and hijack the conversation, I blurt out, "So that's it?" I toss my head in the direction of the SUV Glasses Man vanished into. "He's going to jail?"

"Oh yeah," Officer Espinosa says. "And not just for the killings the past few weeks. He's been all over the country, murdering people for years. He's even been caught before, gone to trial. But there's always someone willing to pay his bail. They give him flashy lawyers that get him off. You have any idea why?"

I shake my head.

"Someone really wants him to keep hunting vampires," Mom says ominously.

I tremble. "So that's why Glasses Man was doing this?"

"Who?" Officer Espinosa asks.

Victor shrugs. "Just what we were calling *him*."

"Want to know his real name?"

"Nah," I say.

"What happens now?" Mama asks. I know what she means. Are we going to be safe? And if Glasses Man has someone helping him, someone who's willing to get him out of jail so he can keep hunting vampires, does that mean we'll never be safe?

"It's out of my hands," Officer Espinosa says. "Just know I'm here to help."

I frown. That's not exactly the answer I want, but, on the other hand, it's a nice feeling to know we've got some allies.

Speaking of friends . . . I step out of the adult conversation circle and go join them. They're all huddled together like they're up to something.

"Adam, look!" Shoshana whisper-shouts. "That schmuck had this *book.*"

Calling what Shoshana is holding a book isn't exactly right. It's not anything more than color photocopies inside a binder. But those pages? They definitely were copied from an old book. Like, medieval ages old.

"Where'd you get that?" I ask.

"Alejandra found it in Glasses Man's van," Luis says.

"Isn't that stealing from a crime scene?" Victor asks.

"Sheket," Shoshana shushes him. "Look at this."

She flips through the plasticky pages. Each one has hilariously awful medieval artworks on it.

"It's a book about *vampires,*" she says. "See?"

"What are they doing?" Luis asks.

The drawing he's pointing to has what I'm guessing is a sick mortal on a bed. Their arm is hanging over the side of the bed. A vampire kneels next to the bed, holding a bowl up to a cut in the mortal's arm, and another vampire is off to the side, drinking from a glass.

"Blood magic," I say. "Like what we did for Alejandra. We used to do that . . . make mortals better, and then we'd drink their sick blood."

"I thought blood magic was, like, sacrificing people to make yourself more powerful," Luis scoffs. "But this is cool. Why would anyone lie about it? Or want to make you *extinct*? Vampires and mortals, it's like . . . a win-win. It's literally free healthcare."

"Yeah, that might be why," Shoshana grumbles. "But we aren't going to figure anything else out unless we know someone who can read Latin."

"Mom can!" I say.

"Mom can what?" Mom asks from her grown-up conversation. I wave her over, pointing excitedly to the book.

"Alejandra found an old book," I say. "And we need you to read it."

"Oh, and every old book is written in a dead language that only Mom can read?" Mom asks as she picks up the binder. She raises her eyebrows when she sees the words. "Okay, so yeah, this old book is written in a dead language only Mom can read."

Mom's eyes get glassy as she flips through the pages, like she might cry. "I've been looking for this for ages."

I remember what Mama told me, about Mom finding a book that made her realize vampires weren't the bad guys. Was this it? "What does it say?" I ask.

Mom crouches down, smoothing out her skirt, and beckons us to sit around her. She places the book down in the middle of our group and smiles.

"It's a transcript of a meeting long ago," Mom says. "It says a council was formed specifically to get rid of vampires. The people on this council believed that if you were sick, it was a punishment from heaven for something you did wrong. The council was angry that the ill kept going to us vampires for help, to get healed by us, and weren't going to the church to pray for forgiveness."

"Even though that couldn't possibly help sick people get better?" Shoshana asks.

"Looks like they started blaming unexplained deaths on vampires." Mom continues reading and flipping pages. "They used the fear they whipped up and slayed every vampire they could find. And then? They gathered up every last bit of proof that talked about vampires being helpful and destroyed it."

Mom has the book open to a page that would have looked scary if the art wasn't so bad: a gaggle of pitchfork-wielding most-likely-mortals and a person (most likely a vampire) engulfed in flames under a (strangely) smiling sun.

"And it took almost no time at all for people to forget what we used to do," Mom says. "They were told their memories were wrong, and they believed it."

"And the vampires that were left?" Luis asks.

"They went into hiding," Mama says. "And the hunting . . . it started in Europe and spread across the globe. Every place they 'discovered'? Every place they colonized, they'd send in vampire hunters to sweep the land."

"Just so mortals would feel bad about getting sick?" Shoshana asks.

"It wasn't just that, though. Remember?" Luis says. "They got everyone on board with getting rid of vampires, but they just used that as steam to go after the next group they didn't like, right?"

"Right," Shoshana says with a blush.

"That is so ridiculous," Alejandra says. "There was only one person trying to kill me this whole time. I'd be dead now if it wasn't for you guys."

"Does that mean no more stakes?" Victor asks.

"Hmm," Alejandra hums. "It might mean we need to go out for steaks."

"What does that mean?" Victor asks.

"Steak . . . you know, the meat?" Alejandra asks.

Victor shrugs. "I don't eat food."

"Oh, *right*," Alejandra says, cringing awkwardly. "Obligate hemovore. Steak. It's like, a dinner you'd eat at a fancy restaurant?"

"Why would you want to take me to a fancy restaurant?" Victor asks. "Just . . . wait, are you asking me out?"

At the mention of "asking out," Officer Espinosa leans back from his "grown-up" conversation circle to peer into ours.

"Not that I'm, you know, trying to turn you into my own personal blood tap," Victor stammers out quickly. "But, uh, a date would be nice."

"See," Shoshana says. "Vampires and mortals can totally get along."

"How *are* you getting your blood?" Luis asks.

I squirm as Victor groans. Great. Old people blood. His favorite thing to complain about.

"Sick people from the hospital," Victor grumbles.

"Mom asks permission to take it," I add quickly. "I mean, I guess they don't realize it's for us to drink, but she always asks if she can take it."

"But if it's sick people, then you're helping?" Alejandra asks. "Like how you helped me."

I glance over to Mom, who has her arm wrapped around Mama's waist. They share a quick look and Mom nods. I perk up, grinning.

"Like how we used to," I say.

Officer Espinosa shrugs. "I learned how to do IVs in the army. I don't mind making donations."

Victor leans back, looking all woozy, and has a dream-like smile on his face.

"No more hiding?" Victor says. "All the hospital-free blood we could ever want? And doing some of that blood magic stuff? Sounds like a good deal to me."

I grin at my brother, and he smiles back. A smile that spreads from ear to ear. A smile I haven't seen in the longest time. And that means more to me than anything else.

I reach into my pocket. My fingers clasp around the rock I'd painted on the bus with my two new friends. I'd nearly forgotten I'd had it. Luis looks over my shoulder as I hold it out.

"*I don't want to be your monster*," he reads, and laughs. "I guess that makes sense."

I didn't get a chance to throw it at Glasses Man, but there is one other thing I can do with it.

I place the rock on the stump next to me, wondering who would find it in the morning. It's not like they'd ever guess that a vampire kid left it there for them. And while I hope mortals find out about us someday, in the meantime, there are other people who are being hunted and attacked and turned into monsters just so someone else has someone to blame. Like Shoshana and Luis said, solving problems by blaming an entire group of people doesn't stop once that group is gone. It just moves to the next group. And the next. And even if it's just words on a rock, hopefully whoever picks it up will see that no problems get solved by treating someone as a monster just for being who they are.

"It's been fun, but it's getting late," Officer Espinosa says. "I told the feds I needed to get my kids home and . . . well, not a lot of room in a squad car to offer y'all a lift."

"Oh, it's okay, we drove," Mama says.

"I'm definitely getting a ride back to the house," Sung says. "You two coming?"

Victor and I share a secret smile.

"Well, you can't walk home," Officer Espinosa says. "They've got their people posted at every park entrance."

Sung grins back. "They don't need roads."

I take a deep breath. It feels like being on the top of a roller coaster, like I'm right on the edge, leaning over, my heart rate climbing in anticipation. The future feels bright— brighter than it ever did before. And I know now . . . no matter where I go, no matter what happens, good or bad, I know where a vampire kid like me belongs.

Victor glances at me and catches my eye. A mischievous smile spreads over his face.

"Race you home?" I beat him to the question.

Victor grins back. "You're on."

THE END

AUTHOR'S NOTE

There aren't actually any real vampires in the world (none that I've met, anyway), yet much of what inspired *Don't Want to Be Your Monster* (DWTBYM) is influenced by how even made-up stories about made-up creatures like vampires can cause very real harm to actual, living people.

The idea for this story started when I read (what I thought was) the source of all vampire lore—Bram Stoker's *Dracula.* As I approached the scene where we meet Dracula for the first time, my mental image was one that was created by movies—the slicked-back hair, the pale face, kind of suave with the cape . . . but what did I read? I almost laughed at first! "Bushy hair growing . . . profusely" that seemed to "curl in its own profusion"? That's not scary! "His eyebrows were massive, almost meeting over the nose." Dracula had a *unibrow*?! He had "protuberant teeth" and "pointed ears" and a nose that was "aquiline," which means eagle-like or hooked . . . and that's when I realized what made Dracula "scary" was something I'd seen before.

Dracula was being described just like a stereotypical caricature of a Jewish man!

As I continued, I noticed more antisemitic stereotypes. Dracula hoarded gold; he could transform into vermin (Jewish people are often compared to rats); the only person who helps Dracula is described as "being of the Hebrew faith"; and at one point, Dracula's hideout is even described as smelling like Jerusalem!

So what was going on? I found out that Eastern European Jews were immigrating to Britain in the late 1800s to escape pogroms (quite literally people going into Jewish communities and hunting us), and antisemitism had become super common in Britain. So common that when Bram wondered "what looks evil and villainous to me?" he ended up describing his vampire in the way Jews are often caricaturized.

It wasn't the first time Jews were described as drinking blood. *Dracula* tied vampiric blood-drinking with an anti-semitic fable called the "blood libel"—an idea from way back in thirteenth-century Europe that claimed Jewish people slaughter Christian children and drink their blood as a part of our rituals . . . which is wild, because as Shoshana says in DWTBYM, Jewish people don't even eat kosher animal meat if there's blood in it!

So why the myth? It comes down to a simple facet of human nature: if you convince a lot of people that someone you don't like does the absolute worst thing imaginable—that Jewish people kill Christian children and drink their blood, for example—then anything you might do to them will always be "better" than "what they are going to do to you." And then you can say that hurting or erasing that group is justified because you're only "protecting yourself"!

Nowadays, many more antisemitic tropes have found a home in vampire lore, particularly the idea of an evil "secret cabal" that seeks to "control the world." Or that vampires can be literally hurt or repelled by a cross or holy water. The connection made between Jews and vampires in *Dracula* became so widespread and accepted that even Adolf Hitler wrote that Jewish people are "vampires and bloodsuckers" and described us as "the race which shuns the sunlight."

A lot of these tropes are so closely associated with vampires that many people think they can't be a "real" vampire unless they include these tropes! And when you are a Jewish writer like me? It's really hard to write about a mythological creature when you know it's full of someone else's hatred of you.

One of the reasons I wrote DWTBYM is because I wanted to imagine what it would be like if the "Jewish vampire" resembled the *actual* Jewish life that I knew. I reimagined why vampires might need to drink blood (not to harm others, but to help!) and invoked a lot of the history of my people—one full of misunderstandings, danger, and persecution. One where we've been made into monsters to serve someone else's purpose. Basically, I took Bram's attempt to hurt us and flipped it to show the reality of what it means to be Jewish—one of many "demonized" minorities.

And I get it! You might be thinking "Lighten up! This is made-up stuff!" It *is*, but you'd be surprised how often people let fictional ideas seep into their concept of the real world.

Even if you know you are only watching a movie or reading a book, it still affects the way you see others— especially when it's an "other" you have only ever "met" in a story written by someone who wants to convince you that that "other" is out to get you. Even if we know it's not real, we all trust storytellers to build a believable story. One of the reasons we are so easily misled into believing entire groups of people are bad is *because* we are never given any other representations of them. And when you only ever see a certain group being shown in bad ways . . . you see where I'm going?

When you think of a villain, who do you picture? If it's someone who looks, or prays, or loves differently from you, ask yourself why you picture them when you think of villainy. Where did that idea come from? When have you seen similar people used as villains? And *why*?

Hate doesn't die in silence— it thrives. The only way to stop it from growing is to call it out when you see it, in whatever form it takes. Ultimately, the only way we know someone is a bad person is when they *do* bad. And even some bad stuff can be apologized for! But if you're told that what makes you "bad" is a part of you that can't be changed, then there's nothing you'll ever be able to do to become "good." So be cautious when someone tells you to make monsters out of an entire group of people based on what they *are*.

Only true villains want you to think that's the way to a better world.

LOCATIONS

Don't Want to Be Your Monster takes place in Olympia and Lacey, Washington—both of them real cities that you can visit!

The Capitol Theater that starts the book off can be found at 206 5th Avenue SE in Olympia. They actually do play old movies, though I haven't seen *The Lost Boys* up on the marquee yet.

The Pioneer Cemetery where Adam meets Luis and Shoshana is at 4178 Ruddell Road SE in Lacey, though the iron banner that stretches over the entry gate doesn't have the quote mentioned in the book. If you want to see that, you'd have to travel to the Maplewood Cemetery at 331 W Haven Avenue, in the Chicago suburb of New Lenox, where I spent a few years growing up.

You won't be able to climb to the top of the crane at the Port of Olympia (unless you're a vampire, of course), but you can get a similar view from the Observation Tower at Port Plaza Park at 701 Columbia Street NW in Olympia.

Saint Martin's University (at 5000 Abbey Way SE in Lacey) D Parking Lot is where Adam, Shoshana, and Luis analyzed the murder scene, and just in the woods to the north, you'll find station eleven of the Stations of the Cross. (Please be mindful that the university is also a working abbey, and that monks live, teach, and worship here. If you don't think you can be respectful of their religious observances and reverence for these locations, please do not visit!)

Wonderwood Park can be found at 5304 32nd Avenue SE in Lacey, and if you explore the grounds, you can find all the places in the book—the open field where Victor got captured by Glasses Man is just east of the tennis courts; Adam and his friends come up with a plan at the giant stump close to the baseball diamonds; and you can even look for painted rocks while you're there. You might even find one that will remind you that no one wants to be a monster!

ACKNOWLEDGEMENTS

This book would not have been possible without a lifetime of love and support, so to kick off my gratitude, I'm starting things at the very beginning. Gleno—you are a twin sister made of dreams! We've shared every story idea, from when we couldn't write and could only make books with folded construction paper and drawings that told wordless stories, to the shaky moment I called you to tell you I was about to become a published author. I never would have gotten here without your critical ear, your sympathetic shoulder, and your words of encouragement. Thank you beyond all words I can think to say.

To Mom and Dad, who got me started with my love of books by reading to me every night. Dad, I still remember us reading *The Hobbit* and *The Lord of the Rings* together. It's one of my fondest memories from my childhood.

To my cousins Josh, Mat, and Jason, for all the years we played in the cemetery. Having my vampire making friends in one is a small nod to you three for creating some of my favorite childhood memories.

To my spouse, a friend forever and wonderful partner, who built me up to be an unstoppable force. We've been on an unbelievable journey together, from our days hitch-hiking around the Midwest to living in Italy. Thank you for always believing in me and following me on every adventure my heart settled on, even though I leap so often without looking. You're a great partner to jump with.

To my kids, my ultimate inspirations. You have so much energy and passion and enthusiasm and my life has been completely upended and enriched with your love. Not a day goes by that you don't make my heart swell with pride. I never knew being a parent could be so powerful, and I can't think of a greater honor in this world than knowing that you were the ones to give me that title.

I could never have gotten this book off the ground if it weren't for my incredible friends, beta readers, and critique partners. Top spots to Louise Willingham, Michelle Timian, Sofiya Pasternack, Jisuk Cho, Joseph Espinosa, Kate Foster, Jessica Russak-Hoffman, Esme Symes-Smith, Ash Van Otterloo, Ally Malinenko, كل اساتنتي في المهعد الدفاع اللغات، حاصتاً أستاذة سلمى, Mason O'Hara, Emily Dempsey, and so many people I'm probably forgetting (I am so sorry!)—your time and insight and dedication in helping me to perfect my craft was positively inseparable from my success. If this book has gone anywhere, it's only with your hard work and volunteered effort. I could not have possibly done it without you.

To Emily Forney, my rock-star agent, who could see the potential in my story and decided to take a chance on me—a thousand million thanks. You are the dream maker. Without you, my life would still be incomplete, empty of this goal I've been pursuing for as long as I can remember. You gave me that dream and for that, no words will ever express how much taking a chance on me means.

To Peter Phillips, my extraordinary editor. The day you asked me if I would be comfortable making the manuscript possibly more Jewish was the day I knew there was no better editor I could have chosen. You've been the most gentle, supportive, excited person I could have ever hoped to have my book in their hands. All the thanks in the world.

To Sam Devotta, the most stellar of all publicists, who has been so fantastically excited about every title (and its inspiration!). You've been such a wonderfully kind and supportive person to have in my corner!

To Matt Rockefeller, for the heart-stopping cover art. For so long, the dream of walking into a bookstore and finding my book on a shelf would end with just a blank cover, and you filled it in the most incredible way. And to Andrew Roberts, whose cover design made me think back to classic horror movie posters. Not even in my imagination did I think my book would look this great!

And ultimately, to the Source of All Creation, I offer my thanks, for keeping me alive, sustaining me, and enabling me to reach this time, to see this dream of mine come true. May my knack for creativity always be a suitable outlet to bring good into this world You've created.

רבה אמונתך